Yossa's Crystal

Sarah M. Scott

Yossa's Crystal
A Lulu Book/ August 2007

Published Through Lulu.com

This is a work of fiction. Names, characters, places, and incidents either are the product of the author's imagination or are used fictitiously. Any resemblance to actual persons, living or dead, events, or locales is entirely coincidental.

ISBN: 978-0-6151-8000-7

Published in the United States

To anyone who wakes up and wonders what it would be like to wander around inside the head of someone who is not sure where her own reality and the reality of the universe are supposed to merge.

To all the family members who ever freaked out because I managed to get this published.

And especially to those who believe romance can happen to us all. You are the ones who give us nonbelievers what we really deserve, an inner laugh and invisible finger pointing when the truth is revealed and we end up looking foolish.

Island of
Yossa

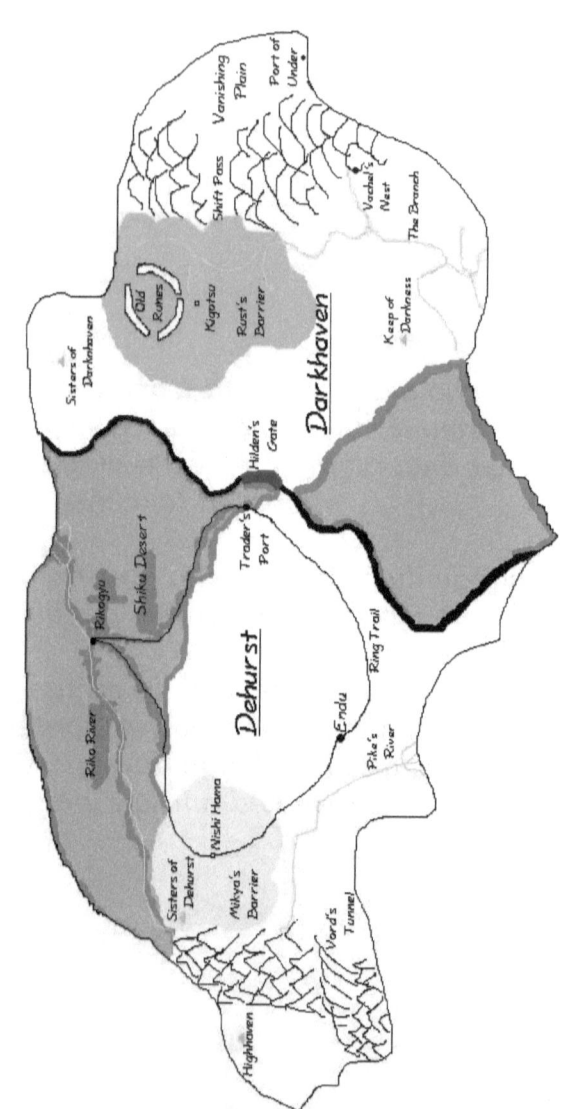

Sisters of
Darkhaven

Old
Runes

Kigotsu

Rust's
Barrier

Skift Pass

Vanishing
Plain

Port of
Under

Vadist's
Nest

The Branch

Keep of
Darkness

Darkhaven

Hidian's
Gate

Trader's
Port

Rihogiu

Shiku Desert

Riko River

Dehurst

Endu

Ring Trail

Pika's
River

Nishi Hama

Sisters of
Dehurst

Mikya's
Barrier

Highhaven

Vord's
Tunnel

Demon Blood

He lies on his side, the sharp pebbles making permanent creases in his shoulder. Still, he does not dare roll over onto his back for fear he will strangle on the blood that rushes up his throat every minute. *It is all the eggs' fault! Blasted, cursed things are the only reason the curse actually works.* They are created from the blood and entrails of human children, and thus, they emit a magic presence that causes these symptoms.

Around his little mound of dirt is a ring of them at least four eggs thick. They are about the size of two human heads stacked on top of each other. The bigger the eggs, the worse the pain. It rages through him as he lies here, the victim of the princess and her sorcerers.

The underground room is so cold his ragged breath appears in puffs before his face. It has to be cold for his demon blood to become the jelly they will purify and feed to the princess to enhance her power to protect the kingdom. In his misery, he often wishes she would discover what it is she is really eating. He would like to be there when she gets a taste of what it feels like to have her insides try to force their way up her throat.

At this thought, he coughs loudly and painfully as another rush of blood adds to the inch-thick cake surrounding him. His black hair clings desperately to his face. It is naturally long enough to fall to the small of his back, but they have hacked it off so that it reaches his shoulders as a symbol of his captivity. Like this, it only just hinders the hard line of his jaw. His elbows and knees are bent so that they are nearly touching. A loose, sleeveless, black shirt covers his chest and shoulders as it is tucked sloppily into his black pants. These too, are loose and cover the tops of his shin-high, black boots that have heels of one inch. All the black serves to hide some of the blood as it seeps into his clothing.

Because of the thickness of the jelly around him, he can tell they will soon come to harvest it. It will be a momentary relief of his misery, but a welcome one, nonetheless. He coughs again, this time causing some of the blood to splatter back into his face. Gasping for breath through the mess, he can hear the familiar clank of chains with his pointed, demonic ears. His green eyes slip open for a moment before drooping back down, as he has not the energy to keep them open. The noise becomes steadily louder until the soldier stands over him.

Black armor covers the man's muscular frame. A red dragon appears on the metal at his chest, marking him as part of the princess's personal guard. The demon thinks it quite ironic that the princess knows nothing of his existence, yet one of her guards is always responsible for retrieving the jelly. The man's dark, brown eyes peer down at the broken form of the demon with only a small twinge of pity, knowing pain like this is something any demon could handle. The brown hair falls to his shoulders in waves.

Before taking a step, the soldier gazes at the red mass in disgust. Still, despite his aversion, he moves forward, careful to step just inside the ring of eggs to disturb as little of the jelly as possible. He takes hold of the demon's wrist to lift him up and out of the circle.

Pain shoots through the demon's body at having been removed from the cluster until the soldier places the shackles around his wrists and ankles: "Nark and the Sisters want to see you. It's about your production." "Not my fault," the demon answers in a voice just above a whisper. "They'll blame you for it anyway. It's just the way they do things. Here, it's from Riko, she's worried," the soldier replies, handing him a strip of meat. The demon snatches it up, stripping pieces away with a ferocity he could not have mustered only moments before.

"Praise to the spirits. I feared I'd have to live in this stinking hole for the rest of my life without ever getting to taste meat from her kitchen again," he sighs gratefully, making certain to get the scraps from his fingers and face. The soldier smiles at the thought. *At least Riko is trying to take care of him.* Not even *he* should be made to live this way. "Can you walk by yourself?" the soldier asks, helping the demon to his feet before he can get comfortable on the ground. Wiping his mouth of the fresh blood, the demon whispers bitterly, "I'll have to either way. Nark has eyes everywhere."

He forces himself forward and begins his slow trek over the mounds with rings of eggs around them in a path toward the heavy, iron door. Without this feature, the room would appear to be nothing but an ordinary cave. The soldier is forced to keep his pace slow as he follows the demon's labored progress. He has a powerful urge to swing the poor creature over his shoulder and hurry to meet Nark, but doing so could get both of them in the worst trouble of their lives. Thus, he contents himself with following close to the demon in order to provide any help.

When they finally make it, the demon stops to allow the soldier to open the door. It opens into a stone corridor where two other soldiers wait with a small cage. The first is surprised to see them here, but does his best to hide it. Nark must have discovered he was treating the demon more gently than the sorcerer cares for. The demon glares at the cage without a word as the soldier gives the other two the traditional nod. Their armor is black as his is, but a dragon of blue adorns their chests.

They are both prison guards, and he knows them to be especially vicious when they have to be and when they just wish to be. The one to the left has a hard jaw and a set of piercing, blue eyes. His blonde hair is held back at the base of his neck and falls to the small of his back. The one to the right has a smooth face, her mouth set in a slight frown as it usually is. Her bright, green eyes are focused on the demon. The braid of her brown hair is slipped forward over her shoulder.

"How was he?" the blonde asks. "You needn't worry about Reno. He always behaves himself," the demon answers with a small smirk. It does not have quite the force it normally would because his eyes keep drooping. "He wasn't talking to you, Vachel," Reno interjects hurriedly, "And, he's been much more compliant with *me*, Coby." "Really?" Coby remarks, taking a step forward and drawing a metal bar covered in bands of the eggshells. It is his item of choice when dealing with prisoners because the presence it emits can cause even the most hardened criminal great pain. However, in Vachel's case, it causes double the pain because of the curse.

Coby places it at the base of Vachel's neck, pressing down.

The magic of the curse takes effect immediately, and the demon sinks to the floor with a cry of pain. Reno winces at the sound of it but quickly straightens his face at the sight of the other soldiers' gazes on him. "I think you'll find that I can make him comply with me just as well," Coby replies, removing the bar, "Lin, get him into the cage."

She barely manages to get the door open before Vachel rushes inside in a crouch, glad to be away from the reach of the bar's magic, as the curse is negated when he is encased in iron.

"See, all it takes is the right amount of *force*, and I could get him to lick my boots clean," Coby boasts with a triumphant smile. "That's what *you* think, stupid bastard," Vachel hisses from the safety of the cage, "I still have *some* dignity left, but you can't say that now can you?" "You need to learn some respect, demon," Lin replies, kicking the bars. Vachel is silent, but a deep glare is perched on his face. Reno knows exactly why he did not retaliate, but there is no doubt Lin believes it was because of her threat.

With a snap of her fingers, Lin causes the cage to rise up three inches and levitate there above the floor. She nods to Coby who returns it to her before turning to Reno. However, without giving him a chance to speak, Reno crouches to look at Vachel as he pleads, "Could you please behave yourself this time?" "Can't," Vachel replies, "It goes against my policy as a demon to give respect to those who refuse to give it to me." Sighing, Reno stands and gives his nod to Coby who returns it before turning and starting down to corridor. Lin follows, the cage trailing behind her.

The stone slips by slowly as they make their trek toward the Sisters' meditation chamber. It is a large, open room made entirely of a green crystal that aids one in picking up mental vibrations. They just want to meet with him in a place where they can easily read his mind. An archway frames the entrance to the chamber. Across the space from it is an area blocked off with a black curtain. Only the High Sister is allowed back there and only if she must call on the ancestral spirits.

Just a few feet before this area is Nark.

Two of the highest-ranking sisters and one of lower rank sit on small cushions to the sorcerer's right. Nark is wearing a long, white robe with gold trimming at the end of the sleeves and the hem. Over his heart on the robe is a green dragon sewn into the fabric. His white shirt has a high collar and long sleeves hidden by the robe. The shirt is neatly tucked into his white pants, but allowed to fold over the gold belt buckle. The only black to him are the shined shoes, and gloves slipped over his long-fingered hands. His blonde hair falls to his waist behind him, not hindering the hard line of his jaw, as he stares steadily at the cage with his bright, red eyes.

The High Sister sits straight with her two aides on either side. Her long dress billows out around her on the floor. She is the only sister allowed to wear white. It is cut low, but the light blue robe of the High Sister prevents it from revealing too much. Her hair has turned silver from the magic of her position and falls to the floor even when she is standing. The blue eyes have slight creases at the corners, showing the only hint of her true age other than the slight wrinkles on her chin. She has her hands folded neatly in her lap, and Vachel instantly notices that her eyes are straight ahead, not gazing at the soldiers as they enter.

On the other hand, both aides are looking directly at him. The one to the High Sister's right he recognizes as Sister Selene, a crafty little monster, who enjoys tormenting him almost as much as Nark does. Her long-sleeved, blue dress billows out around her on the floor. Around her neck is a gold chain bearing a medallion with a blue dragon, symbolizing her place as the High Sister's successor. Her black hair is streaked with silver as it falls to her shoulders in smooth curls.   Unlike most woman in Dehurst, the smoothness of her jaw line is mixed with that of a much harder bone structure, giving her a hard look while she remains feminine.   The violet eyes dig into his flesh, but refuse to meet his.

On the High Sister's left is a girl he has met only once. The Sisters took her in as a small, starving child and named her Crystal for the glittering object she would let no one else touch.   Her blue dress has a tighter fit to the skirt so it slips beneath her with her legs.   It is obvious to Vachel she is of the faerie race.   Even the full-bodied, red hair does little to hide her long, fern leaf shaped ears.   The smooth, flawless skin covering her hands and face could have told him much the same.   Her green eyes shine as she gazes at him with a smile and a small blush.   Could she have waved or rushed up to greet him, she would have.

It makes him feel strange to think a faerie could fancy him, but he has more important things to deal with.   *A confrontation with Nark is mere moments away, and I intend to do my worst to the self-serving bastard.* Just as this thought enters his mind, Lin uses her magic to snap open the cage door and dump him out onto his face on the floor.   He has to grit his teeth to keep from yelling several curses at her.

"Thank you for bringing him," Nark whispers, "We will send for you when this is finished."   Coby and Lin both nod before turning and exiting the room.   With a wave of his hand, Nark brings a solid barrier up from the floor to seal the archway. Vachel is still as the sorcerer gazes steadily down at him.

"So, you are the demon causing Nark so much mischief. I never expected to see one such as you in chains," the High Sister observes with a smile that has a quality to it suggesting she just told a hidden joke. "Well, I certainly didn't even expect to see you, High Sister Margaret," Vachel replies, turning to look at her. It is now that he gets a good look at her eyes, realizes that the poor woman is blind, and understands her joke. "That is not what we came here to discuss, demon," Nark interjects, "You have not been producing at a proper rate, and that has to change."

Vachel acts as if the sorcerer has not even spoken: "Being at such a low point on the authority ladder does not give one much hope for meeting one of your influence." The High Sister is about to speak when Nark hisses, "I will not be ignored by such trash as you. Now, I want to know why your production has been lacking!"

This time, Vachel is silent. It is obvious Nark does not know how to take a hint, but perhaps the High Sister might.

By this time, Nark is hot under the collar; he is not used to being ignored, especially by someone he considers to be so far beneath him. "Stop being stubborn and answer my question, you worthless, little bastard," Nark growls in his anger. At this, Vachel presents him with an obscene hand gesture.

Both Sister Selene and Sister Crystal gasp and hurry to whisper to the High Sister the details of what has been done. A smile comes to her face as the High Sister turns to Vachel's general direction and scolds, "Now, now, Vachel. That was rather rude. Why do you refuse to answer Sorcerer Nark's questions?" "It's simple, High Sister," Vachel replies, "I refuse to speak to someone who does not have the tact to address me by my name. Because my name isn't demon, trash, or bastard, I will not answer." "Just as I thought. You did seem like the type to think that way," the High Sister remarks, "Perhaps you should try calling him Vachel, Sorcerer Nark."

"He is supposed to be receiving discipline, High Sister. He will not learn anything if I am lenient," Nark protests.

"And we will get nowhere if you are not."

"High Sister, we cannot give an inch."

"May I remind you that with two witnesses I outrank you?"

Nark is silent.

"Now, you will address him by name or I will do this myself."

Not wishing to suffer any more of her lecturing, Nark whispers angrily, "Why has your production been low…Vachel?" He has to force himself to speak the final word, but he manages. "Again, it's a simple thing," Vachel explains, "I'm tired, hungry, and I ache like I haven't in twenty centuries. Even a demon body cannot recover under these conditions, and therefore I can't produce."

The High Sister gasps at these words, and her eyes soon narrow into a tight glare. At her side, Sister Crystal covers her mouth with her hand. Only Vachel can see the outraged look on her face as she listens. On the other hand, Sister Selene has a look perched on her face that suggests she enjoys hearing about his plight. The thought makes his blood boil.

"You haven't been feeding him? The body requires energy to do anything. I though you would understand that," the High Sister responds. "We feared he would be too hard to control at full strength," Nark defends. The High Sister shakes her head as she responds, "Nonsense. You're just out to get him for something. Either that or your position has made you believe he is too inferior for such 'luxuries' as food and sleep." Nark shrinks back from the power in her voice as Vachel watches with a smile. Nark might be a sorcerer, but he has gotten himself into much more than he bargained for. *Yes, it seems the High Sister is much smarter than Nark wishes she were.*

Power of a Princess

Lying on her side, she buries her face into the soft pillows. The mattress makes her feel like she is snuggled into a cloud, but she is still uncomfortable. The constant strain of keeping the stone full of magic is making her head throb. A thin, pink veil hides her from those who are not allowed inside. It is a comforting thought, but not one she wishes to dwell on. It blocks some of her concentration.

Her long, black dress trails on the floor behind her as she walks, but now she has the hem pulled up to her knees, for it gets dreadfully hot in this room. Both feet are bare, as always when she is in this room. The sleeves are wide at the ends, and the front is cut low (something she has wanted to be able to wear since she turned sixteen two years ago). Her black hair is equally long and spreads out around her head as she lies there. A few strands brush the rounded cheeks she has yet to lose from her younger years. The green eyes are tightly closed against the pain in her forehead, her arms wrapped tightly around the pillow, as well.

Two maids hurry around the room, straightening drapes and dusting furniture. This can only mean that the Sisters are coming to give her the nasty, red jelly again.

She hates it with a passion, but they insist it will help her to protect the kingdom. It cannot be denied the jelly helps her throbbing head and makes her task of maintaining the barrier easier. Still, it tastes strange and leaves a metallic taste in her mouth. A sigh escapes as she curls up into a much tighter ball. "I don't want them to come today," she whispers to herself, opening her eyes to stare at the veil.

"Princess Mikya," one of the maids call in a soft voice, "Sisters Mara and Ru will be arriving shortly. Perhaps you should get ready soon." Taking the maid's advice, Mikya pushes the skirt back down to cover her ankles. She then returns to her huddled position to wait.

Closing her eyes, she begins to think of what the strange jelly might be made. The first thought to come to her is one she quickly dismisses: blood. They would never feed her something so repulsive. If given the choice, she would rather drink sewer water or eat with the hogs. The thought of having another person's blood in her mouth is too sickening for words. Moments later, there is a knock at the door, which the maid rushes to open.

"Good day, Sisters," the maid greets them with a bow. They nod to her before entering, stopping in the center of the room to wait for her to leave, which she quickly does, closing the door behind her. With a small frown at the thought of eating the jelly, Mikya rises to a sitting position. She gazes through the veil at them as they stand still. Both wear long-sleeved dresses of blue that have long, flowing skirts. All Sisters wear this color as a sign of their position.

Sister Ru stands just behind Sister Mara with the dish of red jelly balanced on her palms. Being blessed with long, blonde hair and sparkling, blue eyes, Sister Mara fancies herself quite the catch. Meanwhile, Sister Ru is not so confident, even though her brown eyes and hair have a distinct shine.

Turning toward the veil, Sister Mara parts it with a wave of her hand. "Good day, Sisters," Mikya greets once the veil is fully open. Both give her a slow bow in response before Sister Ru moves forward with the dish. It seems to be fuller today, as if they are trying to give her as much as possible while they can.

She has the urge to grimace, but keeps her face blank as she takes the dish. Her hand has a slight shake to it as she grips the spoon. A wish for them to be gone so she can make all the necessary faces, grips her for a moment, but she takes in the first spoonful anyway.

It feels slimy as it slides down her throat and makes her want to gag, but she prevents herself from doing it because the Sisters are watching. She really wishes they would go so she can make all the necessary faces. Diligently, she takes a spoonful at a time, battling her urge to vomit all the while. Finally, she is halfway done when a commotion in the corridor takes her attention away.

Both Sisters turn their heads to the door with a frown as the argument becomes louder. It sounds as if one of the maids is trying to keep a man from entering.

Suddenly, the door bursts open and one of the Elder Sorcerers makes his way in, a frantic maid at his heels. He wears a long, white robe, trimmed in gold along the hem, collar, and the cuffs of the wide sleeves. Over his heart is a gold dragon stitched carefully into the fabric and around his neck is a medallion of gold, bearing a red, blue, and green stone. His white shirt is tucked into his pants of the same color so it touches the top of his gold, belt buckle bearing the same stones as the medallion. The pants hide the tops of his black, shin-high boots. His silvery hair is held back at the base of his neck, but falls to his knees regardless.

Red eyes knit in frustration, he glares at the room in general. His jaw is taut as if he is trying to keep himself from sinking his teeth into something. This anger serves to hide some of the fine lines of his face. He does not have quite so many as the others, being that he still looks to be 49. But then, one is chosen to be an Elder based on power and wisdom, not age.

"Elder Gilden, what is happening? What's wrong?" Sister Mara asks once he has stopped pacing. "I'll have that boy's head for this," Gilden replies, shaking a finger at her to show emphasis, "Nark's gone too far with this one, Sister, and I intend to make sure he gets a swift boot up the--well, you know what I mean." "What has he done, Elder Gilden?" Sister Ru asks, confused by the commotion. Gilden throws his hands in the air in disgust as he answers, "Stupid boy's back to tormenting Vachel. As if the poor creature doesn't have enough on his plate to contend with!"

"Elder, mind whose presence you are in," Sister Mara warns. At this, Gilden waves his hand in a dismissive gesture. Sister Mara's eyes narrow, but she remains silent. "Either way, I'll need to borrow Princess Mikya from you,"

Gilden continues, pacing with his hands clasped behind his back.

"For what purpose?" Sister Mara asks.

"He won't listen to me alone, and he refuses to heed the Elders' commands unless we are all present, which is not the case because two left for Highhaven just this morning. So, I have to go above even our heads, to the princess," Gilden explains in a rush, pointing at Mikya when he mentions her title.

"You can have her once she is finished," Sister Mara replies, gesturing to the princess and the dish in her hands. Mikya cannot help but smile as they argue over her, neither one remembering that she has the final say.

"Nonsense! Something so trivial can wait. The barrier isn't going to collapse just because she doesn't eat it right on schedule," Gilden protests, moving closer to the princess. In anticipation of what he will do, Mikya places the dish beside her on the bed.

"Nevertheless, Elder, it is still important for the future," Sister Mara counters, a slight anger in her voice. "Bah! I'm talking about the here and now. If Nark has his way, there won't be any more for her to eat, anyway," Gilden replies angrily, taking Mikya's hand and pulling her to her feet.

Sister Ru cannot help but tremble at the anger she sees in Gilden's eyes; however, having dealt with such more often, Sister Mara retains her bearing. "I told you that you can have her once she is finished," Sister Mara repeats, her teeth gritted slightly. "I'd like to see you stop me," Gilden challenges with a raise of his hand. Both Sisters freeze at the sight of the green light forming in his palm. "Elder, you can't do that!" Sister Ru cries. He smiles at her as the light grows to encase both he and Mikya: "Just watch me." "Elder!" Sister Mara yells just to have them disappear before her eyes.

Mikya can feel a sharp wind tugging at her hair and sleeves, but her eyes refuse to open for her to see the surroundings. Still, she can feel Gilden's hand around hers, so her fear stays hidden. Moments later, her feet touch down on a hard, stone floor. Gilden releases her hand and starts down the corridor, his boots clicking against the stone. Not wishing to be left alone in the cold darkness, Mikya rushes after him.

The torches along the walls cast wavering shadows on the floor and walls. Being here makes her feel as if night has somehow fallen in the last few moments. She is having some trouble keeping pace with Gilden, not only because he is two heads taller than she, but because of the weight of her skirt, as well. Beads of sweat begin to slip down her face from the effort, but she keeps silent in fear of the anger he showed earlier. She can only see the back of his head, but she has the distinct feeling that the glare is still perched on his face.

Then, as if suddenly remembering something, Gilden abruptly stops. Mikya nearly falls to the floor in her effort to keep from running into him.

Glad to have a small chance to rest, she takes several silent, deep breaths. As she does so, Gilden moves over to the stone wall and presses his ear to it. He stands there for some time as if waiting for something amazing to happen. Although, what could happen in such a deserted place is beyond her.

Finally, once she has caught her breath, Gilden straightens, placing his middle finger on a stone block just above his head. Mikya has the distinct feeling he was really waiting for her to recover herself. Pressing against the block, he sends a green spark of light into the surface.

All is still for a moment until the spark returns to the surface and forms a circle at the stone's center. Nodding as if it confirms something to him, Gilden takes three steps back and raises his hand again. This proves to Mikya that he was waiting more for her than a sign of anything. This time, he moves his hand back and forth as if scrubbing a stain from the air. As he does so, the wall begins to fade and disappear, revealing a blocked archway with two soldiers guarding it.

A small cage rests to the right of the female who Mikya instantly recognizes as Lin. The other takes a short time to strike a chord, but she soon realizes he is Coby. Having both of the worst prison guards present sends a jolt of fear through Mikya. If this is where Nark is, then the person Gilden called Vachel must be dangerous. A frown decorates Gilden's face at the sight of the barrier.

"Elder Gilden!" the two gasp, giving him a hurried bow, "We were not expecting you." "Obviously," Gilden replies rather coldly as he takes Mikya's hand again. Without any hesitation, he moves forward through the barrier, Mikya at his heels.

The room beyond is made of a green crystal she has never seen before.

Gazing around, Mikya instantly spies Nark standing straight ahead with a shocked look on his face. It seems Gilden was right in assuming Nark had not expected him. To his right are the High Sister and her two aides, Sisters Selene and Crystal. However, the black-haired man sitting shackled before Nark is a mystery, and the smile perched on his face as he stares at her has a demonic quality she does not like in the least.

"Elder Gilden, good day to you, sir," Sisters Selene and Crystal greet, standing to bow properly. Gilden gives them a nod before turning to Nark who gives him a small bow with a deep glare. Sister Selene gives the High Sister a tap to indicate she should turn her head in this direction. "Good day, Elder Sorcerer Gilden," the High Sister greets, giving his general direction a nod of her head. "Good day to you, High Sister Margaret," Gilden replies, returning the nod, "I pray your students will not give you as much trouble in the future as mine are now."

Nark continues to glare as the man on the floor begins to snicker.

Mikya is quite relieved to have his gaze elsewhere and does not wish to interrupt, so she does not bother to give them a greeting.

"Now, now, Elder. All it takes is the right amount of discipline. Perhaps you should have bent him over your knee when he deserved it," the High Sister responds with a smile. This causes the man on the floor to have to cover his mouth with his hand to stifle the laughter. Gilden does not return her smile, but Mikya can tell the words have helped his mood: "I can assure you that I did, High Sister. However, it appears that I need to do it now, as well."

"That would certainly be an interesting sight to see," the man interjects, "Still, I think the High Sister has held her own in teaching the little bastard his place." A mocking smile appears on his face as he turns to Nark. Mikya blushes slightly at his vulgarity, but otherwise thinks he is not as bad as the shackles seem to suggest. Gilden is in no way amused, and wastes no time in informing him of it: "Mind your tongue in her highness's presence, Vachel, or I will personally remove those for you."

The man, Vachel as Gilden calls him, looks down at the floor with a frown. Again, Mikya is struck by the feeling that he is not as bad as the presence of the two worst prison guards suggests he is. Then, there is the threat. It seems odd to Mikya, for it is her assumption a prisoner would want to be released from his shackles. Perhaps there is a magic to them she does not understand.

She is about to ask Gilden about his comment and the possible magic to the shackles when Nark hisses, "What is it that you want, *Elder*?" Her curiosity flares at the disrespect Nark is giving Gilden, but she is unwilling to ask about *this*. Gilden might take it as her underestimating the amount of control he has over his subordinates. "Because you refuse to listen to me," Gilden responds, "I have brought Princess Mikya here to discuss how you treat your captives."

"And just what is wrong with my methods?"

"He needs sleep and food!"

This strikes a chord in Mikya and anger boils quickly into her brain. *How dare you?! Inexcusable!* "Explain this!" she demands, "Why is he not being fed or allowed sleep?" Nark is silent for a moment as Vachel flashes him a triumphant smile that exposes his fangs. "Answer me," Mikya commands in her anger. "Well...I...that is to say...the truth is--" Nark stammers, unable to think properly in the face of such sudden fury. *It is to be expected from Gilden. But, why would Princess Mikya defend a demon?*

"The truth *is*, Princess Mikya," Vachel explains, turning to her, "He hates me terribly, but he is far too much of a coward to admit that he let that sway his judgment." Gilden does not reprimand him this time, so Vachel leaves it to keep the sorcerer from doing so. "Why does he hate you so much?" she asks, the anger catching a new flow.

Vachel merely shrugs, being unwilling to give Gilden a reason to remove the shackles and bring on the pain. Although, he does know Nark hates demons of any form, especially those with human blood, as well. Little does he know, Vachel did not start out life with only a Halfling's demon power.

"Well, Nark?" Mikya demands, turning her anger back to him. "He's a bloodthirsty demon!" Nark yells in frustration. *I've been ordered to keep him contained! Dammit all!* This does little to deter Mikya who yells back, "I could not care any less! You are to feed him and give him rest or I will not only strip you of your post, but all of your rights as a human being, as well!" *He's still a living creature!*

Vachel's smile only grows wider as the princess storms off with Gilden right behind her. The High Sister stands soon after, and gives Vachel a smile of her own. Sister Crystal gives him a small, hidden wave as she stands to follow the High Sister. Just as hidden, is Vachel's silent desire to be able to acknowledge that wave, but he does not need to give Nark another way to get back at him. She and Sister Selene follow the High Sister from the room in silence as Vachel whispers, "Well, Nark, you heard her highness."

He cannot help but think it is a little unfair to force him to eat with his hands shackled behind him, but he soon decides it does not really matter. Even if he could use his hands, a boiling hot bowl of soup is just that, hot.

Still, it is food, and food made by Riko with tender care. Deciding there is no other way to do it, he takes the edge between his teeth and slowly tilts it to gulp down the steaming liquid. He winces slightly from the burn, but the warm feeling seeping into his stomach keeps him going. The bowl is soon empty and he places it back on the floor with a shake of his head: "Ow...that burns." *Understatement of the year...but no less true.*

Twenty women of the kitchen staff rush around the large room. Knives flash in the light of the fires as various items are cut to proper size. Open fires heat large pots of soups and stews. All the activity is a hint of the large gathering to be served this evening. It makes Vachel smile to know they are taking time from this tight schedule to pay him mind. One notices his bowl is empty and quickly ladles more into it as she rushes by. He is grateful for this and carefully gulps it down as he did the first.

Leaning back to wait, he feels the heat from one of the ovens seep into his back. This one is occupied with the baking of bread, while others farther down are employed with things in the dessert department. Vachel can smell several different gravies being carefully tended as a second woman drops two slices of meat into the bowl. For these he has to use a more dog-like posture, but the taste and feeling of a filling stomach are all worth it. *I'll take humiliation over starvation any day.*

He soon spies a familiar pair of boots and hurriedly sits up to smile at her. Riko has the sleeves of her blue, collared shirt rolled up above her elbows, and a white apron at her waist. The shirt is tucked into her white pants, which, in turn, slip neatly into a pair of soft, brown leather boots that lack heels. Her fists are on her hips as she frowns down at him with her smooth jaw tight. The green eyes are narrowed beneath the few stray, brown hairs that have somehow managed to escape the bun at the back of her head.

"Now, how is that for a demon to look?" she scolds gently, "You've got food all over your face." "Can't help it," Vachel replies, lifting his shoulders to show her he can't move, "I'm no contortionist, and my hands are shackled behind me." She rolls her eyes at him, as she knows perfectly well how flexible he is or is not, grabbing a towel from the rack above his head and taking it to his face. Once she is satisfied, Riko tucks the towel into her belt and marches away.

"Thanks!" Vachel calls after her, with a smirk at the knowledge they both knowing full well it will only get dirty again. A third woman drops a fresh roll in the bowl for him, and he is about to snatch it up as he had everything before it when he spies Sister Crystal moving toward him.

So, that was Riko's angle.

"Good day, Sister Crystal," Vachel greets, bowing as well as he can from his position on the floor. His head nearly touches his crossed legs. She gives him a nod before slipping to the floor beside him, her legs tucked beneath her again. He has a feeling life among the Sisters taught her to

24

do that. "High Sister Margaret sent me to see if Nark kept his promise," Sister Crystal explains with a small blush at being this close, "But can we be friends for a moment?" *Make that a strong feeling...*

"That all depends," Vachel replies with a raised eyebrow, curious to see just how far her affections go. The smile disappears from her face for a moment as she asks, "'Depends' on what?" "'Depends on' whether or not the friendship lasts just a moment," Vachel answers with a sly smile on his face at having scared her just a little. It seems she is , at the very least, determined to have a small relationship. Even friendship will work, as she desires some connection that much. Again, he has a feeling the Sisters had something to do with this mentality. The smile returns to her face and brightens as she nearly squeals, "Really? You would do that for me?" *A very, very strong feeling, that...*

"Sure as I'm a shackled captive," Vachel responds, his smile taking a slightly bitter turn as he jingles the chains. "Then...I really want you to have this," she whispers, delicately taking hold of a gold chain around her neck. As she pulls it up over her head, a red crystal slips from its hiding place between her breasts. "Interesting place to keep a treasure," Vachel remarks, staring at the sparkling surface of the trinket.

"What honorable man would look there?"

"Good point." *Honorable man? Pft. Find one around here for me.*

"My mother gave it to me before she died."

"It must be special to you." *Oh, boy. Where's this going now?*

"Yes, that is why only you can have it."

"Afraid I don't follow." *Shit, now I've done it.*

"She told me to give it to the man I love, whether he shares it or not."

Now it is Vachel's turn to blush as he turns his gaze to the floor.

"What is the matter?" she asks, spying the look on his face. "I've never had anyone say something like that to me before," Vachel confesses in a whisper, "I was usually the trinket being passed. A tool to aid someone with a love of power." Even as he says it, he has to consider how untruthful it is. The fact of the matter is that it has been a long, long time since someone has.

A frown comes to her face as she replies, "That is really sad, you know." Silently, he has to agree, but then, he is the one who has had to live it this long. "Do *you know* that I'm a demon?" he asks, gazing over at her. There is a nagging thought in the back of his mind he just cannot get rid of, and he has to figure out why. She nods, holding the chain in both fists against her chest: "And I...I still want you to have it." "Can you say that this is in spite of my being a demon?" he asks, the flush suddenly intensifying on his cheeks.

Something inside really wants her to give him the crystal, but he has to be sure she is certain and sincere. This is it. This is what was nagging at him.

"Yes, I dismissed it as a whim of my lonely soul, at first, because I knew you were a demon," Sister Crystal whispers, sounding oddly ashamed to be saying it, "But, when I saw you today, in that cage, I really wanted to attack them, just to get you free. And it made me realize how much I really did care, which is why I blushed."

"That's really sweet you know?" Vachel responds with a smile.

"So, will you accept it?" she asks, looking into his eyes. He is caught in her gaze for a moment, but he manages to reply, "If you're still willing to give it." With a nod, she places it around his neck, slipping the crystal into his shirt: "This way you will always feel a part of me close." He has the sudden thought that he would rather have much more of her close. It makes the smile widen until his stomach growls loudly in protest against his dawdling. Sister Crystal giggles softly as he blushes from embarrassment.

Taking the roll from the bowl, Sister Crystal pinches off a piece, offers it to him, and says, "It looks like you might need some help with that." Vachel does not answer as he takes the offered piece, being wary of her fingers. The women must have noticed because, when the roll is finished, Vachel notices a spoon in the bowl with the stew.

That night, as he sleeps soundly in the first bed he has been on in years, his fist is closed tightly around the crystal. *"My sweet, darling one,*

Power of a Princess

You are my only melody.
You are my favorite rhythm.
You are my soul's rhyme.
May you be the only song
I ever crave to hear."

Messenger

He made it through the barrier easily thanks to his master's magic. However, he is uncertain whether or not he will even be able to get into Nishi-Hama with all of the guards stationed in his path. *Not even Master's magic could help me with this part. After all, he's still at home.*

Perched atop a small bolder, he sits eating a slice of melon for its juices, spitting seeds when necessary. Traveling through the Shiku Desert, even using Ring Trail, is not something one does because one enjoys it. In order to keep suspicions down he had to. Otherwise he cannot say he is merely a trader from Rikogyu sent with a message for the princess. It is essential he gets inside the castle, but keeping such a ruse will be difficult.

He rubs the back of his neck in frustration, causing the four links of chain attached to the thick, black-leather collar to clank against each other. *No, not a collar!* He has to remember it does not appear to others as a collar, but his master neglected to tell him what it looks like to them. He does know it will appear as some sort of jewelry, for traders of Dehurst tend to be much wealthier than those on the other side of Hilden's gate. Then again, he is not really a trader and does not have to worry about the money situation for the moment. Of course, this fact is the reason why he has not been questioned about the gold bands around his upper arms.

His tanned skin should aid him in the ruse on the basis that he spends most of his time in the desert. The brown shirt has no sleeves and is loose to shift in the light breeze and help to prevent him from overheating. A black belt with sharp, gold studs adorning it is tight against his waist to hold the baggy, white pants in place. The pair of black combat boots reaches his shins where they cause the fabric of his pants to bulge out around the rims as they are tucked in. His hands are hidden by black gloves, the thumb of his right slipping behind the pack on his shoulder. A white, traveling cloak is draped around his slim shoulders.

Frowning, he glares at the wall of Nishi Hama with a pair of violet eyes. His black hair is short, yet shaggy, as it flutters in the wind. A pair of gold earrings slaps against his face in the wind, as well. He finds himself wishing the line of his jaw was much harder every time he feels their touch. Each is a small hoop attached to a dangling, triangular plate that nearly reaches his shoulder. He is silently glad he has been blessed with a pair of human-shaped ears instead of those that resemble demons' or faeries' like other Hybrids.

Spitting his final seed into the sand, he stands and tosses the stripped rind over his shoulder. It is time to begin the mission. He thrusts a hand into his pocket as he starts off toward the city. The sand makes a slight crunch beneath his boots with every step, announcing his presence to the sharp-eared guards. He watches the whole column straighten through the sand picked up by the wind.

A smile comes to his face at this sight. In the real world, a lack, or perceived lack, of discipline almost always works in the enemy's favor. When he finally makes it to them, he stops before the largest one with a smile on his face.

"State your name and business," the guard demands, gazing down at the boy over his mound of black armor. "Ven Heoshin. I'm a trader here to give Princess Mikya a message from King Nisho of Rikogyu," he replies, his smile never wavering. The guard does not seem pleased with this answer, as he demands, "Why would a king need a trader to send a message?"

Here comes the best part. "Weird things have been happenin' in the desert. There are some strange shadows roamin' about with magic powers," Ven answers, lowering his voice, "Most people are afraid to go near it anymore. Guess the king thought I could handle it because I've been through it all my life." "So, he was correct, then?" the guard asks. "Sorta. But, this little trinket keeps me protected, too," Ven replies, gesturing toward his neck. *It is time to find out what the master disguised it as.*

"A ring protects you?" the guard asks in disbelief with a raised eyebrow. *So, it's the old ring on a chain trick.* Ven nods as he says, "Yep. I've no idea why, but it does." The guard still looks suspicious, but finding nothing reasonably wrong, he slowly turns to the large metal door and taps once. The sound rings through the air, and there is a pause before any other is heard. After this pause, the sound of a lock turning is heard as the door moves up just enough to allow Ven to slip underneath. Once it is closed behind him, Ven smiles to himself for accomplishing the first objective of his mission. *I've infiltrated the territory of Princess Mikya of Dehurst.*

Spread out along the dirt road are several small houses made of what appear to be mud bricks. The red, tile roofs give off heat waves as a testament to the rising temperature of the morning. Women in simple dresses move about through the small, neighborhood market, buying necessary items for their families. Goods are much cheaper on the outskirts, but one rarely sees a respectable person taking the time to venture out into these poorer neighborhoods.

The gold coins in the pouch at his hip make Ven feel all the more important as he makes his way through them, searching for a piece of fruit he can eat as he walks. Deciding on a pair of apples, one red, one green, Ven drops a coin in the vender's hand and walks away before the man has a chance to argue about its worth.

Sinking his teeth through the green skin of the apple, Ven has to be wary of the juices. As always, the better produce is to be found in the out skirts. One is not going to get a good piece of meat bartering with worthless fruit and vegetables; it has to be the best it could possibly be.

As he makes his way deeper into the city, he has to move to the crude, stone sidewalks to avoid the horses and carts. The buildings are made of wood in this part of the city. Things are becoming more "civilized" and he receives several prying looks until they spy the jingling pouch at his waist, the gold on his arms, and at last the earrings. Of course, could they see the collar, their opinion would instantly revert back to the first: *trash, lowlife.*

No, the correct term is servant.

He finishes the apple, core and all, so no one will see the fanged markings and raise an unnecessary panic. Soon the very sidewalk becomes better done. The women's dresses come in every color and style imaginable, and even the men are dressed as sophisticatedly as they can in the heat rising up from the sand. Gold peaks out at him everywhere the eye can see and even from several places where it should not be able to. His presence is met with upturned noses and a general disdain. He meets every look with a steady violet gaze. Even with this determination, he is thankful when the castle wall comes into sight.

He immediately steps up to one of the guards. Both are done in black armor with a red dragon splashed across their chests. The one before him demands, "State your name and business." "Ven Heoshin. I've come to give Princess Mikya a message from King Nisho of Rikogyu." He leaves out the part about being a trader just to make the exchange easier. If he explains that to the guard, he will have to do so with Mikya as well, and she will be surrounded by Sorcerers and Sisters when he tries it. The guard turns to the other who looks skyward in thought. Ven is silent as he waits, unsure if this is a good sign or not. If things do not go right he will have to use his magic, which he does not want to have to do.

Finally, the second guard gives the first a nod. "You may enter, we have been expecting you," the guard explains, taping his chest three times in signal. There is the sound of a lock clicking, and the wooden doors open in their stone frame. Ven strides through into an immense room packed with people. It appears as if half the nobility of Dehurst is packed inside.

In an effort to keep his eyes from popping out of his head, Ven moves forward into the crowd in search of Princess Mikya and the sorcerer his master called Gilden. He has been shown what they look like, but it is still some time before he spots them. However, when he does, Ven sees something he really does not want to: she is surrounded by several Elder Sorcerers, and the High Sister along with her two aides.

He recognizes Mikya by her green eyes and the gold tiara resting atop her long, black hair. Her black dress is a little too revealing for one of her stature, in Ven's opinion, but then he never has understood royalty. Gilden's back is to him, yet Ven recognizes him by his long, silver hair. Suddenly, Mikya spots him and pushes past the sorcerer to rush over. Seeing as she has been expecting a messenger and he sticks out like a sore thumb amongst all the finery, Ven is not surprised to watch her doing it. Remembering himself as she stops before him, Ven places a fist over his heart and bows: "Strength to Princess Mikya."

When he rises and spies the confused look on her face, he instantly regrets the bow. He acted without thinking and gave her a greeting from the other side of Hilden's Gate, a Darkhaven greeting. "Forgive me, your highness. I have been around these parts only a short time and keep confusing this land's customs with those of my homeland," he apologizes quickly.

He spies the glint of recognition in Gilden's eyes. Now he has spent all this time only to be found out at victory's doorstep. He waits for Gilden to speak up, but the sorcerer never does.

Princess Mikya gives her nod in response with a smile as she says, "That's understandable. I've only recently become fluent at it myself." Inwardly he breathes a sigh of relief. She probably has no clue Darkhaven even exists. So as to keep from attracting any more attention to himself, Ven gives Gilden the proper bow and greeting, which the sorcerer acknowledges with his nod.

"Have you eaten yet?" Mikya asks once he has given a greeting to those gathered around her. "No, your highness, I came here directly," Ven explains. "Excellent," she replies with a smile, "We're just about to have dinner. You should join us." The others smile in agreement, but the look in their eyes tells Ven he needs to be more careful.

Suddenly, a bell sounds, and the room becomes louder as the people begin making their way into the next and pushing past him. Taking hold of his hand, Mikya leads him through an open set of immense doors into the dining hall. He has to hold himself back to keep from curling his own fingers around her warm hand. That is something reserved for family and lovers, not those who outrank him. His hands are to be kept as far away from these as the royalty will allow him to have them. He glances up in time to see the large table where he will have to see to his next meal. The high table stands in the center of the room on a raised platform.

It is large enough to seat twelve comfortably, while those positioned around it have room for only four. Mikya gives him the seat to Gilden's right who sits at hers. When they arrive, the table is already laden with bowls of fruit and rolls. Ven watches silently as the Sorcerer Elders and High Sister take their seats before gazing over at the princess. She is smiling as she whispers something into a maid's ear. *People around here smile too much.*

"So, how has Nisho been lately?" Gilden asks, leaning forward to take a piece of fruit from the bowl. Following suit, Ven replies, "I don't know. He sent one of his advisors to have me deliver the message. I was on my way out of the city when he caught up with me." Gilden takes a bite, gazing off in thought. Noticing that his hand is tensed too tightly around the fruit, Ven quickly takes a bite, as well.

This time he is wary and turns it so the mark is down.

"Perhaps he wasn't feeling well," Mikya suggests. Gilden nods at her, no doubt having just considered the possibility. Gazing over at the princess, Ven notices a woman placing a bowl on the table before her.

She does the same for every person at the table before slipping away as quietly as she came. Ven shifts his gaze to the contents of the bowl. It is a soup consisting of little more than a thick broth with vegetables. Still, he is grateful there is no meat to be found; he does not wish to have to explain his aversion to it just yet. He continues to hold the fruit in his hand, but because he has not had a chance to rid it of the incriminating marks, he deposits it in one of his pockets.

Picking up the soupspoon, he beings eating in silence. It is a habit, for the master does not allow him to speak at the table unless spoken to. "I like your necklace," Mikya says, interrupting his thoughts, "Where did you get it?" Swallowing his mouthful quickly, Ven answers, "The ring is a gift from my mother, but I bought the chain." The master also expects a prompt response from him.

Gilden's eyes narrow slightly, but not enough for a mortal to detect. Ven, however, sees it as if the sorcerer were mouthing the word "liar". *Perhaps, even for an Elder so young, he has the power to see past the master's spell. Will he be able to tell what the collar is used for if he can?*

Soon, however, they take their focus off of him and begin to speak to one of the other elders. Ven takes this opportunity to finish the soup, struggling to keep his hand steady. Just as he manages to finish, another woman comes forward to remove the bowls and place empty plates before them. Right behind her is a line of women carrying large trays and bowls. These replace the fruit as each moves forward quickly and departs to serve other tables. Ven cannot help but find this odd. The master does not allow women the chance to do much for him at the castle. Most of the positions these women occupy are reserved strictly to men. He prefers a more silent, hidden place for the she-demons of his court.

Ven gazes at it all with apprehension.

Several of the trays bear large pieces of meat. Just looking at them reminds him of the things he has seen his master do to the insides of people, has helped the master do to the insides of people. A wave of nausea washes over him, so he looks down at his plate.

Those around him begin to fill their plates and pass items around to each other. Ven takes special care to avoid all of the meat unless he absolutely has to help pass it. Once everyone is settled, another woman steps forward to fill their glasses. Ven notices she is the only one of those he has seen who is wearing pants, another thing the master would not have allowed. Her brown hair is pulled to the back of her head in a bun, and even though she is smiling, her green eyes remain severe. He feels her gaze pass over him and linger at his neck for a moment. She gazes up at Gilden, who shakes his head, before moving on to the next person.

Once again in silence, Ven takes his fork to the vegetables and gravy he has amassed on the plate. No one bothers to speak to him during this time. However, when the food is passed around a second time, Gilden takes notice of his refusal of the meat.

"What's the matter?" he asks, taking a drink. Ven stabs a potato before he whispers another lie, "I don't like meat. I've hated it ever since I had to help slaughter one of the family hogs." "Understandable. I haven't been able to trust bread since I saw an Elder killed with it," Gilden replies, "The poison did horrible things to that poor man." At this, Ven reaches forward and plucks a roll from the pile.

"I can see you have no such aversion," Gilden says with a smile. Ven pulls is apart and uses it to soak up some of the gravy as he explains, "I can't afford to give up the energy in it." He takes a bite of the gravy-soaked roll as if that ends the matter. Deciding he is not getting anywhere with this, the Sorcerer resolves to be more direct: "Would you like to tell me why you're wearing a Shiku Hara?"

"What?" Ven asks in a whisper, having never heard it called that before. "They can't hear us, so I want you to be truthful with me," Gilden replies, "Now, why are you wearing a Shiku Hara?" "And how do I know you won't try to discredit me with the princess if I tell you?" Ven demands. "I could turn you in right now for lying to Princess Mikya and have you hanged for treason," Gilden threatens.

"I didn't lie to her...she's the one who assumed."

"No, you lied to her guards, which is the same."

"I already said I'm not from around here. What more do you want?"

"Yes, you are of Darkhaven. What business do you have with Mikya?"

"It's her demon I have the business with, if you must know."

"Good. Now, tell me about the collar."

"My master makes me wear it, but I'll tell you nothing more."

"Thank you for the cooperation. But, she'll not allow you to kill him."

Crystal for Curses

He lies amongst the eggs again, the pain made all the worse from his temporary separation from it. The blood refuses to allow him to even breathe properly now. It must be Nark's doing, to pay him back for causing Gilden and the princess to side with him. The fact he did nothing to gain their aid makes his blood boil and forces him to tremble from the ache in his head caused by this new tension and the pain he feels in the rest of his body.

He hates them all with a vengeance, and the blood pouring out of him because of their stupid curse does not make it any better. Still, knowing he has not only her crystal, but Sister Crystal's love as well makes him feel somewhat better. The problem really lies in removing the curse so he can be with her. He coughs loudly in pain as he grips the crystal tightly through his shirt. A sharp, ragged breath is all he can muster before the blood heaves its way up his throat.

If she could see him now, what would become of her feelings? Even he is repulsed by the condition of his blood-coated face and hair. A small tear is spared for her that she chose him, but something inside refuses to let him give any more.

When dinner is at last finished, Mikya leads Ven and Gilden away from the rest. The three make their way out of the large room and down the corridor to a small wooden door. Behind it lies the room containing the crystal she uses to produce the barrier that protects them. When Mikya moves to the center, Gilden follows close behind, protectively. "So, I understand you have a message for me," she begins, looking at him with a smile.

It is only now that she sees the faint shadow of something around his neck. For a moment, it seems as if the black ring she sees is being pulled to the surface by some magic, making it hide the gold necklace from view. However, just as suddenly as it appeared, it disappears.

Ven smiles back, but there is a sly, mischievous air to it. "It seems you're even slower than your elder here," he replies, moving forward to smile directly into her face. "What?" she asks, confusion spreading out on her face. This sudden change has her frightened; Ven isn't the man he was only moments ago. "The only message I have to give you concerns your demon. I--" he begins. "Wait! What do you mean 'my demon'?" Mikya interrupts, becoming even more confused. Ven gives a long, ringing burst of laughter. "So, you've been keeping secrets from her, as well," Ven accuses Gilden.

She turns to him, shocked, as he stands silent, avoiding her eyes. "What is he talking about?" Mikya demands quietly. "He's speaking of Vachel. The one you ordered Nark to take better care of," Gilden whispers. "Heh. And he's being used to create that magic jelly," Ven adds with a much more demonic smile, "It's made of--"

42

"Don't!" Gilden interjects in a pleading voice, his eyes even begging Ven to keep quiet, "It'll hurt her!"   "So, Vachel's pain means nothing to you?" Ven asks with a raised eyebrow. Gilden falls silent, his gaze slipping back to the floor. He is shamed by his divided loyalty; it is obvious on his face. Mikya is still trying to divine what they are really talking about. She cannot understand what pain Vachel is suffering that a prisoner should not.

"I thought so," Ven replies, turning back to Mikya, "Your magic jelly is made of blood…demon blood…Vachel's blood."

Blood? Demon blood?! Vachel's blood?!!

The words freeze in her mind as she stands still, staring wide-eyed at him. *No…they wouldn't do this to me, to him. They wouldn't!* His smile of triumph makes her skin crawl. "Now that you know this, I can really give you the message," Ven whispers, "I'm here to take your demon."

There is something in the castle that does not belong, and he can sense it moving about. The aura has a strange feel to it, as if several types of being exist within at the same time. It is not a Halfling, of that he is certain. He has sensed Halflings before. He's been one for some time now. *Hell, my own sister is a Halfling; I should know.   The only other explanation is a Hybrid, but I sincerely doubt that is the case. There have been no Hybrids in Dehurst for quite some time. Try four bloody centuries! The mortals saw to that, now didn't they. But then, what of those in Darkhaven? It is possible. Not at all*

probable, but possible, certainly. It is also possible that the king himself is running around Dehurst in broad daylight stark naked!

Still, he has not been there for nearly five centuries, and it is impossible to get any information from in here. *A psychic could not get any information from here!*

A cough racks him, allowing his thoughts to break away from the past. Now, he can clearly tell the creature is on the move. Surprisingly enough, Mikya and Gilden seem to be traveling with it. Other than that, he cannot tell anything. Curling up against the cold, Vachel pulls out the crystal to look at it. The red surface sparkles in the magic-made sunlight of the cave. It is oddly alive, as if telling him that it somehow wishes there was something it could do to help. *Yeah right! Maybe the pain is just beginning to affect my brain. The Crystal of Yossa is the only one I've ever had speak to me.*

Still, it makes him smile to think Sister Crystal cared enough for him to give him her most precious possession. It makes him wish he had something to give her in return, like more of his time and energy. Presently he does not have much of either to spare. Sighing, he shakes his head with a small smile at the crystal. He kisses it, wishing he could do the same to Sister Crystal's sweet lips, before replacing it beneath his shirt so as to keep the blood away.

Suddenly, he hears footsteps coming from the door. A sigh slips from him before a rush of blood pushes its way up his throat. All the muscles of his abdomen are tense and aching from the almost constant heaves. He can still hear the footsteps and tries to curl up farther against the cold surrounding him, but it only causes an extremely large amount to force its way from him, nearly choking him.

It takes a few minutes, but finally the footsteps cease above his head. He turns his head slightly to gaze up and finds Riko standing above him. "Yes?" he asks without trying to hide his confusion. Her face is contorted in worry and disgust as he brings up another rush of blood, coughing uncontrollably. She waits for the sound and trembling to stop before saying anything.

Then, "There's a Hybrid roaming around. He's from Darkhaven and has a Shiku Hara." "Wearing it or having it?" Vachel asks in a whisper. It is all he can muster presently. "Wearing it, but there was a spell over it, masking its presence. Gilden knows and has been keeping an eye on him," Riko explains.

Vachel suddenly feels a spark of energy take him as he gives her a demonic smile and, pulling himself to a sitting position, says, "If he's from Darkhaven and wearing a Shiku Hara, he has to be one of Rust's. Meaning, his real interest lies with me, and not the princess."

Riko nods as she requests, "Just make sure you take special care of yourself. If not for me, then do it for Sister Crystal." "What about for both of you? I think I can handle it for two people. I've not gotten quite that pathetic, dear sister," Vachel replies with a warm smile. He has to turn away and empty his mouth of new blood only moments after.

"I still can't believe you get me to eat this stuff," Riko remarks, "Just watching you makes me want to vomit." Vachel gives her a blood-coated smile, as if saying it is just a gift he has. "But, it's best this way: fresh. Hasn't been squeezed through intestinal lining coated in wizard's sand," Vachel adds to the smile, poking a freshly hardened blob. "That's what they feed the princess?" Riko asks disgustedly. Ignoring her question, he grabs a handful and advises, "You should eat some now, while there's an opportunity." "But, wouldn't that put you behind?" she asks, eyeing the handful with distaste.

Slamming his fist as hard as he can into his stomach, Vachel brings up twice the normal amount of blood. "There, it's been compensated for. *Now eat it,*" he commands, holding up his hand. Knowing she will not get out of it now, Riko takes it from him and quickly swallows.

She makes a twisted face of disgust, shivering slightly.

He nods to her before saying: "Good. Now go worry about your kitchen." Riko slowly returns his nod before turning away and moving toward the door. It is obvious she does not want to leave. She never does. Of course, knowing this fact does not change his mind. If her information is correct, the Hybrid is coming to him, and from what he sensed, it will be bringing Mikya and Gilden. She does not need to be found down here. It is off limits to anyone without the proper access, and no one even knows they are related (which he wants to remain true), so she does not have it.

The energy of his excitement expiring, Vachel lies back down. He closes his eyes and thinks, trying to decide his course of action for when the three arrive. An odd scent reaches his nose, and his eyes instantly snap open. *The Hybrid is already here!* Jerking to his knees, Vachel cries, "Riko!" However, just as the words escape, the doors fly open before her.

The Hybrid is right in front of her with Mikya and Gilden right behind him. Vachel reaches out only to receive a jolt of pain shoot through the arm extended out of the circle of eggs. Giving a small growl of protest, he glares at the scene. The Hybrid grips Riko's forearm tightly, spinning her around as he marches her back toward the center to Vachel.

When the group makes it to him, the Hybrid pushes Riko forward to the ground. "I understand from this one that you're Vachel," the Hybrid whispers with a triumphant smile. *Great, a mind reader on top of it all!*

"Perhaps," Vachel replies coldly, "Who are you that wishes to know?" "Ven Heoshin, it's a pleasure. We have some things to discuss," he answers. "Destroy the eggs first," Vachel responds, pointing to the ring around him, "I will discuss nothing as a prisoner."

As he speaks, Vachel casts a glance to the princess. Her eyes are wide as she stares, trembling. He finally has his wish, but it does not have the effect he wanted. All this trembling is too benign a punishment for what has been done to him thus far.

Then, he turns on Gilden and says, "You know how to do it, Elder, get rid of them." Quickly, Gilden raises a hand above his head then brings it down with a jerk. Vachel can tell he only heeded the request because of guilt. Still, all the eggs disappear into the green light and the pain lifts.

With the eggs gone, Vachel begins the task of ingesting the solid blood around him. It has part of his demon power within, which he needs. The others look on in disgust as he bolts it down as quickly as possible. It sounds like a large beast devouring another's insides. Mikya is forced to close her eyes and clamp her hands over her ears. As usual, Gilden rushes to her in an effort to soothe her. As she gazes on, Riko has to hold a hand over her mouth. Only the Hybrid, Ven as he calls himself, is able to keep a steady gaze on the proceedings. As he swallows the jelly, Vachel can feel his scalp tingling. His hair is lengthening back to reach the small of his back, where it belongs.

When he is finally finished, Vachel realizes he feels better than he had when he woke this morning. Having missed the ability to do it, he runs a casual hand through his hair. Then, with an impish smile on his face, he comments, "Now that was good. And to think they made the princess eat it only after it's been pushed through wizard-sand-coated intestinal walls."

Mikya gives a distressed squeal as Gilden stares at him wide-eyed. "Vachel! That's absolutely disgusting!"

Riko cries. Vachel stands and brushes himself off before he replies, "Isn't it though? I mean, who wants to eat wizard's sand?"

Ven smirks at this, but remains silent.

"You know what she meant, Vachel," Gilden bursts in his anger. Licking his lips in thought, Vachel whispers, "You know, I think I might have just missed it. Sorry, not as quick on my feet as I used to be. Five centuries of living in the same circle, covered in blood, will do that to you." His smile is demonic in nature and spares them no hint of his blood-covered fangs: "I'm not one to complain, but I really needed a reason to get the hell out of this stinking hole in the ground."

"Does this mean you're willing to discuss my reasons for coming to you?" Ven asks, staring into Vachel's eyes. In response, Vachel gives him a shallow nod. He has to know what Rust has in store for him this time. "Good to hear. I need your aid to find the Crystal of Yossa. My master wants it and advised me to find a demon 'living' in Dehurst. You are the only one I have come across," Ven explains. *Liar. You knew very well that I am the only demon alive in Dehurst. Rust is the one who helped put me here...through* her.

"You should have known there would be one if any at all. Demons come from Darkhaven. It is the faerie race that accumulates natively in Dehurst," Vachel responds in a flat voice as if it is common knowledge, "Now, what's so special about this crystal?" He will follow the ruse for now.

"It's a crystal for curses, put simply. But, there are other uses."

"Cure or cause?" *As if I have to ask.*

"Yes. It can also give power."

"No doubt the reason your master wants it." *I knew the Sisters wouldn't give it back to him once it was in their clutches. But he doesn't listen to his servants.*

"The populace of Darkhaven cannot be ruled by a weak king."

"A babe would know as much."

Vachel can tell the others are listening intently, and he is struck by the fact that he and Ven have cut them from the conversation. Still, he has to know more before he will make a decision. He has to know exactly what Rust wants him to have forgotten over his long centuries in captivity. "What of the princess and elder?" Vachel asks, gesturing toward them. Ven smiles as he replies, "They have agreed to follow." Vachel looks to them and they nod, avoiding his eyes. *Fools. Complete and utter idiots.*

"Why bring them?" he asks. *Has Rust finally gotten his head out of his ass and realized what he could control?* "Their power will be useful," Ven answers, "And my master will reward me for bringing them." *Just as I thought. Rust wants Mikya in his clutches.* "'Much easier to conquer a country when you have its queen-to-be and her most trusted advisor in your clutches,'" Vachel responds sourly, "A wise warrior once said that of an enemy. Heh! And that enemy beheaded him. I believe he was your master's first and only challenger." *I also believe I was the one to behead him…*

Ven nods in recognition, a smile on his face. "I also recall him declaring he would fight to the end," Vachel continues, "He did…to the end of Rust's sword, anyway." *Ahem, yes…to the ends of my claws, anyway.*

A small snicker escapes him at this thought.

"How do you know the king's name?" Gilden interjects. Vachel gives him a smile full of pity. The man is even more stupid than he first thought he was. "He's the bastard who stripped me of half my demon power and turned me into a bloody Halfling," Vachel replies, only a hint of venom in his voice, "Of course, it saved me from loosing a few things when the sorcerers put this curse on me."

Gilden winces at the thought in silence. *It seems he already knows the details of said curse. Interesting…* "Why don't you share with the audience? They seem so eager to learn," Ven suggests, his smile taking an impish turn. Vachel smiles, as well; it *is* time they heard the truth.

"'*Tishoku Denav* is a blood curse of the highest order, requiring the most care and patience to perform properly'…or so the book goes," Vachel begins, doing his best to make this a perfect quote just to give that added little punch, "'First, find a demon or Halfling between the ages of 1500 and 2700 years. It must be male and posses the ability to wield some sort of elemental magic.' Mine happens to be a lovely little grouping of all of them, if you want to know.

Anyway, 'be advised'…heh, heh, what a way to put it…'be advised, a demon requires the removal of the testicles, while a Halfling's may merely be injected with a liquid metal, preferably lead.' You see? They might be useless, but at least they're still attached." For added effect, Vachel shifts his weight to his other hip, making his thighs brush slightly.

Now, Riko is forced to close her eyes tight as she trembles. Mikya has fallen to the ground and Vachel can see tears slipping from her chin even though her hands cover her eyes. Having difficulty with the explanation himself, Gilden does not try to comfort her. Ven's smirk has grown in size as he listens. Seeing the half-hidden tremble of the Hybrid's hands, Vachel can tell it is only an act, which gives him more reason to continue.

"The next step is just as nasty, but I want you to imagine what it feels like. Still, don't let your imagination get too carried away with you," Vachel continues, "'Second, take special care to select four children, two female, two male, who are as pure as possible. Put each to sleep as you need them, then cleanly remove their heads. With each, remove all the blood and entrails, but save half the blood for a later step. Now, grind the solid and liquid together until it has become a slippery paste. This is to be applied to the demon, or Halfling's, skin until the paste is gone.' Let me tell you, that's quite a layer once its all said and done. 'Bury him three feet below the surface, horizontally, in wizard's sand to be left for a period of twenty-four hours.'"

Finally, the smirk slips from Ven's face, and his hands are clenched into fists at his sides. Riko has emptied the contents of her stomach over the ground. He warned her not to let her imagination run wild. Mikya has slipped into a shock as she sits hunched over, gripping her middle. A look of mingled disbelief and horror is spread over Gilden's face as he trembles, still on his feet. He might have known about the curse, but hearing it first hand is still too much for anyone.

Vachel notices his valiant effort to remain calm, but also knows it is futile. The whole process is just too sickening, which is why Vachel is so valuable. No one wants to have to perform the curse.

"Now, for the final touch," Vachel adds, "Last, 'begin to boil the blood an hour before the demon or Halfling is to be removed from the sand. When the time arrives, the "victim" is to be thrown, headfirst, into the liquid.' It hurts like a bitch, I'd like you to know. 'He is to be left for exactly three hours, any more or less is dangerous'…for the victim anyway. 'As a test, place the victim in a ring of the Blood Eggs for two days. If it is too long, the victim will begin convulsing and blood will seep from every orifice. However, if it is too short, the victim will not produce. Be warned, to prevent the knowledge of this procedure from spreading to any unnecessary ears, those whose time is too short should be immediately disposed of.' End quote."

The finality of it gives even Vachel goose bumps. *Or, it could just be the cold.* Either way, it is still a little frightening to think about. There is no room for error, and no turning back. The curse is just plain dangerous, and there is nothing else to it. "What kind of sorcerers would do such a thing?" Riko whimpers, tears in her eyes. Vachel has the urge to take her in his arms and comfort her, but he knows she would not appreciate it in front of the princess and Gilden, let alone in front of a perfect stranger.

"Fourteen generations of elders ago, there was a small sect who had a fetish for curses," Vachel explains, "The *Tishoku Denav* was one they all enjoyed. They just couldn't find a reason to perform it." "Until the fall of the empire," Gilden whispers, shuddering at the thought. "The new king needed help keeping up the barrier," Vachel replies, "*I was their twenty-seventh attempt.*" The color drains from Gilden's face as he slowly mouths the words.

"Yep…it was always that last step. Three men I came to think of as brothers were killed by it. All three had been left in too long," Vachel whispers, shaking his head.

Not wishing to let the others see his trembling hands, Ven turns away: "I propose we leave tomorrow evening. That should give you enough time to plan." The words are spoken just a little too quickly to hide how he really feels. Just as the words escape his mouth, Nark bursts through the doors in a rage. Gilden quickly steps behind the princess to hide her trembling, tearstained form even though his pale face can tell the same story. At the sight of Nark, Ven stiffens as if he were a soldier whose commanding officer has just come into sight.

Vachel watches this with a raised eyebrow as he bends down and slowly scoops up an egg that fits neatly in his palm. As Nark brushes past Ven, he demands, "What's the meaning of this? What's happened to the eggs?" "They're gone," Vachel answers, moving forward with his hands behind him. Having the egg in his palm is causing him pain, but he hides it.

"What do you mean 'gone'?" Nark demands, turning on him. "Magic was used to do this," Vachel replies, smashing the bloody, slime-filled egg into Nark's face, "Only it wasn't so messy." Fury spreads out on Nark's face through the slime as he stands stunned. Only Vachel laughs as he leads the way out of the room, calling back to Nark, "See ya later, bucky!"

Vachel's Crystal

She makes her way down the corridor to her room, a small yawn escaping. Spending a party following the High Sister around gets tiring after a while. It might be an honor to be her aide, but it is still extremely boring. Even Sister Selene seemed agitated at having to spend the evening with the High Sister, and she is next in line for the position. What she needs right now is a good night's sleep. When she arrives at her room, she slowly opens the door to have a hand grip her wrist and tug her quickly inside.

She is about to strike out when she sees the person's smiling face. "Vachel?" Sister Crystal gasps, "Did anyone see you? You could get into big trouble for being here."

"No one sees me unless I want them to," Vachel replies, trying to reassure her, "Besides, I really missed you, and this is worth any kind of trouble." It is more the smile than the words that are reassuring, but she feels better, either way.

Moving forward with a smile, she leans against his chest as he wraps his arms around her. She can feel the crystal beneath his shirt as she whispers, "You know, I have really missed you, too." Looking up at him, she watches as his smile grows wider. "I'm going tomorrow evening to get this wretched curse removed," he whispers, leaning his head down so that their foreheads touch. She blushes without meaning to as she asks, "What then?"

"Then I'll return, and you'll be mine for all of eternity and even longer," he answers with a smile. "You know, that is really sweet," she replies, leaning up so that their noses touch. Her arms slip up and around his neck as he pulls her closer.

Finally, she allows herself to take the next step and presses her lips to his. He gratefully accepts the kiss, returning it. They break away slowly only for him to cover her mouth with his again. Soon, his kisses begin to slip down her throat. Each travels farther down until he reaches her collarbone and she stops him.

"Vachel, I cannot do this here. If we get caught, they will hurt you," Sister Crystal whispers dismally. He smoothes her stray hair from her face as he asks, "What about if I take you elsewhere? Or do you want me to wait? I'll be fine either way." This is a lie, but he is hoping she will feel as he does.

"I *am* afraid for you, but I do not think I can bear to wait now," she confesses, looking away. Inwardly, he breathes a sigh of relief. "Then, follow me," he replies, taking her hand. Pressing his ear to the door, Vachel determines the hallway is empty and slips out, leading Sister Crystal behind.

He picks his way carefully to the room the princess gave him to use for the time being. It is out of most people's way so they do not meet up with anyone until they make it close to the door. Vachel releases her hand and pushes her back a step. The person is a Sister, so he gives her the greeting before pretending to continue. Because this Sister is of higher rank than she, Sister Crystal gives a greeting, as well. When she catches up with him, Vachel whispers, "Well done, little one," as he slips his hand around hers.

Slipping inside, Vachel closes the door behind them and runs his finger over it to draw an "X" as he says, "Aesdel." He whispers, "That should keep anyone passing from hearing something they shouldn't," to Sister Crystal's raised eyebrow. It is now that she notices the length of his hair. "How did your hair get so long all of a sudden?" she asks. "Magic. When I was freed from the eggs, it grew back to its proper length," he explains, deciding to spare her the gruesome details of how he ate his own blood. "I like it this way," she replies with a smile, "It gives you a regal look."

Secretly, she wants him to stop talking and take up where he left off. However, before she can let him know, she realizes he is digging into the closet. She gives his back a confused look, but does not voice it. Soon, he produces a short, thin nightgown and hands it to her, saying: "I don't want you to strangle yourself."

Sister Crystal nods, unzipping the back of the dress and slipping it off. She then pulls the nightgown over her head. It is now that she realizes that it falls to the middle of her thighs. Being bare besides the small garment makes her feel uncomfortable standing all alone. Gazing over at him, she finds Vachel waiting across the room for her. He has removed his boots and shirt, but the crystal remains on its chain around his neck, as if he is determined to keep it with him at all times.

Smiling at the sight, she moves over to him. He takes her hand again, leading her over to and finally onto the bed. She snuggles in close to him as he wraps his arms around her again. The coldness of his skin startles her and she asks, "Why are you so cold?" "It has to be cold in the cave for my blood to turn to jelly," he whispers slowly, "The only reason I was warm the other day was because I was leaning against that oven." She smiles before kissing his chest and replying, "Then, let me be your oven, this time." At this, he turns her head to face him and whispers, "Sounds good to me."

It makes her face flush again.

With a small laugh, he covers her mouth with his. In response, she pushes against him, challenging his force. He smiles against her skin, his fingers tracing a line up her spine. As he progresses down her throat, this time, his hands find their way to her shoulders and slip the thin straps from them to gently push the gown down and out of his way. She slips her fingers into his hair, running her fingers through it and sending a tingling sensation from his scalp through him.

As he slowly moves down her chest, she stiffens, accidentally pulling his hair as she does. He smiles against her skin as he feels her release his hair for a moment. "Do…not…stop," she whispers in response to his pause. He slowly moves back up, running his tongue over previously kissed areas. Her fingers are now tangled in his hair, and she jerks hard against his scalp. This time, he does not take the time to pause, but instead continues his work.

Slipping down all the farther, he slips his tongue gently into her belly button. He takes the time to run his tongue gently around it, causing her to giggle in protest to the tickling. As he trails his mouth down to her thigh, his fingers search between her legs. Her fingers are still tangled in his hair, and they pull insistently when he slips one of his own inside her. Nipping at her thigh, he strokes her, listening to the soft cries slipping from her throat. This is all he can give to her for now, and he nuzzles against her skin, taking pride in her pleasure.

Unable to stop himself when he feels her tighten around his finger, Vachel slides his fangs into her skin. It is only enough to have a small taste of her blood, but he knows she feels it because of the extra gasp that spills from her throat. When she is finished, he gently licks the two small wounds before turning his eyes to hers. There is a small look of wonder on her face, and he can guess why.

The Sisters of Dehurst are known mostly for their purity, or at least a sense of it. While among those of their order, they would rarely dare to be with a man. That his fingertip met no resistance other than the usual tightness, tells him she is not as pure as she appears, and he knows she is not one to break her oath. This says to him that Sister Crystal was taken before she was rescued by the Sisters. No doubt, it was a traumatic experience. And no doubt that was more why she hesitated when confronted with her feelings than because he was a demon.

With that, he slowly pulls the gown back up to cover her, helping her to untangle her fingers from his hair. "What is it?" she asks when he lifts his eyes to hers. "Any more is bad luck for the first," he replies. In truth he does not want her to discover one of the side effects of the curse through closer scrutiny. It is bad enough to know it exists himself.

Snuggling in closer to him, she pretends to be disappointed as she replies, "Fine then, I guess I can content myself with this." She can feel his heart beating rapidly beneath her fingers and realizes he is forcing himself to stop, as well. She finds herself regretting what she said, even if it was only a joke. "Oh, don't sound so disappointed," he whispers, kissing her again. She suddenly finds that the sweat on her skin is making her cold. Without meaning to, she begins to shiver. In response, Vachel reaches down and pulls a blanket up over them both. "Thank you," she replies with a smile. He merely nods his head as he slips his arm around her again.

Departure

He lies silent for another hour after Sister Crystal leaves to tend to her duties. The crystal digs into his palm as he grips it, trembling slightly. "I really don't want to leave her behind," Vachel whispers to himself, "What if we're all killed? She'll never know what happened." He curls up into a ball as he continues, "I don't like Darkhaven as it is, and now I have to go there with three people I wouldn't trust with a pet rock, let alone my life. Still, she doesn't need to know it's even out there. I'll not put her in danger for my selfishness!"

It comes out as more of a growl than he intends it to, as if he were staring into the face of a beast that was trying to kill her. Reaching over to the side of the bed she slept on, Vachel runs his fingers gently over the mattress. He can still smell her scent, even as it slowly seeks to fade away.

"She wasn't there long enough," he whispers, explaining it to the air with a note of regret tingeing his voice, "Why did it have to be me of all people? She should have chosen someone more deserving...more like her...perhaps her own species."

The last part stings, and he buries his face into her pillow, taking in as much of her scent as he can. *What is wrong with life being simple for once? It would be a nice change of pace.* He breathes a sigh into the pillow, wishing she were here now to explain it all to: "Still...I really need to get going." With that, he throws the blanket off and climbs out of the bed. His shirt and boots are still on the floor where he left them. These he pulls on in a rush, not even bothering to tuck the shirt in properly. Dashing out the door, he sprints all the way to the kitchen.

Again, they are all rushing about, tending to their various duties. Most are employed with cleaning messes from breakfast. The others are already starting those dishes that must be cooked for an extended length of time and are to be served at dinner. He spies Riko dashing about between the two groups, helping where she can and giving instructions where needed. Vachel watches from the doorway, wondering how she can keep up. However, his stomach soon begins to growl as the scent of the food reaches him.

As if called, Riko rushes past him, thrusting a plate into his hands.

Heaped on it are four eggs, three strips of bacon, two pieces of buttered toast, and a cut of ham. A bright smile rushing to his face, Vachel slips to the floor and begins to devour the food. Out of habit, he does not even bother with the fork. He is nearly finished when Riko drops another egg and two more strips of bacon on the plate.

Slipping to the floor beside him, she remarks, "One would think you wouldn't be very fond of eggs after what you've been through." "These were created the way nature intended: from birds," Vachel replies after bolting down the final one. "Speaking of nature," Riko continues, "If you're going to fulfill your natural desires with a Sister, make certain no one finds out."

At this, Vachel chokes on the piece of bacon he is chewing. Riko smiles at him as he struggles with the coughing fit.

"What? Who found out...and *how*?" Vachel demands, swallowing hard. "Luckily, just me. So, I placed a charm over the subject so anyone else who catches wind will forget it immediately," Riko answers. Giving her a searching look, he asks, "And how *did* you find out?" "Remember the 'Sister' you guys met up with?" Riko begins, continuing after Vachel's nod, "I was afraid you two would get caught, so I disguised myself to follow you."

Vachel gazes at her as if he does not believe a word of it.

Then again, it sounds too much like her for him not to.

"Not cool! But, I wouldn't call kissing and fondling 'fulfilling my natural desires'. Mine tend to be a little more involved," Vachel replies. "I was just making an assumption based on the smile. You were almost like the cat that has just gotten into the cream. Still, I'm sorry for playing the part of the nosey little sister," Riko explains, giving him a small kiss on the cheek.

"Yeah, well I haven't exactly been the best big brother," Vachel confesses, glaring down at the floor, "We wouldn't even be here if I'd used my head and not gotten caught." But then, he would not have met Sister Crystal, either, and that stings to know.

"I'd say you got the worst of the punishment," Riko replies, leaning her head on his shoulder for a moment. Her eyes search the room just in case there might be a wandering eye belonging to a certain Sister she knows. She does not want the poor girl to get the wrong idea, seeing as how no one knows they are even related. Then, smiling, Riko asks, "Can I be nosey some more?" "About what?" Vachel replies, picking up his last piece of bacon in anticipation of a question he will not want to answer.

"Why didn't you go farther than kissing?"

Yep! Vachel shoves the bacon into his mouth to keep from answering.

"Didn't want her to notice your lead rocks, huh?"

"That's not a topic of conversation I enjoy."

"Just answer the question."

"Yes! Are you happy now?"

"No. You shouldn't have to worry about things like that."

"Well, I do. There's nothing anyone but I can do about it."

"How can you fix it?"

Vachel stares at her for a moment before he asks, "Weren't you listening to the Hybrid before?" "Yes, but he's wearing a Shiku Hara. He could just be bluffing to get you back to Rust," Riko protests. Smiling furtively, Vachel whispers, "I doubt Rust will be too happy to have me in his court again." "He could be after your demon power again," Riko counters, concern evident in her voice.

Vachel would like nothing better than to laugh, but he knows she would not appreciate it. "I know the Crystal of Yossa is real," Vachel explains, choosing to be kind to her presently, "I've seen it. I just don't know where it is, now." This is a lie on his part, and, had he not tampered with her memories of the crystal, she would know it. "Fine, fine. I'll let you have that one. Just remember to take special care of yourself for us, alright?" Riko pleads. With a smile, Vachel replies, "No problem."

He has spent the last three hours sitting in a meeting with the other elders. They all insisted it would be no problem for them to take care of things in his absence. That was until they learned Princess Mikya would not be staying. Sadly enough, he knows more about the goings on of Dehurst than even the High Elder.

The first two hours were spent filling them all in on what is happening and who to go to in order to get updated information. The final one was used to tell them how the princess wanted things done. By this time, his head is throbbing and his nerves are fraying from all the frustration. He is not at all looking forward to having to review it all with them.

Even being the youngest of them, he is too old to have to run around in the same circle this many times. However, before he can begin to ask them anything, the High Elder commands, "Gilden, go tend to your other preparations. We can handle it from here." Standing a little more quickly and excitedly than he intends, Gilden replies with a bright smile, "Yes, sir. Thank you for your generosity." The High Elder waves him away with a smile.

He lies on his side, his head propped up on his fist. The cloak has been abandoned to rest folded over his pack. His other hand is employed in the task of holding the apple as he eats, watching the princess try to reason with two Sisters. Then again, most of his focus has been on the one Mikya calls Sister Ru. The other, Sister Mara, as she is called, is nice too, but given the choice, he prefers the dark-haired beauties.

They have paid him little mind, except to throw agitated glances at him. There can be no denying it now; they all know him for what he is. He should have taken more steps to hide it, but that can't be helped now. He will just have to continue the mission with them all in the know.

Still, there is no reason for the argument over whether she should travel with him or not. Neither one of the Sisters seems to understand that she has already made up her mind about it. And she has complete authority. Finally, after getting tired of hearing them bicker, Ven interjects, "Why are you two even bothering to discuss this?"

The Sisters peer down at him with a glare, but do not answer. Ven keeps his gaze into their eyes steady as he whispers, "She is the princess. Therefore, in this land, her word is law. If she has decided to accompany me on this journey, it is no business of yours to try and change her mind."

Once the words are out of his mouth, Ven wishes he had not said them.

A sudden hatred for his words springs to his mind as it does to their faces. He just let himself defend a royal, and it makes his insides boil. Royals have caused him only trouble, and now he is trying to keep one from it. The look of gratitude on Mikya's face does nothing to quell the heat. Tired now of looking at the Sisters, Ven closes his eyes, poising the apple before his mouth as he adds, "That's just the way things work. I assumed you would have figured this out already. Forgive me for giving you some credit." With that, he takes a bite as if to tell them the matter is closed.

Time is slowly ticking by, and he has yet to hear from the king. He has half a mind to take things into his own hands and force both Ven and Vachel back into Darkhaven with much more than Shiku Hara around their necks. Lin is presently off seeing to her duties before he can get his hands on her. If the king does not send word soon, he will be too preoccupied to get the message if it does come. However, the thought of simply neglecting his duty to go after her has its merit.

Bribing her into keeping Coby in the dark about his connection to the king is often as rewarding, if not more, for him as it is for her. As the thought begins to take hold, however, the spark of violet flame appears before him.

"Has he arrived, yet?" a wavering, deep voice asks. "Yesterday. He's gotten them to free Vachel, and they intend to leave tonight," he answers, a smile coming to his face, "Half the castle already knows he is a Hybrid, yet Princess Mikya has no idea." "Excellent. Still, it is not likely to stay that way for long. Gilden will no doubt spill the information all over himself in an attempt to keep it from her. For now, I need you in Dehurst, but I will contact you when I want you home," the voice replies. He nods, whispering: "Understood, sire." "Just one more thing, Reno," the voice adds, "When you are to return, get rid of your nightly visitor."

Again, he nods his understanding.

At this, the flame disappears.

He sits silent in the darkness of this back room. He has three, being part of the princess's personal guard, but enjoys this one most because of this darkness. There are no windows to this small, stone chamber, which makes it all the better to conduct *business* in. Still, alone it is somewhat cold, and the chill strikes at his bare chest. She will be here soon, so it does not bother him as much as it would normally. Again, just as the thought crosses his mind, she opens the door and steps in, closing it behind her.

She wears a loose pair of white pants and a shirt to match, having abandoned her armor in one of the front rooms already. Smiling, he notices she has taken the time to let her hair down. Something she has not done before. As she strides across the room to him, it seems she is much more serious this time. This he notes with a wider smile as she slips up into his lap.

The time is nearly upon them, and Vachel finds himself wishing he could see Sister Crystal once more before he has to go.

Leaning against the wall with his arms folded over his chest, Vachel glares at the floor in frustration. Ven, Gilden, and Mikya are all fussing over the items packed. Luckily for all of them, Riko gladly gave the princess some of her old things to wear. The dresses would have slowed them down quite a bit. Thus, Mikya wears a white, collared shirt with the sleeves rolled up to her elbows. A pair of black pants is secured at her waist by a white, cloth belt. The pants slip easily into a pair of equally black, heelless boots at her knees. Her hair had to be braided and then tied up again to create a loop that still falls to the small of her back.

Gilden has given up the white shirt for a sleeveless one of black. The amulet has been slipped beneath his shirt in an effort to conceal who he is momentarily. Of course, he has refused to give up the robe, which is just as much a symbol as the amulet. The pants are now securely tucked into his black boots. He has also pulled on a pair of black gloves.

Vachel has not bothered to bring anything but himself and the crystal, hidden beneath his shirt. He has yet to even think about doing anything with his hair. It is not high on his priority list at the moment. How he will survive this encounter is. Suddenly, he is brought out of his thoughts by a familiar scent and gazes up to find Sister Crystal standing before him.

Giving the others a glance over her head, Vachel decides they are too preoccupied to notice and whispers, "I thought you were afraid of getting caught, little one." "Not by them," Sister Crystal replies, "It is the other Sisters I am worried about."

With a smile, Vachel pulls her close and kisses her on the mouth. It has more urgency to it than he intended it to have, that is, until he feels the one she returns. He now realizes that he did them both an injustice last night. As they slowly part, she slips a thin, black ribbon from her hair. Vachel gazes at it in confusion, having not even noticed it before.

With a smile at his look, she turns him around and carefully pulls his hair back at the base of his neck with it. She makes certain not to pull on it too hard as she tightens the hair into the ribbon. Of course, Vachel would not have cared either way.

"Thank you, little one. I hadn't thought of that," Vachel whispers, turning back around to face her. "Think nothing of it. Still, it is my very favorite, and I want to see it again sometime," she replies with a slight blush. He gives her a knowing smile before he suddenly glances up to find the others watching. To prove to them he does not care,

Vachel takes her head in his hands to kiss her fervently again. As intended, this one is much lengthier.

"Make sure to come back uninjured, too," she requests once they part. *Is everyone determined I'm going to get myself into trouble?* With a smile, he replies, "No problem, little one." Returning the smile, she dashes away to get back to her duties. He watches her go, leaving the smile on his face for the moment. She deserves to see it if she happens to look back, after all. However, once she is out of sight, he lets it drift back into the frown for dealing with the others.

Vachel crosses his arms again before moving over to them. They are oddly silent as he stands staring at them. It makes him wonder if any of them have ever been kissed before. *Geez, what are you, two-fucking-years-old?* Soon however, Ven bursts, and a steady stream of snickering slips from him. Mikya blushes slightly and turns away, hiding her mouth with her fingertips. Gilden whispers, "I didn't know you liked her, Vachel." Vachel has the urge to counter, "That would just add to the list of things you don't know", but he curbs his urge before it can make it to his lips. He has to travel with these people.

"She wanted the secrecy, but I wouldn't care if all of Dehurst knew," Vachel replies instead, "It isn't something I think needs kept secret." *Love isn't something to hide from people...well, except for Rust. He can die thinking I don't love anyone.* "I can understand her caution. The Sisters would not approve of either the relationship or what you are...and that's dangerous," Gilden explains. *He sounds almost concerned. Yeah, right.* Flashing a smile that reveals his fangs, Vachel whispers, "So...am I."

"That sounded suspiciously like a threat, Vachel," Gilden observes, narrowing his eyes. *That might be because it was, you idiot!* "Who says it wasn't...*Gilden*?" Vachel answers, running his tongue slowly over his fangs, "I don't even need half my true power to eat you and the entire court of Sisters." "Are you two going to act this way the entire trip?" Mikya interjects, her eyes narrowed as well. Gilden immediately falls silent and gazes away, but Vachel openly yawns at her. She has no real authority over him now, and she needs to learn that quickly.

Stretching his back and arms as he turns away, Vachel places his hands on his hips and replies, "If you all will kindly remember what I am, I wouldn't need to keep reminding you. I'm a demon first, keep that in mind." All three nod solemnly at his back, but remain silent. He doesn't bother to make them voice their understanding; he can sense it in the surface thoughts of their minds. Vachel does not speak for a while as he tracks the life moving around the castle.

Finally, he adds, "We should get started. I suggest we take the back way." "Why?" Mikya asks. Shaking his head in pity, Vachel replies, "It's the most direct route to the trail, and I don't want to dance with the guards presently. I might kill one just for spite." "You certainly seem to be traveling light. Any particular reason why you're not bringing anything?" Gilden asks, quickly changing the subject. This proves to be the wrong way to do it. Unable to understand exactly why the sorcerer's voice is irritating him other than the desire to be rid of all three and snatching the crystal to cure himself, Vachel still gives over to the anger that pulses into his brain.

Vachel turns around quickly and hisses, "Do I have to pull your tongue out of your head to keep you from asking stupid questions?" "You don't have that kind of power," Gilden replies defiantly, taking a step away from the others, toward Vachel. In response, Vachel jerks his arm up, parallel to the floor, his half-open palm directed at Gilden's chest. The demon's eyes glow red as black chains burst forth, wrapping themselves tightly around Gilden. They pin his arms to his sides before jerking him forward.

A smile befitting his species on his face, Vachel takes Gilden by the throat and lifts him so his feet dangle. The chains drop away at this, as if having Vachel's aura that close frightens them. Out of instinct, Gilden wraps his fingers around Vachel's wrist and seeks to pull the demon's fingers away. It does not help him in the least; Vachel's hold proves too true for that.

He continues to struggle against the fingers.

Still, the fear in his eyes betrays his attempts at resisting.

Vachel runs his tongue over his fangs again, much more slowly this time, whispering: "Would you like me to tear out your throat with my fingers...or with these?" Gilden's eyes widen only minutely, but Vachel's own catch the subtle movement. The sorcerer is terrified of him now. *Perfect. This makes things so much easier.* "Vachel! Leave him alone!" Mikya commands in a yell. *And the princess has to ruin it all for me. Damn.* Glaring, Vachel drops his captive, as he whispers, "As you wish, yakim[1]." Shocked, Mikya is silent as she glares at him. Ven snickers softly, but Gilden is too busy catching his breath to offer any comment.

Slipping quickly from his laughter, Ven observes, "That was too much demon power all at once to go unnoticed. We should leave now." "At least one of you is paying attention," Vachel remarks, jamming his hands into his pockets. He makes a measured trek across the room, as if he does not want them to be able to follow but knows they have to. Shouldering his pack, Ven takes off after the demon, sparing the others only a half-glance. Still shaken, Gilden moves ahead with a gesture telling Mikya to follow suit.

---

[1] This is a derogatory name for a woman that insults not only her intelligence, but her purity, as well. It is all the worse because Vachel is a demon, and demons are considered to be the most impure creatures in Yossa.

On Ring Trail

As promised, the back way leads them almost directly onto Ring Trail.

It is a pitted, ruin of what it once was at best. Now, after having had no rain for close to a month, the soil drifts around in bursts of dust. Vachel remains in the lead with a considerable gap between him and the other three, not even bothered by the circling wind and grit that catches in his hair and brushes against his face. *But then, is he really being hit with it?* Mikya has to wonder to herself, as the boys will offer no observation on the situation. Still, Ven, Gilden, and Mikya are all uncertain as to whether Vachel is actually being brushed against by the wind and dirt that smacks them hard in the face.

Vachel is walking far too straight-backed and unconcerned for that.

Several times, they could have sworn the clouds of dust were avoiding him. He did say his elemental powers included all of them. That would mean Vachel has enough power to keep the grit-filled wind from touching him, let alone bothering him, even with only half the power he would have had in his usual state. It would also give him the power to create his own wind within his tunnel of protected space.

Oddly enough, Mikya is the first to gather the courage to confront him about it. She has the sudden urge to try to get him back for the name-calling before they left the castle. She knows it's childish, but she can't help it. That name was completely uncalled for. Rushing to catch up with him, she asks, "Vachel, you're protected against this wind, aren't you?"

"What of it?"

"The rest of us are having a hard time of it. You could at least help."

"Either that…or you want me to get rid of my barrier, correct?"

"Yes. It isn't fair. You're the one who kept claiming power."

"'Claiming power', princess? You should mind your words."

"So, make your decision."

"Fine."

Immediately, the barrier surrounding him falls away, as if dissolving in the air around it. The dust slams against his face, but he does not even flinch. Instead, he walks just as straight-backed and unconcerned as before, a small smile coming to his face this time when he notices the frown on hers: "I would rather the discomfort than aid any of you." "I'm sorry you feel that way," Mikya replies, allowing herself to slip back in the ranks. Shaking his head, Vachel answers, "Not sorry enough, princess."

Even though the night is creeping in on them, Vachel continues to lead the way. Trying to stifle it and failing,

Mikya gives a broad yawn, which she covers with the back of her hand.

By this time, the wind has decided to ease up, but it is still powerful enough to give the occasional burst and toss grit into their faces. Mikya keeps her gaze on Vachel, and suddenly realizes he has not bothered to even speak to them for close to two hours. She has a feeling her performance earlier is the reason for this silence.

Suddenly, she feels guilty for trying to seek vengeance on him. Of course, he's going to be callous, he's been slowly dying each day she has lived, and she didn't even know he existed. She finds herself wanting to make him speak to her again. However, she has no idea how to ease it. Finally, she forces her way up next to Vachel again and is about to speak when he stops abruptly. She takes two more steps before it sinks in that he is truly intending to stand still.

Ven and Gilden catch up to them before Vachel whispers, "This is far enough away for tonight. We can always get a head start tomorrow morning." "Tired, Vachel?" Ven teases with a small snicker. Grinding his molars together, Vachel curbs the urge to hang the ingrate by his Shiku Hara. "No," Vachel replies shortly, "But, *her highness* is." He speaks her title as if it is leaving a bad taste in his mouth.

Mikya is about to protest when she feels the aching in her legs. They have not gone very far and already her body is beginning to tire on her. "I'm sorry, you guys," she apologizes, hanging her head. "Don't apologize," Vachel responds, snapping before his voice softens to explain, "It's not your fault there is such a skewed view of the proper ruler nowadays."

"What do you mean?" Mikya asks, bringing her head back up to look at him. Sighing, Vachel replies, "Never mind." And he'd felt bad for her a moment earlier, too.

Moving to the side of the trail, Vachel drops to the ground, lying back and balancing his head in his hands. The movements are almost too smooth to seem natural. Ven drops his pack to the ground and pulls the cloak from his shoulders. He lies down on his back, his head coming to rest on top of the pack. It does not make the best pillow, but it is better than having a stiff neck from sleeping all night without it. Carefully, Mikya slips to the ground, but does not lie down. Instead, she asks, "Shouldn't someone keep watch?"

"No," Gilden replies before Vachel can answer, "We have a demon in our midst. If he can't sense something that is creeping up on us, then it won't matter whether we're awake or not. The thing will kill us either way." "That's certainly comforting," Mikya whispers, rubbing her arms as a sudden chill climbs up them. "I'm sorry, *your highness*, but it wasn't meant to be," Vachel interjects mockingly, never leaning up to even pretend to look at her as he says it. Mikya does not answer, gazing over at Gilden for support as he, too, slips to the ground.

Sighing, she removes her own bundle and lies down. Sooner than expected, she begins to drift to sleep. However, it feels as if only minutes have passed when she is woken by the sound of boots. Her eyes snap open, and she is ready to seek escape when she spies Vachel pacing back and forth. There is a red crystal, secured with a gold chain, hanging from his neck. His arms are crossed over his chest as he mumbles to himself.

Sitting up, she asks, "Is there something wrong, Vachel?" He jerks like he has been shot in the back with lightning and spins around, fists ready. However, when he spies her sitting there, he drops them and whispers solemnly, "No." "Then, why were you pacing?" she asks with a raised eyebrow. She is uncertain whether he can see it or not, but it remains out of habit. "It is nothing that concerns you or yours, princess," Vachel replies slowly, "I am the only one who can fix this, so you need not know anything about it."

"Have you been betrayed before, Vachel?"

"That's a personal question, princess."

"I know, and you don't seem very trusting."

"I've spent centuries spewing blood, princess; I've every right to be."

"I know, but couldn't you at least give me a chance."

"No."

"Why not?"

"You didn't even know I was there. How do you expect me to trust you could keep it to yourself? You just don't have the qualities of a person I'd be willing to trust," Vachel explains, turning away. Standing, Mikya asks, "Does this mean you think I'm too incompetent to even keep a secret?" "Yes," he answers, placing the crystal back inside his shirt, "I really do." "Keeping a secret isn't as hard as you make it sound, Vachel," Mikya replies, moving up to stand at his side.

As he gazes out into the darkness, his eyes seem to take in the moonlight, making them shine green. Still, most of his face is in shadow, making them like two lights in his face. "How do you do that?" she asks. "I can't explain it," Vachel replies slowly, "The only way you could understand is to become a demon, but even then it's hard to understand." "Does it make you feel inhuman, Vachel?" she asks, gazing up at the shine. He turns his head to face her and the shine suddenly vanishes. A smile slips to his lips at the look of confusion on her face: "I'm only reflecting the moon's rays. It doesn't work if they can't get to my eyes."

"Do you enjoy feeling inhuman?"

"What is it with you and personal questions?"

"I'm just curious to understand the person I'm traveling with."

"It would be easier for you if you didn't know."

"Why don't you let me be the judge of that?"

"Fine. Yes, I enjoy feeling inhuman. Makes me feel powerful."

"Does the trick with your eyes make you feel that way?"

"No. It happens to everyone's eyes without their knowledge."

"But, it looks like your eyes are stealing the light from your face."

"It's how I was holding myself. You're on the wrong side of my face."

"So, it was just this side that was in shadow?"

"Yes, that is why I said I was only reflecting the moon."

"A reflection of a reflection…"

"*That* makes me feel inhuman," Vachel confesses, gazing back out into the darkness so that his eyes catch the light again, "It makes it seem worse than just a reflection…like something I have to think about to make happen…like when I hurt things." The last has an edge to it she doesn't understand after all the boasting his has done about the ease with which he can kill.

Turning her gaze to the surroundings, as well, Mikya replies, "It's hard to think of you as inhuman with eyes like that." "Like what?" Vachel asks immediately. "They're so deep, but they still have a certain shine to them that has nothing to do with moon rays," she answers, shaking her head as if it does not make any sense to her. "Why don't I just take it as a compliment, and we let it go?" Vachel suggests, "Besides, you should really get back to sleep."

"I have another question, first," Mikya adds, just now realizing that he contradicted himself. "Shoot," Vachel replies. "When I first asked how you did that, you said it had something to do with being a demon," Mikya explains, keeping her gaze off him, "Now, you're saying that it is actually something we all do. Which is it?" "The first answer was based on the thought that you were talking about how still I was standing. So, the trick of the eyes is really something anyone can do," Vachel explains, as if speaking to a child.

"Why do you consider me a little girl, Vachel?" Mikya asks, finally turning her gaze back to him. Sighing, he whispers, "I've lived for over twenty-two hundred years, but I've been a captive for five hundred of them. It tends to make one feel much older than he is. Even Gilden seems a little boy, now." "Why do you look so old? I thought demons took millennia to age," Mikya asks, the confusion evident in her face. Smiling in pity and bitterness, Vachel replies, "It's nice to know you think I look old." "I'm sorry, I didn't mean for it to sound that way," she apologizes quickly, "I just meant you looked older than I would have thought you should being only twenty-two hundred."

"Demons only take millennia to age after their first eighteen years. In those first we age as any mortal would. Besides, it takes a Halfling a century to age a year, which is why I look five years older than I should. And don't worry about it, princess. I've been called much worse, and it doesn't really matter to me what you think of my appearance," Vachel explains. She turns her gaze to the ground in an effort to keep him from seeing the flush springing to her face as she replies, "Is that because of Sister Crystal?"

"Go back to bed, princess."

When she wakes the next morning, the boys are already up, and Gilden and Ven are speaking in a hushed tone farther up the trail. Vachel stands with his back to her, most likely scanning the horizon for threats.

Getting to her feet, Mikya moves up next to him to ask, "Why didn't anyone wake me if you were all ready?" "You'll slow us down even worse if you're tired, princess," Vachel replies. Mikya has the distinct feeling that he is trying to get her to forget their exchange the night before. Still, she has no time to make him aware she knows because Gilden and Ven stand to join them.

"We're finally ready to get going, then?" Vachel asks, turning to face Gilden and Ven. They nod in unison, and Vachel passes by them without another word. Mikya rushes to grab her pack before she follows him, leaving Gilden and Ven to resume their conversation at the back of the group.

Once she makes it in line with Vachel, Mikya asks, "Why are you avoiding me, now?" "Just because I talk to you, does not mean that I enjoy it," Vachel replies in a whisper. "If it bothered you that much, why did you even do it?" Mikya asks, her eyes narrowing. Slipping his hands into his pockets, Vachel answers, "Fine...I might enjoy the company, but I don't want them to know it. I'm supposed to be mysterious and aloof because I'm a demon and a walking power magnet." "'Power magnet'?" Mikya questions, raising an eyebrow. *Oops, slip of the tongue. Ah, hell with it. Everybody else knows by now.*

"A power magnet can call someone's power and allow the wielder to use that power against them. They are usually an object, like a crystal or sword, but I can do it without the aid of an object, so I'm a living power magnet," Vachel explains, not even bothering to look at her.

Mikya gazes out at the surroundings and realizes suddenly she cannot feel the grit against her skin despite how hard the wind is blowing. "Vachel..." she whispers, turning her gaze back to him. "Don't worry, princess, our tag-alongs aren't getting beaten around, either," Vachel replies.

As soon as he says it, she notices the hint of red in his eyes. The majority of the color is still green, but there is a ring of red hugging the pupil.

"Why do your eyes do that? Is it something all demons do?"

"Only the more powerful demons can keep their power calling reserved to their eyes. Every demon has something that happens to them that let others know they are drawing on demonic power. It's nature's way of giving a small aid to those who do not possess our gifts," Vachel replies, "Why the sudden interest in my species, princess?" "Like I said: I'm just curious to understand the person I'm traveling with," Mikya answers, giving a small smile. "Interesting," Vachel whispers, more to himself than to her.

"You once lived in Darkhaven, didn't you?" Mikya adds when the thought suddenly occurs to her.

"Again with personal questions?"

"Will you just humor me, please?"

"Fine...yes, I once lived in Darkhaven."

"That's where all demons come from originally, right?"

"Yes."

"Could you tell me what a Hybrid is?"

"Strange topic change, don't you think?"

"Vachel...please."

"Alright, alright. A Hybrid is a creature created from the melding of all three races: faerie, human, and demon. One parent has to be a Halfling, usually part demon, part human, while the other must be a pure breed. When the child is created, he or she is given a special gift that is never the same between two different ones. These powers are usually invoked by a mere touch, but even then, the place where the Hybrid must be touched is unique. The only way to keep the effect from happening is by giving a sign of trust. This sign is chosen by the Hybrid, and the most often used is a kiss on the wrist. If the Hybrid is submissive enough, he or she can be forced to give a certain sign. Ironically enough, the Hybrids are actually weaker than the elements that make them up. They are neither strong enough to take on a faerie, nor are they even close to being powerful enough to take on a demon. Their powers can only aid them against humans and Halflings, depending on the person's strength. Happy now?"

"That's a lot of information to think about."

"Isn't it though. I only know because Rust has a Hybrid servant."

"Did you live in his castle at one time, Vachel?"

"If you can call being in his presence living…"

"Why did he steal your demon power?"

"I was becoming too powerful to control."

"Is there anything I should know in case we have to deal with him?"

"Keep out of his way. He will only deal with people he believes are powerful enough to be in his presence. It's caused him to truly hate humans. He views them as weak…well, all except the sorcerers; they have magic to make them powerful," Vachel explains, gazing up for a moment in thought.

"But, you knocked Gilden around like he was nothing…how will Rust see him now?" Mikya asks, a little fear springing to her voice. "I was only able to do that because I was channeling power from him, taking his magic and using it against him. I'm a power magnet remember," Vachel replies, turning his gaze to her. He has no qualms about lying to her, and she doesn't need to know about the reserves of power he has kept all this time. He only let the surface energy deteriorate, thus he has kept the majority of his power since they started draining him with the curse.

"So, the more powerful the source, the more powerful you are?" Mikya asks, giving a glance over her shoulder at Gilden and marveling at the power he must have to allow Vachel to have used that much demonic power at once. He is still absorbed in his conversation with Ven.

Nodding, Vachel adds, "That's why Rust feared my power. I could take his and use it against him. It's also why he brought me into his court of protectors in the beginning." "If he's that powerful, why does he need bodyguards?" Mikya asks. "He doesn't want to have to do the dirty work himself; he views it as beneath him because of all that power," Vachel explains, "There were six of us, and he made us do all of the killing of his enemies. I refused to kill my family, so he decided to punish me by stealing half of my demon power."

"He asked you to kill your own family?"

"He asked the first time…then he threatened me with my life."

"Couldn't back it up, could he?"

"I think it was more of a change of heart. He wanted me to suffer by taking away the only thing that kept me safe from other people. Being a power magnet made me very popular with the sorcerers of Darkhaven, so I fled to Dehurst. Of course, that turned out to be just as much of a problem," Vachel replies. He also knows who was responsible for that change of heart. Because he stood up against what she was doing, she gave Rust the keys to crippling him, and he still has to even the score.

Nodding, Mikya falls into silence, unable to bring herself to ask anything more. She is not certain she will be able to handle any more of the answers. Vachel is content with allowing her to fall into silence as they continue.

They spend the next two weeks in this fashion, Gilden and Ven bringing up the rear as Mikya learns as much as she can from Vachel. At one point, she asks him to teach her some of what he knows about wielding elemental magic. He refuses quite loudly. When she asks for a reason, he merely explains that his techniques could kill her. In response to her question of how, he explains his use of demon aura, which could kill a human in large enough doses.

Mikya does not bother to ask about any of his other magic.

After these two weeks, they come across Endu, the halfway point of this side of Ring Trail. Gilden, Ven, and Vachel all agree that stopping here would be a waste of time, so they continue past. It takes them another three weeks, due to an accident with quicksand, to finally reach Trader's Port, the final city before they must cross Hilden's Gate.

Trader's Port

Once they enter the city limits, Ven naturally takes the lead. He has been here several times more in the past than the others, or so he claims. Behind Ven's back, Vachel is quick to point out to Mikya that a Hybrid has the memory capacity to be able to know a place after only one visit.

The dirt streets are lined with wood buildings, most of which are at least two stories. People rush about the street even at the late hour at which they have arrived. In Nishi-Hama, everyone would be moving in for the night at this hour. It is close to eight in the evening, but still the streets are full and busy with activity. Most of them are wearing simple clothing designed for travel, marking them as the traders for which this city is named. Still, some are decked out in finery or armor, suggesting they are merely passing through on their way along Ring Trail. Ven pays most of it no mind as he makes his way down the middle of the street.

As Mikya watches, crowds of people move away so Ven can pass through, almost as if they are afraid of him. It doesn't seem to bother him, either; in fact, he appears to expect it from them. She does not bother to ask, but Vachel explains it to her anyway, most likely seeing the confused look on her face, "Most traders have at least a small amount of magical talent. This allows them to sense the power of his aura...and mine." "Why does yours have anything to do with their moving for him?" Mikya asks, still gazing ahead. "They think he is mine, and do not wish to anger me," Vachel replies. Turning her gaze to him, Mikya now realizes that he has been holding himself unusually straight-backed even compared to what he was doing on Ring Trail.

"What's with the soldier routine?" she asks, gesturing to let him know she is speaking about his posture. "It's all for show. I want them to think I have the power to consider them below me," Vachel whispers, "Now, no more questions until we're settled." Mikya does not ask why he wants her to stop questioning him because she can see the accusations in the people's eyes.

If they are not looking down on her for being in the presence of three men who do not appear to be family, it is because she is walking this close to the demon of the group.

It seems none of them understands who she truly is, but then, they have no need to. Most people of her kingdom have never even seen her, and she looks like little more than another traveler wearing Riko's clothes. Gilden obviously spies their reaction as well, for he reaches forward and pulls her back, closer to him: "It's more appropriate for the lady to be under the protection of a sorcerer, not a demon." "But, Vachel wasn't even protecting me," Mikya protests. "I know, as do they," Gilden replies, "That's why it isn't appropriate for you to be walking beside him. They think you're his...servant." He uses the last word as if he is unsure whether that is the right one to use or not.

"You mean they think I am only with him to serve his natural urges?" Mikya asks, a little disgusted. Humans will do just fine for her. "Yes," Gilden answers simply. Wrinkling up her nose, Mikya turns her gaze to the ground, unable to believe they could think that way.

When they finally make their way into the inn Ven has chosen, Mikya is ready to spin around and yell at everyone that she is not a demon's toy. The accusing eyes were bad enough, but now they are even turning their noses up at her. She is silently grinding her molars together as they enter the four-story, wooden structure.

The first room they come to is filled with wood tables, each one holding at least a group of four around it. The walls are painted a light blue, and several pictures of past owners are hung at various points. Worn and scuffed, the floor appears to have gotten quite a bit of use. On the opposite side of the room is an open archway leading to another room full of tables. It is not quite as crowded as this. To the far left is a bar where several men are sitting, having a deep discussion with the bartender.

Ven makes his way over to it, standing at the end so the man has to move away from the group he is talking to in order to see what Ven wants. The man is massive enough as it is, but when he steps up before Ven, it makes him look all the bigger. His white, collared shirt is tucked neatly into his black pants and he has the sleeves rolled up to his elbows, exposing his massive forearms. There is a cigarette balanced neatly between his teeth. His brown eyes have a piercing quality, but Ven meets the gaze from them without even flinching. His shoulder-length hair is brown as well, but it is about a half-shade darker than his eyes.

"What can I do for you?" he asks in a deep but somewhat gentle voice. He understands Ven is a creature who could tear him in half despite his obvious size advantage. As Mikya, Vachel, and Gilden make their way up behind him, Ven replies, "I need to get two rooms for the night." The man glances up with a raised eyebrow at Mikya, but lets it go and asks, "What name do I put these under?" "Ven Heoshin," Ven replies, leaning forward onto the bar's edge.

Reaching below the counter, the man brings out a pad of paper and a pen. There are numbers in one column and signatures in another. The man runs his finger down the list, looking for two rooms close together. He has to turn two pages before he finally comes across two that satisfy him. "There are two open on the second floor...208 and 207. I'll warn you, though, 208 has a faulty lock. Sometimes it works, sometimes it doesn't," the man explains, looking up.

"We'll take them," Ven replies, a smile on his face. It is not entirely pleasant, but it does not suggest danger, either. This seems to ease the tension in the man's shoulders slightly. "Before we actually accept this offer," Vachel interjects, "May I have the owner's name?" "Sure thing. My name's Hirron," the man answers with a smile. He is being extra polite to Vachel simply because of the demon aura, as

Mikya knows a human rarely gives his name to a demon because of the superstition a demon can steal one's soul if he has the name.

Vachel gives him a nod before he crosses his arms again, reverting to his silent, perceptive state. He can trust the man for the time being. Hirron does not *seem* unnerved by the demon's silence, but his hand is somewhat shaky when he produces the keys and hands them to Ven. Ven smiles at him before he leads the way through the open archway.

This room is painted the same blue as the first, but it is filled with people who are more interested in food than drink. There are at least seven women weaving between the tables, each wearing a skirt that is as short as it can possibly get without flashing anyone when they are standing still. However, once they are on the move, every step gives a small peek of what they are wearing below, or not wearing in some cases.

Each wears a bright smile, and one moves up to Ven to ask, "Can I offer your party a table, sir?" "Perhaps in a minute," Ven replies, his voice immediately becoming something closer to a purr. Even frowning, Mikya catches the flash in Vachel's eye before he moves. Vachel steps forward at the sound of Ven's voice and takes the Hybrid's upper arm in a tight grip. Forcefully, he pulls his captive forward, hissing in his ear: "You can flirt after we've gotten upstairs first."

Ven makes no move to pull from Vachel's grasp, but the look on his face suggests he is not at all happy with being forced around. Odd for someone with a Shiku Hara to show so openly. In the far, right corner is the set of wood stairs leading up to the second floor. Vachel marches Ven up them as quickly as he can without tripping them both.

Once they are all up the stairs, Vachel releases Ven's arm with a small jerk and allows him to lead the way down the corridor. Each wood door has a metal number worked into the surface at eye level. Their rooms are at the end of the corridor, across the hall from each other. Before Ven can offer the key, Vachel decides to test the lock on the door to room 208. The knob turns easily and he pushes the door open to reveal a small room.

There are two beds done in blue against the far wall. On the right wall is a small window and to the right of the door is a place for coats. To the left is the door leading into a small bathroom. Vachel glances over his shoulder and demands, "Open the other." Taking the key from his pocket, Ven unlocks the second door to find it is a mirror replica of the first. "Is everything in this building done in blue?" Ven responds with a raised eyebrow.

Shaking his head, Vachel makes his way into the first room with Mikya and Gilden right behind. Ven takes the time to lock the second door again before following. Standing in the center of the room beside Vachel, Gilden asks, "How do you suggest we divide?" "You and the princess should stay together. I'm certain no one would

95

want her to be seen in the presence of either Ven or myself," Vachel answers, a somewhat bitter smile coming to his face, "Of course, for safety reasons, you two should take the room with the functioning lock."

Gilden nods his agreement before moving over to Ven to retrieve the key. Mikya follows after him when he makes his way into the second room to drop off his things. Pulling off his cloak, Ven drops it and his pack on the bed farthest into the room. He keeps his gaze on the floor as he passes Vachel, determined not to meet the demon's gaze.

"Are you frightened of me, child?" Vachel asks, his smile baring his fangs. Ven still refuses to look at him as he answers, "Yes...you were a member of the court of protectors. I have every reason to be afraid of you." This isn't true, considering how Vachel treated Ven when he was still part of Rust's court, and they both know it. Either way, he decides to play along with Ven's ruse. For some reason, he and Rust don't want Vachel to remember that he knows the Hybrid.

"Still, I have but half my strength. What do you have to fear from me now?" Vachel pushes, his smile slipping to a frown. "My master saw fit to strip you of half your power because you were too strong for him to control. If you were too strong for my master at full strength, I know you will still be stronger than *me* at half," Ven whispers as if he is afraid of being struck for speaking. *No doubt, Rust and Nera's attention turned him into a proper slave.*

Vachel moves forward and slips his finger underneath the edge of the Shiku Hara as he replies, "It is only because of this that you are not powerful enough. How do you think it is used to make those with demonic aura submissive?" Ven shakes his head as if to say he does not know. "It prevents us from channeling power properly," Vachel answers simply, removing his finger from the collar with a slow movement. His nail gently scrapes against Ven's skin, a small sign of affection between a demon and one who is beneath him. Before Ven can reply, Gilden and Mikya make their way back into the room.

Vachel sits with his legs crossed in the chair opposite from Mikya, his hand playing along the stem of his glass. He has a rather perturbed look on his face as he gazes at Ven who has found himself two ladies. Of course, judging by their attire, Vachel would not call them that.

They are both wearing black skirts short enough that they cannot sit down without flashing the room. The one on Ven's right is wearing a red shirt that barely covers her, while her counterpart wears one of blue. Both have a slight tan to their skin and brown hair. The one in red has brown eyes and the other has blue. Their shoes are open-toed, black, and have dangerous heels. The three are seated at a table in the corner, and every eye in the room is on them. The girls have positioned their chairs so they are as close to Ven as they can get without getting up off them. Ven has them so full of liquor that they are both giggling at every word he speaks. Of course, that could also be the only reason they are practically sitting in his lap.

Mikya cannot help but blush every time she gazes over at them, so she has decided to keep her focus on the tabletop before her. Sitting with her back to them has definite advantages. Gilden sits at her right with his hand resting next to his full glass. He has not touched it since Ven decided to take off with the two women. Vachel, Gilden, and Mikya sit in silence as does the rest of the room, all their attention focused on the three in the corner.

Finally, Vachel breaks the silence as he takes a drink: "Pitiful…it's rather sad when the only way you can get a girl is by pumping her full of mind-numbing chemicals." For a moment, all eyes turn to him, as if interested in what he might say next. "Of course," he adds once he is certain he has their attention, "It makes one sick to know that a respectable lady would allow such a poor soul to trick her that way." A few heads nod, but the room remains silent other than the noises of the three in the corner.

Vachel has to force himself to set the glass down gently in order to keep from breaking it as a suspicious scent reaches his nostrils. The alcohol must really be working for them to be that excited by Ven's presence. Then, a particularly loud giggle brings everyone's attention back to Ven and the girls.

A small, knowing smile slips to Vachel's face as he watches one of the girls try to pull Ven's glove off and take his hand. Before she can accomplish her task, he takes her wrist and turns her hand palm up to give the wrist a gentle brush of his tongue. The other girl giggles all the harder at this and presents her own wrist to him. He happily presents her with the same trust sign and allows them to slip the gloves from his fingers.

Mikya turns her gaze to Vachel and asks in a whisper, "Is that what you were talking about when you mentioned 'trust signs'?" "Yes, and it appears as though his medium is his hands," Vachel replies, "That would explain why he wears the gloves." Of course, Vachel already knew that, and this proves he is not mistaking anything. This is the same little one he met in Rust's court, the same Hybrid servant he was having Nera train.

"I thought it was just because he was pretending to be a trader," Mikya responds, leaning forward to rest her crossed arms on the table. "No trader wears gloves unless there is something wrong with their hands," Gilden answers before Vachel has the chance, "They're superstitious about such things and think that by hiding their hands, others will think they are hiding more."

He is beginning to feel as if he knows nothing because of all the questions Mikya has been asking Vachel.

Sighing, Vachel adds, "And there's no way I'm going to get out of this without it embarrassing the hell out of me." "Why do you say that?" Gilden asks with a raised eyebrow. He has a suspicion he knows what Vachel is thinking, but he wants to make certain. "I've no doubt the stupid boy is going to bring them back upstairs with him, and we're sharing a room," Vachel answers, massaging his forehead. "I certainly feel sorry for you," Gilden replies sarcastically. Removing his hand to gaze up at Gilden, Vachel responds, "I'm not interested in a drunk whore, sorcerer. In fact, he's making me sick at the moment." "You can't tell me you've never been with one, Vachel," Gilden answers, an accusing tone to his voice.

"Actually, I can. When I was in Darkhaven, Rust forbade any of us from having anything to do with them. We were allowed to have steady lovers, but never just a one-night stand. And out of Darkhaven I've been stuck in a hole in the ground," Vachel counters, a glare coming to his face, "Does this mean that because you've been with one the rest of the world has to have, as well?"

Gilden glares back at him, but does not answer.

Mikya immediately interjects into the conversation at this, "Does this mean that you had a lover, Vachel?" "Personal questions, princess," Vachel answers in a warning tone, turning his gaze to her. Catching the discomfort in Vachel's words and wanting to spite him, Gilden backs up the princess: "It would be nice to know, Vachel."

Vachel glares at them both, but does not answer.

He knows the only reason Gilden is pressing.

Otherwise, he wouldn't have bothered to find out.

"What could it hurt to tell?" Mikya asks in response. She, he knows, is just curious about him. It seems she's trying to make up for not knowing he was a prisoner in her castle by discovering everything she can about him. "It's none of your business. I can understand your wanting to know about Sister Crystal, but what I did in Darkhaven is nothing you need to concern yourselves with," Vachel snaps, suddenly angry. "Does this mean it was something you regret?" Gilden asks, a smile coming to his face. "Yes, I regret it. Stupid wench got me locked away for five hundred years," Vachel answers, his voice heated.

"So, this is about pride?" Gilden asks.

"No, it's about the fact that I don't have to answer these questions."

"What have you done as part of Rust's court that you don't like?"

"None-of-your-business."

"It has to be something bad to make *you* not want to talk."

"You're pushing it, sorcerer."

"What are you going to do, start something with all these witnesses?"

"I don't give a damn who sees."

"People are staring, you guys," Mikya interjects uncomfortably.

At this, both Gilden and Vachel gaze up to find that all eyes are on them, again. "What are you all staring at?" Vachel growls, his temper suddenly flaring. Quickly, they return their attention back to their tables, giving him small glances. Vachel utters a string of curses under his breath before emptying his glass: "I'm going back upstairs."

Gilden does not say anything as Vachel pushes away from the table and makes his way across the room.

He is at the stairway when he feels all the eyes on him again, and he spins around, flashing fangs at them and hissing. Every head turns away in a rush as he makes his way up the stairs. Mikya and Gilden give each other a small glance before getting up to follow. None of the people follows them with their gaze, afraid that they will do worse than the demon.

Mikya and Gilden make it to the top of the stairs to watch Vachel rush into his room, slamming the door shut behind him. Both take their time walking down the corridor as if afraid hurrying will make Vachel all more upset. However, once they make it to the door, neither one wants to be the one to open it. They stand in silence for several long moments only to decide there is no safe way to find out what is really bothering the demon.

Finally, Mikya takes the initiative and gives the door a gentle but firm knock. There is only silence in return.

"Vachel?" she calls, unsure if he will even answer. He does, but it is in a muffled voice, as if something besides the door is blocking his mouth: "Leave me alone. I'm through talking to you people." "You can't just hide from us, Vachel. We have a mission to complete, remember," Gilden adds. "I told you to leave me alone...all you'll do is make it worse," Vachel answers in that same muffled tone.

Narrowing his eyes, Gilden takes hold of the doorknob. Mikya is about to stop him, fearing for both Vachel and them, when he forces it open. Gilden gets only a step inside the room before he stops in his tracks. Mikya has only to peak around him to understand why.

Vachel lies on his side in a tight ball in the middle of the floor with his back to them and a pillow clutched tightly to his face. Mikya pushes past Gilden to kneel at the demon's back, but she does not dare touch him. Instead, she reaches out, allowing her hand to hover over his head as she whispers, "Vachel, what's wrong?" He does not answer at first, and Gilden makes his way into the room, shutting the door behind him. Once the door clicks shut, Vachel replies, his voice still muffled, "I want you two to go away. Why can't you just listen to me for once?" *Because that would make sense.*

"We want to help you," Mikya protests, still unsure about touching him. At this, he gets to his feet in a single, fluid movement, somehow avoiding her fingers and keeping his face hidden even as he drops the pillow. With is back to them, Vachel growls, "I don't want you in here." "Why not?" Gilden asks before Mikya has a chance. He has a sudden fear of what Vachel might be upset about. If it's upsetting a demon, what will it be like if he actually reveals it to them? Moving away, Vachel wraps his arms around himself in a makeshift hug as he shakes his head. "Just tell us why you don't want us near you," Mikya replies, getting to her feet.

"I don't like having people around me when I'm upset..."

"Why not?"

"What is it with you and questions?!" he nearly yells.

"Vachel...just answer, please."

"I don't like groups of people."

"Stop being evasive and answer the question," Gilden interjects.

"No."

"Vachel..."

"I said no! I'm not answering any more of your questions!"

"Vachel!"

"It scares me, Ok! Are you satisfied now?" Vachel bursts, unable to stop himself, crouching and lacing his fingers on the top of his head. Mikya moves in front of him, but he has his head bowed so she cannot see his face.

"Why would groups of people scare you?" she asks, bending down in an effort to see his face. He crouches lower to avoid her gaze as he whispers, "I'll tell you nothing...just get out of here." "You're the one who forced me to do this, Vachel," Gilden whispers dangerously, grabbing a handful of the demon's hair from behind. Vachel pulls against the hold only to have Gilden jerk his head back and place two fingers on his forehead.

A growl issues from the demon, his teeth clenched tight, making the fangs all the more prominent. In response, Gilden sends the spark of green light into the skin. Vachel's eyes pop open, but the green has overtaken his pupils. His jaw loosens as he stares blindly toward the ceiling. "Now, Vachel, explain to us why you're afraid of having groups of people around you when you're upset," Gilden commands, his voice firm. "They frighten me...too many hands reaching for me. I don't want to...to be touched," Vachel whispers, his face still blank.

"Why don't you want to be touched?" Gilden asks, his fingers loosening their grip on the demon's hair. "Just too many...it's crowded...no room to breathe...can't get free of them all...feeling trapped," Vachel whispers, a sudden pain coming to his face. Gilden tightens his hold again and demands, "Stop hinting, Vachel, tell us what you're really frightened of."

"They'll touch me again...I-I'm sorry master...I'll never disobey again, just don't let them have me...please. It hurts when they touch me...they've done nasty things to me...I don't. I won't! Stop it! Stop fucking with me!" Vachel answers, rage bursting to the surface as he struggles against the hold of Gilden's magic. His teeth are clenched again, but his eyes are still lost in the green pools. "What is he talking about?" Mikya asks, turning her gaze from Vachel to Gilden. What she sees on his face is not comforting, or pleasant for that matter.

His face is contorted into something between rage, fear, and pity, and it makes his features into a twisted mask of what they usually are.

Finally, he commands, "Answer the princess's question, Vachel." Vachel is silent for a moment as if he actually has to think about the words. "Vachel, I told you to do something, now do it," Gilden commands, his voice suddenly heated. "No, no, no, no, no...I won't tell...I'll never tell...I promise, master...I promise...I'll never tell...I don't want it to happen again...it hurts too much...I won't tell if you won't send me there again, please," Vachel mumbles, his words becoming more scattered as fear slips to his face.

"Vachel, just tell me. I won't let your master know that you told," Mikya whispers as if she is the one casting the spell. Vachel sucks in a deep breath as if having trouble getting enough air before he whispers, "They made me love them...over and over and over and over...I couldn't catch my breath...I couldn't find a way out...they just kept coming...and touching ...and making me touch. I don't...I won't get angry again, master...I promise I won't...just don't let the Sisters have me again...they scare me."

"Do you understand?" Gilden asks, turning his gaze to Mikya. Biting her bottom lip as if ashamed for her ignorance, Mikya solemnly shakes her head. "Vachel, you're still hinting, answer the princess so she can understand," Gilden commands in a whisper, afraid of hearing what will come out of the demon's mouth next.

"But...I didn't tell, master...I swear I didn't tell...no, no, no, please no...I didn't tell! I didn't tell! I didn't! Master, no! Don't let them have me again, please! Please,

I'm begging, don't give me to them, please!" Vachel begs, his chest heaving in fear, "They'll make me give myself to them...they'll make me give them everything...they'll make it hurt. Master, don't let them do it! Master! Master, help me! Don't let them, Master! Master, I'm scared! Master, don't leave me alone with them!"

"Vachel! Stop it, don't tell me anymore," Mikya cries, holding her hands over her ears. "I don't want to go in the coffin again! They locked me in the coffin with a corpse! They made me take the corpse and left me to drown in her rot! They chained me up and sliced me open...just to listen to me scream...just to know I was still afraid of them. No, master, no please! I'll do anything! Please!" Vachel screams, his hands coming up to grip the sides of his head in fear.

At this, Gilden jerks his hand back from Vachel's head like he has been burned by the touch. His own chest is heaving as he slips to his knees on the floor. Mikya still has her hands clamped firmly over her ears, taking deep breaths that make her entire frame shudder.

"You bastard...how dare you," Vachel whispers dangerously, slumped forward again. "You refused to tell us without it, Vachel. What would you have had me do?" Gilden counters breathlessly. Growling deep in his throat, Vachel replies, "I wanted you to leave me alone. That's why I told you to go. Instead, you paraded my pain like I was some kind of toy for your amusement."

"That isn't why he did it, Vachel," Mikya counters, forcing herself to look up. "Bullshit!" Vachel growls, "If there was another reason, he would have left it alone." She begins to protest: "Vachel, we just--" "Shut up! I don't want to hear your voices! Get out of here, now! Get out!" Vachel yells, his head jerking up so that she can see pure hatred and fury in his eyes.

Mikya scrambles to her feet, but is too afraid to pass by the demon. At this, Vachel slips to his feet, taking a step toward her. Mikya takes a step back in response, her eyes going wide with fright. Vachel continues to move forward, and Mikya takes a step back for each one he takes forward. Eventually, her back makes contact with the far wall, and she can no longer get away. His eyes ablaze with hatred, Vachel stands back to glare into her eyes.

Mikya makes a small, frightened noise before looking to Gilden for help. However, before he can make it forward, Vachel takes Mikya's arm and flings her around toward the sorcerer. She collapses on the floor at Gilden's feet, her legs refusing to work for her.

"Now, get out of here before I make certain you never come near me again," Vachel threatens, his entire frame trembling. Gilden grabs Mikya's upper arm and pulls her to her feet, careful to keep her balanced with his arms as he slowly makes his way back toward the door. As they make their labored progress, Vachel stands silent, but the heated aura is strong enough to be seen in a flaming cloud around him. At the sight of this, Mikya's legs suddenly decide it is time she gets out of here.

In response, she turns in Gilden's grasp and begins pushing him back, causing him to nearly stumble his way to the door. When they finally make it out into the corridor, Mikya pauses only to close the door quickly behind her. Satisfied they are out of harm's way, she all but collapses to the floor at Gilden's feet. Her shoulders tremble with silent tears, and Gilden can do nothing but watch. He lets her cry for a few minutes before he decides it would be wise to get her out of the hallway.

At this decision, he unlocks the door and opens it before picking her up like one would a sleeping child with an arm around her shoulders and the back of her knees. She makes no protest as he carries her into the room and shuts the door with his foot. Once inside, he lays her down on the first bed, smoothing the hair out of her face before giving her some space. She breaks out into sobs, unable to keep them back any longer.

It seems as if only minutes have passed when Gilden wakes to the sound of a gentle knocking on the door, as if the person doing it does not really want anyone inside to hear. Looking around, Gilden realizes night has slipped over the world as he slept. Stretching, he gets to his feet and makes his way over to the door just as the knocking ceases. Still, Gilden opens the door. He finds a distressed-looking Vachel about to turn away.

"Is something wrong, Vachel?" Gilden whispers, trying to get the demon to look at him. Vachel stands silent with his head hung low, and Gilden can tell he is either ashamed or unsure of something.

Standing silent for a moment, Gilden decides to press, but gently this time: "What's wrong?" "I know you probably think I deserve to be tormented right now...but I wondered if you two would mind if I slept in your room," Vachel whispers as if he does not really want to be asking. "Did something happen with Ven?" Gilden asks, pulling the door completely open but not stepping aside. Swallowing hard, Vachel replies, "He's brought them both up with him...I can't handle the noises they're making at the moment." Gilden is about to ask why when he remembers the confession he forced Vachel to make.

"The princess is already asleep, but I don't see the harm in it," he answers with a small nod more to himself than to Vachel. "Thanks...I-I'm sorry about blowing up at you two earlier," Vachel apologizes in a whisper, "I should have controlled myself better." "No, I shouldn't have let my curiosity evolve into something so dangerous. I didn't mean to hurt you with it," Gilden answers, gazing away in shame. "I've had worse done to me to get information, sorcerer, and the one who did it wasn't sorry it hurt, either," Vachel replies, hinting again. Sighing, Gilden pleads, "Please don't do that. It makes me want to know."

"Perhaps...after we're through with this...I'll tell you both," Vachel answers, running a hand through his hair. Nodding but unsure if he truly wants to know now, Gilden steps aside to allow Vachel to make his way into the room.

Gilden carefully closes the door so as not to make enough noise to wake the princess. When he gazes back into the room, Vachel is already sitting on the floor, slipping off his boots. At the sight, Gilden thinks of his own and pulls them off before hanging the robe up beside the door.

As he turns around, Gilden pulls the gloves from his hands and gazes up to find that Vachel has removed his shirt, revealing his back. The skin is smooth and untouched until one gazes below the shoulder line. This is where the scars begin. They are not the kind that one gets by being whipped or swiped with a sword, either, no these are far more intricate, as if someone took the time to carefully etch the designs into his back.

There are symbols representing different forms of magic, each one unlike the others. Above each of these symbols is a handwritten name, all carved neatly into the skin like one would sign into a logbook. None of the scars is nearly as prominent as the one that rests just above his pants. The symbol is a serpentine dragon in a spiral formation, and just above it is the name "Selene".

This one is by far the largest and demonstrates a kind of intimacy the others do not, not only because of where it is positioned, but also because of the fact that this one is more carefully done, as if the person was making certain it would stand out for years to come.

"Did the Sisters do this to you?" Gilden asks tentatively, trying his best not to tread on a particularly sensitive area. "Yes," Vachel answers simply, slipping the ribbon from his hair so it covers all of the scars except that final one in a curtain of black.

Dropping the gloves on top of his pack, Gilden climbs onto his bed before he asks, "Is Selene the lover you regret?" "Yes...she betrayed me to the ones who placed the curse on me," Vachel explains, sighing bitterly, "I hate her so much...almost as much as I used to love her." "Are you going to need anything?" Gilden asks, changing the subject abruptly before he can ask a question that will get Vachel mad at him, again.

Vachel gazes at the floor for a moment, seeming to be in thought before he whispers, "If you've got an extra pillow..." Without a word, Gilden tosses it to him before slipping beneath the sheets and blanket. Vachel slips to the floor and wraps his arms around the pillow, cuddling with it more than resting his head on it. The crystal falls forward to rest before his face, twinkling innocently in the dim moonlight streaming through the window. Smiling at it, Vachel gently kisses the red surface before closing his eyes and curling up around the soft pillow on the floor.

Across Hilden's Gate

Ven wakes to find himself jammed between the two girls from the night before. He lies on his right side so the brown-eyed girl is pressed against his chest. His arm has found a natural resting place across her waist. Even this close her hair can barely brush against his chin. At his back, the blue-eyed girl is tight against his skin, her fingers resting against his shoulders. He smiles to himself that he got more than his master would ever allow, all in one night, and all it cost him was the price of those seven or so drinks apiece.

His gaze falls on the bed Vachel was supposed to sleep in, and he realizes that not only is Vachel not there, but he never slept in it, either. Perhaps he and the girls scared the demon off. This thought makes the smile on his face widen, and he closes his eyes again. However, moments later, the door crashes open, startling him so he jerks, and his eyes snap open.

Vachel stands in the doorway, a deep glare perched on his face. "What do you want?" Ven demands as Vachel moves farther into the room. Not bothering to speak, Vachel takes hold of the edge of the mattress and pulls it up, spilling Ven and both girls to the floor on the other side. If the two girls were not awake before, they are now.

Gently placing the mattress back in its proper position, Vachel sits carefully on the edge, crossing his legs as he glares down at them. Both girls scramble to cover themselves, leaving Ven with nothing for his defense.

"What's this all about?!" Ven demands angrily, glaring back up at the demon. "If you haven't forgotten, we have a mission to complete. I've been more than patient with your natural urges," Vachel replies in a controlled whisper. Taking this as a hint to leave, the girls snatch up their clothes and dart out the door, taking the sheet with them as cover.

Vachel watches them go with a crooked smile on his face, remarking: "That's pretty sad...you made all that noise last night, and for the likes of those two." "That's none of your business!" Ven bursts angrily. Gazing back down at Ven, Vachel replies, "I want out of this town before nightfall, so get your ass moving and get ready to go." His voice is still controlled, as if he is fighting to keep himself from yelling.

"You can't order me around, demon!" Ven growls, not moving. He won't let another one of them take control of his life. Two masters are more than anyone should have to serve. "Well, not unless I invoke the magic of your little trinket...I know how to use a Shiku Hara just as well as Rust does," Vachel threatens, a scheming smile coming to his face. *If not better.* Ven still refuses to move. At this, Vachel flicks his wrist at the door, causing it to slam shut as if wind has pushed against it. He holds out his hand toward Ven as if offering him a hand up.

At this call, the chain on the collar springs to life, jerking Ven forward as it seeks out Vachel's outstretched hand. Pulling Ven's face close enough to touch, Vachel threatens, "I have but to whisper the proper words, child, and you'll regret disobeying a direct order." "You don't frighten me," Ven growls, the fear slipping to his eyes even as he says it. "Your eyes tell me differently, child," Vachel replies, his smile flashing fangs now. "I'll not let you treat me this way," Ven answers, pulling against Vachel's hold on the chain. "Pain...anger...torment. Teach this child what it means to be mine," Vachel whispers, his eyes flashing red at the end.

Slowly, the fear in Ven's eyes deepens as his fingers jerk up to wrap around the edge of the Shiku Hara. Out from underneath it, a violet flame peaks out and slides across his skin. It slowly makes its way up to cover his face and neck before the color changes to black. Ven has only a second to take in a deep breath before the flame plunges into his skin, drawing blood in three places as it rushes deep into the muscle. He gives a mighty scream when the fire wraps itself around the nerves.

His fingers jerk up to his face and dig into the skin in an attempt to take some of the pain to another part of his body. Tears stream steadily down his face as he seeks to hunch over in pain, only to have Vachel jerk on the chain, reminding him that the demon still controls the magic digging into his nerves. "Are you ready to heed my commands?" Vachel asks with a demonic smile. "G-go to hell!" Ven bursts through the pain. At this, the pain spikes before dancing through his fingers and down his arms to rush over his shoulders and connect to the pain in his neck.

The screams increase in volume and he pulls back as hard as he can against the chain. This only serves to make it lengthen in Vachel's hand and cause him to fall back on the bed. The jarring makes the pain all the worse, and he hunches up against it, trying not to let his fingers touch anything more as they throb. Vachel watches coolly, not a hint of regret on his face or anything to suggest this performance is affecting him in any way.

Finally, he asks again, "Are you ready to heed my commands?" "N-none but my m-master can order me to do anything!" Ven cries, gritting his teeth against the pain already shooting through him. In response, the power spikes again, pouring down his chest and back until it rests over the upper half of him. A near shriek is brought from him as he jerks against it. The tears are now joined by sobs that rack his frame and cause the pain to spike all the worse. "You are the only one who can stop the progress, Ven," Vachel whispers in a voice almost too low to hear with the screams in the background. The only answer is another scream as the sobs bring a spike of pain that knifes through him.

"This is your last chance," Vachel warns finally, "Are you ready to heed my commands?" "N-n-never!" Ven almost yells. He immediately regrets it as the pain shoots through the rest of him. This time, he actually does shriek.

His back arches against the pain, and he makes a wet sound deep in his throat, suggesting something inside has started to bleed. The smile still on his face, Vachel leans forward, resting his fingertips ever so lightly on Ven's chest. Ven responds with a shriek like the demon's very touch is burning him. "You merely have to do as I told you to ease this," Vachel whispers in a soothing voice as if he were consoling a small child who has fallen. Still defiant, Ven forces himself to shake his head slowly.

This causes the pain to rush all the more violently through his head. Still smiling, Vachel removes his hand to climb up onto the bed and straddle his captive at the waist, careful to keep his full weight off Ven's stomach. The pressure of his body pressing down would cause the magic coursing through Ven's body to attack that place and most likely kill him. Immediately, the chain shrinks, so, even as Vachel holds the end between them, it strains against the leather. Even the light brush of Vachel's knees against his sides causes the burning in Ven's skin to escalate.

He screams, and a small rush of blood forces its way up to his lips before spilling over them and down his chin. Bending forward, Vachel carefully runs his tongue over the line of blood, making certain to stop just shy of touching Ven's lips. The pain springs to the surface like a hot coal being dropped on his face. A shriek comes this time, and Ven digs his fingers into Vachel's chest, succeeding only in causing the burning pain to shoot along his arms and hands because his fingers cannot find bare flesh to react with.

"Remember, child, if you'll just do as you're told, all of this will go away," Vachel whispers, a smile still on his face. Ven opens his mouth to speak, but a new rush of blood blocks his words. He tries again only to find his throat does not want to work for him; his tongue and mouth are willing to form the words, but the other necessary equipment does not want to function properly.

Finally, he resorts to gritting his teeth and giving a slow, determined nod. Immediately, the pain recedes, leaving him aching, his chest heaving in an attempt to get as much air as possible. "There now, if you'd just done that in the beginning, we could have avoided all of this," Vachel replies, dropping the chain so that it slams against Ven's chest. He gives a grunt of protest but does not move to retaliate

Smiling so his fangs flash, Vachel slips off to the floor as he adds, "You might want to clean off your face before we go." Still trembling, Ven forces himself up to go about the task of getting dressed. It is only now that the screams have stopped that either of them can hear someone pounding on the door. Vachel makes his way over to it with a sudden, fluid grace Ven has not seen before.

He pulls open the door just enough for him to catch a glimpse of Gilden's face. "We heard screams. What the hell is going on in there?" Gilden demands, a look of both anger and concern keeping shop on his face. Smiling as if he is thoroughly pleased with himself, Vachel replies, "I was just teaching a little lesson that our friend let get out of hand.

You've nothing to worry about, sorcerer." "Lesson? What did you do to that boy, Vachel?" Gilden counters, the anger pulling forward. "We can discuss this later," Vachel answers, his voice still pleasant, "I have a few things to see to first." "What are y--" Vachel slams the door in his face before Gilden can finish, using his wind to keep it that way. Immediately, the pounding resumes, but Vachel pays it no mind.

He turns around in a smooth, flowing movement, nothing like the jerks he has exhibited before. It is almost as if calling the magic that allows him to control the Shiku Hara has allowed him to call some of his lost demonic characteristics, as well. By this time, Ven has pulled on the necessary clothing. His sleeveless shirt is identical to the first except this one is red. His pants are black, baggy, and secured at the waist by a tight, black belt. At his shins, the pants are tucked into his boots, so they bulge around the rims. Once again, his hands are covered in the black gloves. Over his shoulders, he has draped a black cloak.

He crouches next to his pack in a defensive position as he gazes up at Vachel. His eyes are nearly double the size they should be, and tears still stream steadily from them. The blood running down his chin is still present, for he has not had the chance yet to clean it from his face. Still smiling as if he is pleased with himself, Vachel makes his way across the room to Ven.

Again, his movements have a grace to them they did not before, as if something about the spell has returned a lost part of him. It is a smooth, fluid quality to his movements most demons cannot perform without years of practice, but by just watching, Ven can tell this is actually an inherited talent. No amount of practice could make one as fluent in the ability to move his body in a steady rhythm that makes him appear to glide across the floor rather than walk.

Once he is in position next to Ven, Vachel smiles down at him in silence. Ven gazes up into his face as if expecting the demon to change his mind and strike him around the face. Vachel slowly reaches forward, causing Ven to flinch in anticipation of a blow. Instead, Vachel bends down and slips his fingertips along the line of Ven's jaw. The confusion is evident in Ven's face as he gazes frightened at the demon's. Vachel gives nothing but the same smile as his fingers slowly feel along the jaw before slipping down to the neck. It is harder to feel here because of the Shiku Hara, but Vachel can still tell there is something wrong with what he is feeling.

"Open your mouth," he commands, gazing directly into Ven's eyes. Ven does as he is told, confusion still rushing through his brain. Placing his thumb on Ven's chin so as to be able to control where his head is positioned, Vachel gazes inside his open mouth. It is too dark for a mortal to see inside, but Vachel can both see it and smell it: blood is slipping from the flesh deep in Ven's throat. "That would explain why you couldn't speak earlier. The spell's gone and torn the parts vital to speaking all to hell," Vachel explains, closing Ven's mouth for him.

There is a new fear on Ven's face at this news, and a tentative hand slips up to touch the skin visible just below the Shiku Hara. "Not to worry, child. I'm an elemental remember," Vachel explains with the same smile. He runs his tongue along the tips of the index and middle fingers on each of his hands before slipping them behind the collar. Gently, he begins to run his fingertips against the skin, as if trying to massage the damage away. Vachel closes his eyes in concentration, and Ven begins to feel a soothing heat slip along his skin where the demon's fingertips touch.

Soon, the twinge of pain in his throat recedes, causing Vachel to slowly slip his fingers away. Gazing at the relief on Ven's face, Vachel asks, "Can I assume this means you feel better?" "Well, my throat does, at least," Ven replies in a somewhat hoarse tone, the muscles of his legs trembling now that he thinks about the ache in them. "We don't have the time to heal every little ache and pain," Vachel responds with a small shake of his head. Ven does not respond, and Vachel gets to his feet. It is only now that he pays Gilden's pounding any mind as he points to the bathroom to hint that Ven is to clean his face now.

As Ven is rushing to get to the bathroom, Vachel makes his way to the door and opens it completely this time. "What's the idea of slamming the door in my face?" Gilden growls angrily. Gazing past Gilden for a moment, Vachel spies Mikya looking frightened right outside the opposite door. He has no doubt the screams she heard have made her fear him. He turns his attention back to Gilden as he replies,

121

"You were interfering with something important." "Just what were those screams about, Vachel?" Gilden demands, his eyes narrowing.

"I wasn't committing any kind of sacrifice if that's what you think," Vachel answers almost casually, "I was teaching a lesson that needed to be taught if we're going to get anywhere on this trip." "And what might that be?" Gilden asks. "I have ultimate power in this group, and I will be treated as such," Vachel answers slowly, controlling his voice again. Gilden stands in silence, having been taken aback by the statement. Just as the words slip from his mouth, Ven makes his way back out into the room, the blood and tears gone from his face. However, the fear is still evident in his movements and the way his eyes keep flicking to Vachel's back as he moves to retrieve his things.

Gilden spies Ven over Vachel's shoulder and demands, "What exactly did you use to teach your lesson?" "The Shiku Hara...I know how it works just as well, if not better, than Rust. I want that to be clear so we don't have any mishaps involving anyone thinking they can outdo me and keep their heads," Vachel explains as if it is something everyone does. "You used the Shiku Hara?!" Gilden exclaims, his hands balled into fists at his sides, "Do you realize the implications of that?!" "I'm as evil as I want to be, sorcerer," Vachel replies calmly, "If I want to dabble in dark magic, it is no business of yours."

"Are you daft?! That's illegal!"

"So is holding someone against their will without just reason."

"I wasn't the one who did that, Vachel!"

"Perhaps...but you never stopped it even though you knew."

"You actually committed the crime!"

"Guilt by association, sorcerer."

"You tortured him, Vachel! No one deserves to be tortured!"

"I'm glad everyone with even a third mortal in them is a person when I'm not," Vachel counters, the first hint of bitterness in his voice. "I never said you weren't a person!" Gilden protests angrily. "You said that no one, implying no person, should be tortured, yet you allowed Nark to torture me for close to two centuries and observed the entire term of my imprisonment without lifting a finger to stop it. Now, when I'm the one doing the torturing, just because he isn't even half demon, tormenting people is wrong," Vachel answers, heat coming to his voice.

"Can we please get out of here before you guys take this any farther?" Ven interjects timidly. Vachel glances over at him, curious to see the look on his face that goes with the frightened voice. Despite his attempts to hide it, Ven's eyes scream fear. Not only are they trembling, but they are also still too wide for his face. Spying this, Vachel turns away from Gilden, still fluid and graceful, and makes his way over to where Ven crouches beside his pack. Once he is standing right beside Ven, Vachel reaches down and runs his hand gently through Ven's hair: "Sure thing, child. We can leave now." A small, cautious smile slips to Ven's face as he gives a nod before climbing to his feet.

Turning away, Vachel declares, "You heard the man, he wants to get out of here just as much as I do." "What did you do to him to make that so?" Gilden accuses, his eyes narrowing again. Pushing his hair from his face with a casual hand, Vachel replies, "Ask him." Gilden gazes over at Ven but does not speak the question.

Taking a deep but shaky breath, Ven whispers, "Is it so wrong to want to get back home?" "No, but I wanted to make certain he didn't force you to make the decision," Gilden replies slowly. A glare slips to Ven's face as he protests, "Just because I'm not powerful doesn't mean I let other people make my decisions for me." Gilden falls silent at the comment, having not meant to touch a sore spot.

Shouldering his pack, Ven stalks past Vachel, pushing his way through the door. It is expected for him to be angry for being underestimated, but he just dug himself a hole by giving Gilden ammunition about his lack of power and how much it bothers him to be under someone's thumb. Vachel flashes Gilden a fanged smile before taking off after Ven, sparing only a small glance for the princess. She still looks frightened, and Vachel has the feeling the fear is being directed at him more and more.

When Vachel makes it to the top of the stairs, he finds Ven standing silent and still about half way down, his back pressed against the wall as he raises his face to the ceiling. Tears are streaming down his face again, and he is trembling. Without so much as a glance back at Mikya and Gilden, Vachel makes his way down the stairs as if nothing is wrong. However, when he makes it to Ven, he stops and turns, so they are facing each other. "So, what is it, child?" Vachel asks in a whisper.

Ven gives a small whimper and shakes his head, but does not speak. Crossing his arms, Vachel presses, "Does this have something to do with my using the Shiku Hara?" Still trembling, Ven gives a small nod and whimpers, "I don't want any more masters...I can't please the ones I already have."

"I only want you to listen to me until we finish this mission," Vachel explains, gazing away, "I've made certain that I am my only master because I hate having one...why would I want to be the master of someone else if I hate the position so?" Ven merely shakes his head. At this, Vachel makes his way to the bottom of the stairs, giving a small gesture for Ven to follow. Wiping away most of his tears, Ven rushes after him just as Mikya and Gilden appear.

Ven is forced to wait for Gilden to make his way down in order to turn in the keys. He has to be careful to keep his eyes on what he is doing, so he will not start trembling again. Simply being in Vachel's presence, no matter what the demon says about not wanting to be his master, is making his very skin tighten with fear.

Throughout the entire ordeal, Hirron is still polite and smiling, nearly as frightened of the demon as Ven is.

Eager to get out of such enclosed quarters now, Ven quickly gives Hirron four gold pieces, but does not bother to get his change. Vachel notices this, but does not speak up to remind Ven of the mistake because he understands it is not one, not really. He even goes so far as to give Gilden a stern warning look when the sorcerer is about to point it out. Of course, Vachel also takes the time to notice Mikya is unusually silent as they take their leave.

Once they are outside amongst the people, Ven allows Vachel to walk ahead. If they moved for Ven the day before, they scramble from Vachel's presence like they believe he is some disease they do not want to catch. The demon pays it no mind as he makes his way through the city. This time, Mikya makes certain to keep herself as close to Gilden as she can. Ven stays between them, almost like a walking barrier, and, even though he does his best to walk as if he owns the city, Mikya can see the trembling in his hands. She does not point this out, however, most likely because she knows her own hands are trembling just as much, if not more.

The people's eyes are still on her, but not because of who she happens to be walking with. No, they are more focused on the pale quality of her face. Her fear keeps her from being concerned that they noticed, but the stares are making her uncomfortable. Sensing her discomfort, Gilden takes her hand in his and gives it a gentle squeeze. She is grateful for it, but does not trust her voice enough to tell him so. Eventually, they near the outskirts of the city, and Mikya finds the stares are not so frequent here, as if the population is more concerned with themselves than the goings-on of the people around them. She is grateful for this as well, but she nearly breathes a sigh of relief once they finally make it out of the city.

Once they hit the sandy expanse of terrain outside the city, Ven rushes up so he is nearly in line with Vachel. Gilden moves forward in the line, bringing Mikya with him and causing their group to seem more compact. Mikya does not protest at being this close to Vachel because her hand is still firmly secured in Gilden's, and she can already see the line on the horizon she assumes is the gate. Glad this mission might soon be over, she contents herself with gazing at the flat expanse of sand that passes for scenery. It is not much to look at, but she would rather gaze at this expanse of nothingness than think about Vachel or Ven. Of course, as the time wears on, she is forced to think about what is really bothering her.

It is bad enough to know Vachel had been taken advantage of, but it hurts even worse to know she and Gilden had to use magic to force the information out of him. She can still see the fury and hatred in his eyes when he rounded on her once Gilden released the spell. It scares her to know that there is magic out there that could force someone to tell everything no matter how painful or gruesome. Silently, she admits it scares her more to know

Gilden was willing to use it on someone, even if Vachel is a demon.

Now, she knows the vision she saw at the castle was actually her magic trying to tell her something was wrong. She knows what a Shiku Hara is used for, and it makes her uneasy to know she is in the presence of someone who's master would force them to wear one. On top of it all, Vachel actually used it on Ven without it bothering him in the least. The screams were terrible, but knowing Vachel was the one who caused them makes them all the worse. She continues to mull it all over in her mind, but she can make no more sense of how this could be happening than when she started. All she can figure out is that she is in the presence of men who can take steps she could never bring herself to take.

After some time, she gazes up to find the dark line on the horizon has grown into a wall before her eyes, a wall she had no idea was even out here. The shock must have shown on her face because Gilden responds, "You've been silent ever since we left. I thought you might want your privacy."

Interesting, he considered her privacy enough to stay silent, but not enough to release her hand. Of course, if he had let go she probably would have gone into hysterics.

Pushing this from her mind for a moment, she gazes up at the gate to find it is more of a wall built with stone that has a set of wooden doors worked into it. The wall itself is close to the height of a four-story building, and the doors fit into an archway that is close to a story taller than that. One would think the wood would not have a chance to keep anything close to a demon in power at bay, that is, until one spies the markings carved into the surface.

Each one is the symbol for a specific charm or spell (that much she can tell from her own lessons in magic as a girl), and there are close to fifty different symbols. Blood trails from some of them, suggesting the person who drew them needed more than just some words to make it work properly and suggesting that person was desperate enough to invoke a blood spell to keep Dehurst and Darkhaven separate. Still, with this much magic on one set of doors, it could keep out many things of close ilk with demons.

Abruptly, Vachel stops, forcing the rest to stop as well. No one speaks as he gazes up at the doors in thought before he finally makes up his mind. Stretching, he suggests, "Perhaps we should save the actual entry until tomorrow...when the sun is up." "I didn't know you were superstitious," Gilden comments, trying to make a joke. "I'm not," Vachel whispers seriously, "I just know what kind of things lurk beyond those gates after dark."

Silence falls over the group for a moment, as if each is thinking of what might come out to attack them. Finally, Ven breaks the silence: "Maybe we should find a more sheltered place to sleep for the night." His voice is low, but the silence prevents him from having to speak any louder. Gilden takes a sweeping look at the expanse of ground before he asks, "And where do you see anything that even resembles a sheltered area?"

"I can make a hill for you if you really wanted it," Vachel replies with a smile. They didn't have much more than a mound of sand on Ring Trail, and he felt no fear. Vachel has a feeling being near Hilden's Gate is what has caused this change of heart. Shaking his head at himself, Gilden answers, "Sorry, I keep forgetting you're an elemental. I've been trying to rid myself of the memory of how I found out." "Did it shake you up that much, sorcerer? Aw, I'm flattered," Vachel responds in a mocking voice. "Can we skip this stuff tonight?" Mikya interjects, her voice hollow.

"Sure thing, princess."

"What's in this for you, Vachel?" Gilden accuses.

"I want to see if she's as frightened tomorrow, and I hate waiting."

Liar! Liar! Vachel hisses inside his head.

"So, you want to sleep until you get an answer."

"Yep...I can dream about it this way."

Stop it! Tell him the truth! Vachel snarls at himself.

Before Gilden can respond, Vachel turns his back and waves his hand over the sand at his feet. He won't tell the truth and show any sort of compassion to these people. That's much too dangerous with his power only at half what it should be. In response, the sand forces its way up from the flattened position and builds into a large mound. Smiling triumphantly as he turns around, Vachel declares, "See? I told you I could make a hill for you." Gilden scowls before moving forward to join Ven and Vachel near the

130

mound. Mikya follows close behind, only now noticing he has released her hand. *Perhaps hysterics was a little overboard.*

Stretching his back and arms, Vachel slips to the ground before stretching out on the sand. Ven lies down near his feet like a well-trained dog. Gritting her teeth against the days events, Mikya tries to keep her thoughts away from the Shiku Hara. Of course, Ven's behavior toward Vachel presently is not helping her focus. Finally, she decides the only way to keep her thoughts in order is to keep her brain from working on them.

Sighing, she slips to the sand, making certain to keep as far away from Vachel as she can without being out in the open. Seeing this, Gilden slips down between them to act as a kind of living barrier. Mikya smiles at him before closing her eyes and slipping to sleep from the exhaustion of mind.

Mikya wakes from the dream, her chest heaving as she tries desperately to take in enough air. It had certainly been much less than pleasant. Throughout she was forced to relive the horror she felt yesterday. Sitting up and drawing her knees to her chest, she hugs herself close, shaking her head as if trying to fling the thoughts from it. Just as she gets her breathing back to normal, she realizes there is someone else awake, and that person does not sound like he is having the best of times, either.

Getting shakily to her feet, she only has to take two steps to see Vachel hunched over in the sand. It takes her a moment to realize the sound she heard was the sound of him letting everything he had eaten during the day come up on him.

A shudder passes through his back, and he brings up another rush, coughing loudly. He takes several deep breaths and swallows hard only to have everything come up again. Mikya stands shocked watching for a few more minutes before he stops. The trembling is still there, but he is no longer struggling against the heaves to breathe. He gives a mighty cough before wiping his mouth roughly and grabbing a handful of sand. He uses the sand to hide the remnants of his stomach's protest against something.

Heaving a sigh, he gets to his feet and turns around to find Mikya standing there, staring. A dark look comes to his face as he asks, "What is it, princess?" "I...I didn't mean to intrude, but I woke up and heard a noise," Mikya explains quickly. "Well, now you know what it was," Vachel whispers, the darkness slipping to his voice, "So, go back to sleep." "I can't do that knowing something is making you feel that badly," Mikya answers, gazing down at the sand. Turning around quickly, Vachel nearly growls, "I'm not going to relive it for you, princess." "Did it have something to do with being this close to Darkhaven?" Mikya asks tentatively. "Yes," Vachel replies simply.

Hugging herself as she gazes back up, Mikya asks, "Did what Gilden and I did bring back the memories of the Sisters?" At this, Vachel tenses before dropping to the ground to be sick again. When he finishes this time, Vachel does not bother to get up as he whispers, "Does this answer your question, princess?" "Yes...I'm really sorry to have given you so much trouble," Mikya answers, tears evident in her voice.

Sighing, Vachel adds, "But, I would have had to be reminded anyway. We have to see them tomorrow to get anywhere in Darkhaven." Mikya is silent as the tears slip down her face. Just as she feared, her actions and Gilden's are making him miserable when all they wanted to do was help. *Why does everything I do have to turn out so wrong?* "They'll expect..." Vachel whispers more to himself than to her, swallowing hard enough to hurt, "...payment for their trouble."

"Vachel...you can't let them have you just for a mission."

"I have to...it will only be for a night or two, but..."

"No one should have to go through that, for any reason."

"Princess, you don't know what you're talking about."

"No! I mean it. We'll find another way to pay them."

"There is no other way, princess."

"There has to be."

"No. The Sisters must be given a gift that has to do with death, magic, or sex. We can't let them kill one of us...and we don't have any magic in our arsenal that they will be interested in. That leaves us with only one option, and I'll have to do it because of the marks on my back," Vachel explains, gripping the sand as if he is trying to force it into a single ball. "What marks? And what do they have to do with anything?" Mikya demands, a shock coming to her voice.

"They used blades dipped in their own blood to etch their names and symbols of power into my back. Because of that, I am obligated to present myself as the gift when I am in their presence," Vachel explains in a whisper, "I don't like it any more than you do, but that's just the way it's worked out." "But--" Vachel glares up at her as he interjects, "Don't argue with me, princess! We're going to do things my way whether you like it or not. Now, go back to sleep, and leave me alone!"

Mikya does not sleep the rest of the night, so she is one of the first to actually get up. It is obvious from the look of her face she has been crying, but she denies it when Gilden asks. Vachel does not even bother to look at her as they wait for Ven to wake. Once he finally does, he gives a rushed apology about being tired from the previous days events. The thought makes Mikya cringe, but she does not harbor quite as much of the fear now. If Vachel notices, he does not show it.

After his hurried apology, Ven gazes up at the gate before making his way over to it, standing so that he merely has to lift his hand to touch the wood. Mikya eyes Vachel's face, and notices he is not surprised by what Ven is doing. Apparently, this is the key that unlocks the gate. The others come up behind him as he slowly removes the glove on his right hand.

Sighing, he lifts the bare fingers up to the surface of the wood and gives it the barest of caresses. He has time only to pull the glove back on before the symbols carved into the wood shine violet. Mikya and Gilden gaze up at it in awe, but Vachel keeps his gaze on Ven's back, as if the sight holds no interest to him.

As soon as the light fades, a creaking sound breaks into the silence as the doors begin to creep open. They are far enough apart to allow one person to walk through when Ven presses forward. The others follow in a single-file line behind him, noticing immediately the doors are no longer moving.

Once they are on the other side, the doors slam shut as if angry at having been opened in the first place. The sand around them is no longer the brown that can be found in Dehurst. Instead it is a sparkling black. Mikya gazes up at the sky in shock, wondering what else could be different about this place. It is as if they have crossed more than just a breach in a wall.

She gazes intently at the violet sky, and the only thought that occurs to her is that they must have at least crossed a dimensional barrier, as well. Swallowing hard, she turns her gaze to Gilden to find him staring up into the sky just as she had; however, when she turns her attention to Ven and Vachel, they appear to consider this passage as having merely stepped through a door to their homes instead of passing into another dimension. Neither one is paying even the slightest attention to the sky or color of the sand beneath their feet, instead, their gazes are focused on the horizon, as if expecting something to come charging at them. When nothing appears, they seem to relax slightly. A smile on his face, Ven turns back to them and announces, "Welcome to Darkhaven!"

Sisters of Darkhaven

"That's certainly laughable...'welcome' is not the word I would have used," Vachel responds, gazing at his surroundings as if extremely upset to even be here. Sighing, Ven whispers, "But, I like it. It might not be so much fun inside the castle, but outside is nice." At this, Vachel gazes over to him, watching a sadness fill the boy's face. The Hybrid wolf has been caged for too long, and it shows. Still, he does not point it out. Instead, he stretches his back and replies, "Well, we had best go see the Sisters before we have to spend too much time around here."

"What's wrong with here?" Mikya asks, gazing hard at the horizon. Vachel takes a step forward before he answers, "Stay put and you'll soon find out, princess."

"How are we going to get to the Sisters without another tedious journey?" Ven interjects, turning his gaze to Vachel. Smiling his best, pity-laden smile, Vachel replies, "We'll just use a bit of magic. I could take us anywhere in Darkhaven without any difficulty if I had the Sister's support. Now, I just have to go get it, and we'll have no more problems." "I really don't want to have to visit them," Ven whispers with a shudder, hugging himself tightly, "They're really dangerous, and that's without the magic." "I know that, child, and I don't particularly want to go, either. Still, we need their permission if we want to be able to get anywhere without their allies ganging up on us," Vachel explains, shaking his head in a mellowed version of Ven's shudder.

"Then, let's just get it over with, please."

Nodding, Vachel turns to Mikya and Gilden, gesturing for them to come forward. They immediately comply, moving up until they are less than an arm's length away. Vachel crosses his arms in the center of their small circle, closing his eyes in concentration. As the time slowly slips by, the wind picks up around them, forcing grit up in a cloud that masks their figures from their surroundings.

Finally, Vachel's eyes pop open, the red invading even his pupil. He gives a deep breath before his entire frame jerks stiff. Mikya is about to reach out for him when she feels the magic close in around them, blocking her senses. Despite this, she can still tell the others are there, as if somehow their presence still calls out to her magic. Her chest begins to burn like she has been denying herself air until she feels a jolt to her body. It is only now that she feels the magic slip away and the ground solid beneath her feet.

They slowly open their eyes to find the gate is nowhere to be seen. Instead, there a towering, white structure made entirely of towers jutting up from the ground. It is a stark contrast against the black sand that surrounds it. "This is where we meet the Sisters?" Gilden asks, forcing his gaze away from the structure. It is so much like that of the Sister's of Dehurst, he has to keep from asking himself what it means concerning the Sisters back home. "Yes. So just let me do the talking," Vachel replies, moving forward.

The grace is still in his steps, but there is a more hunched look to his shoulders, as if he is blocking against a blow that is sure to come. Ven follows after him, a quick glance behind him at the others. There is fear deep in his eyes that he is desperately trying to keep from his face, with little success. Gazing over at Gilden for a moment, Mikya takes after them, her heart racing in her chest. She hears rather than sees Gilden follow, for she keeps her gaze straight ahead in an attempt to keep her pulse from jumping up into her face.

Vachel makes it to the large, wooden door before he turns around to wait for the rest. His shoulders now hunched as well, Ven moves in beside him, but keeps his gaze on the wood surface. It is too soon for both of them when Mikya and Gilden catch up with them. Sighing deeply, Vachel spins back around and rests his palm against the door. Immediately, it begins to open with a loud creak. However, Vachel does not make a move to enter.

Instead, a woman appears in the opening, smiling sweetly at them. The black dress is cut low, billowing out around her from her waist. Only thin straps at her shoulders keep the garment from slipping down to reveal anything more. Sleeves that are not attached to the dress cover her arms from wrist to just below the shoulder. Her blonde hair falls in waves to her waist and frames her face in gold. A pair of piercing, violet eyes gazes out at them, holding no hint of the smile that has captured her face, that is, until she spies Vachel.

"Trinket?" she declares, speaking to Vachel, "I've not seen you in so long. Ooh...the others will be so happy to see you!" "We're here to get permission to travel Darkhaven undeterred, Sherri," Vachel replies in a flat tone. Taking his hand in both of hers, Sherri smiles up at him and answers, "Well, you know that we have to receive proper payment, Trinket."

"Sherri? Did I just hear you say 'Trinket'?" another woman calls as she rushes forward, her skirt gathered in her hands so as not to trip herself. Hair the red of blood falls to her shoulders, and there is a sparkle in her green eyes as she forces her way in beside Sherri. Her dark skin is perhaps two shades more brown than the tan of Sherri's skin. "Yes, yes, Niko. He's come again at last!" Sherri declares, turning to the other woman for a moment. At this, Niko takes his other hand and begins to pull him inside. For a moment, Vachel resists her; then Sherri joins in.

He gives the others a glance over his shoulder, trying to draw attention to them. Even though Mikya knows there must be fear shooting through his brain, Vachel lets none of it peak out. This one glance causes the two women to peak around Vachel's shoulders to see Mikya, Gilden, and Ven staring at the proceedings. "Oh, pardon us," Niko apologizes, blushing slightly, "We have to take you to the High Sister before we can have our fun."

Ven cringes openly at the word "fun", swallowing hard.

"Come along. We'll bring your proposal to the High Sister, and she'll tell you what you have to give us," Sherri explains, "But, Trinket gets to stay with us while you're speaking with her."

At this, both she and Niko pull Vachel after them, gesturing for the others to follow. Vachel retains his straight-backed posture as they lead him through the stone corridors, even though it feels as if his fear is humming along his skin for them to see. However, Ven cannot keep his composure enough to even prevent himself from shaking as they travel along. His eyes keep flicking around him, as if he is trying to be prepared for an attack. Mikya has an urge to take his hand but fears how he will react if she touches him. Her gaze falls on Gilden for a moment, and she immediately notices the sweat slipping down his face, despite his effort to keep it blank and unreadable.

She has only one idea of what could cause this change in him: he has sensed some great power that is not sitting well in his stomach. Still, she is unwilling to ask him about it. Finally, the Sisters lead them to a set of black metal doors that tower over them. Sherri smiles back at them before releasing Vachel long enough to knock on the doors. The sound rings on for a moment after she strikes it.

There is a moment of silence before a voice replies, "Enter." Nearly giggling with glee, Sherri and Niko guide Vachel along as they push open the doors. This seems odd to Mikya because they look too heavy for even ten such women to open. Still, they accomplish this feat without so much as a protesting sound.

Inside, the room is made of a blue crystal. Across the expanse is a platform of the same material that bears a gold throne large enough to comfortably seat six people. A silver cushion with gold tassels at each corner is draped over the expanse of the gold seat. Lounging on this cushion is a girl who appears to be close to fifteen years of age.

Her dress is black as the other sisters', except for the gold cloth wrapped firmly around her waist so an end falls to the hem of the tight skirt. There is an opening in the side of the skirt, which allows the full length of her pale leg to be seen. On her exposed foot is a black sandal with a spiked heel of three inches that appears to be more of a tool for stabbing than an actual heel. Her black hair falls around her face like a veil, obscuring her left eye. Still, her blue-eyed gaze has force, despite it only having half of its strength to work with, especially since the blue has a shine to it that is not caused by the light around her at all.

Pushing herself up to a sitting position, she whispers, "Why, Trinket, I did not expect to see you again. I thought you were gone from Darkhaven." Even without volume, her voice carries throughout the room, as if somehow the air is seeking out the sound of her voice and projecting it.

"Trinket's traveling, High Sister Selene," Sherri explains, "He and his companions need safe passage throughout Darkhaven." "Interesting…do his companions understand our rules?" High Sister Selene asks in the same whisper. However, as she responds, Vachel catches it as something sparks in her eye. He isn't certain he wants to know why. Vachel is quick to reply, "They understand the policy of exchanging something for your aid." "Really...well then, I think there is no need for us to negotiate over payment. Trinket has so graciously given his presence, and therefore he belongs to us for three days. After that time you may continue on your way," she responds with a smile, slipping from the throne.

Stepping forward, Mikya demands, "Why three days?" Vachel gazes over his shoulder at her in an effort to get her to keep silent, but she shakes her head at him. "'Why three days' she asks...I've never heard such a question," Sherri and Niko burst together, dissolving in a fit of giggles at the princess's expense.

Making her way down from the platform, the High Sister replies, "It is quite simple, little one. One day is designated for me, and the other two are for my ladies. It is only fair, considering I do not think you have the time to wait for each to have her own night." Mikya swallows hard at the thought and falls silent. High Sister Selene gives her a smile full of pity in response. "Excellent. Now, we must seal the agreement. Messenger! You are part of this group, so I must share the seal with you," the High Sister declares. Still trembling, Ven drops his pack to the floor before making his way forward.

He stops before the High Sister with just enough room for her to raise her hands. As he stands silent, the High Sister pulls a knife from the cloth at her waist. Carefully, she presses the blade against his lips, just enough to draw blood. "Now, Messenger, you know what is to happen next," the High Sister replies, holding her hand out to him.

Taking a deep breath, Ven takes her hand and kisses her knuckles to leave a light imprint of his lips in blood on her pale skin. The pressure stings slightly, but he refuses to let her see him wince against it. Next, he raises his head, kissing her on the lips. This time, she pushes against the kiss until he gives a small whimper of pain. When he does, she pulls away from him and whispers, "You may join your companions again."

Nodding more to distract himself from the events than to actually agree, Ven turns away and makes the trek back to stand with the others. His hands are still trembling as he reaches for his pack and pulls it over his shoulder. "Sherri, Niko, see our guests to their rooms, then you can take Trinket to the others. I will give you the first two nights, this time. I want to be the last person he sees before he leaves," the High Sister directs, a scheming smile coming to her face.

Giggling all the worse, Sherri and Niko spin Vachel around as they pass by the others. Gilden keeps close to them as they lead the way again, but Mikya hangs back with

Ven. "Are you alright?" she whispers, gazing at him with all the concern she can muster.

Ven merely shakes his head, unable to trust his voice at the moment. Against her better judgment, Mikya slips her hand around his, giving it a small squeeze. Ven makes no move to pull away, but he does not press his fingers around her hand, either.

"Why does she frighten you so?" Mikya asks gently, afraid to make him any more upset. His lip quivers for a moment before he whispers, "She's pure evil...even Master has more mercy in him than she does. She'll do horrible things to you...and laugh." "Do you know if this is the Selene Vachel referred to when he was talking about a lover who betrayed him?" Mikya asks, trying to keep the subject away from what the High Sister might have done to *Ven* in the past.

"I...I don't know for certain. But, she is the only Selene I know of who had the power to keep Vachel's attention when he was part of the court," Ven explains, turning his gaze up to stare at Vachel's back. If the demon knows they are speaking about him, he gives no hint of it.

"Why would she betray him?"

"She was becoming more sadistic, so he dropped her."

"You mean she wasn't always like this?"

"No...it started when Rust appointed her as the new High Sister."

"Why then?"

"To be a Sister of Darkhaven one must be willing to torture people."

Mikya is silent.

"To be High Sister requires a willingness that...that..."

"You don't have to explain it if it hurts."

"She was the reason Master took an interest in me. She decided that I would make a good pet and convinced him to let me live. Master agreed as long as I became his slave by the Shiku Hara, and the High Sister allowed him to use me as his messenger," Ven explains, tears coming to his eyes, "He couldn't keep me until he found a way to bind me to the Shiku Hara. I tried to keep my sisters away from him, but he found them and told me he'd kill them if I didn't submit to the collar." "That's horrible," Mikya responds, her outrage showing on her face. Smiling weakly against his tears, Ven replies, "You don't know the half of it."

After seeing Mikya, Ven, and Gilden to their rooms, Sherri and Niko shift their hold to Vachel's upper arms before leading him away. Sherri leans her head against his arm as she whispers, "You know, it would be so much more fun if it were just the three of us tonight." "If the others weren't expecting us, I'd say we skip out on letting them have a cut," Niko adds, a scheming smile coming to her face. Straightening again, Sherri peaks around at Niko with a smile to match: "You know...I think the High Sister will be able to forgive us one night."

Niko gives her a small nod before pulling Vachel along faster, parting ways with the path they were supposed to have taken. Vachel lets nothing appear on his face, but a tension has begun to build in his shoulders.

Finally, they force him into a small room. It is dark, but he can still make out the outline of a large bed in the corner. Niko releases him to tap the door twice, forcing it shut until she decides to open it. Meanwhile, Sherri takes the time to force his shirt over his head, revealing the crystal hanging around his neck. "Look here, Niko. Trinket's gone and got himself a faerie's crystal," Sherri responds, turning him around to face Niko. Smiling, Niko remarks, "That he does. Did she confess her love, Trinket? Or did you steal it from her like a bad little demon?"

"It was a gift," Vachel replies in a whisper. "A gift he says! Well, well. It seems Trinket's been having some fun with the ladies over in Dehurst," Sherri taunts, jerking on the chain.

Running her fingers along Vachel's spine, Niko purrs, "Was she good, Trinket? Did she make you scream?" Vachel remains silent, the tension building all the more. "Enough yammering. I want my fun before the night's over," Sherri interjects, jerking the chain again. Vachel has to grit his teeth to keep himself from yelling at her to stop.

Niko bends down behind him, wrapping her arms around his ankles so that, when Sherri pulls him forward, he has to step out of the boots to keep from tripping. "Ok, Trinket, you're on first," Sherri directs, pointing to the bed.

Narrowing his eyes slightly, Vachel moves forward and climbs up onto the bed, leaning back against the pillows to stare out at them. He knows what is coming next, and it is making his stomach tighten up in fear, yet he keeps his face blank. He has to, or they will use the fear against him.

"I get first because it was my idea," Sherri declares, bending down and retrieving a knife from her boot beneath the skirt. Giggling, Niko teases, "Just remember to save some clean skin for me." Sherri gives her a nod before slipping her own boots off and climbing up on top of him, resting her weight on his stomach.

"So, Trinket, where do you want to hurt first?" Sherri asks, her voice becoming a purr. Sighing finally, Vachel whispers, "You know the answer to that question." "Yes," she purrs, holding the hilt of the knife against her chest. Still smiling, she leans forward, kissing him as the blade slips into his chest.

Shortly after the Sisters show them their rooms, Mikya and Ven creep out into the hallway and force their way into Gilden's room. He is sitting on the floor with his back to them, his gaze fixed firmly on the large window across the room from the door. His robe lies curled around him as if he just slipped it off and left it there in a pile.

A large bed is positioned on the far, left wall from the door, and the door to a small bathroom is positioned on the right. The walls are black, causing the lack of light within to be all the more prominent. Even with the large window, no light seeps in. This is most likely do to the fact that it has been charmed to reveal a night sky. Even the carpet covering the floor is black. However, the bed is done in gold and silver, as if the person who decorated wanted it to stand out from the rest of the room.

As Mikya stands gazing at Gilden's still form, Ven scrambles around her, seeking the corner farthest from the door. With his back to her and the hood of his cloak pulled up over his head, he appears to melt away into the color of the room. Only the trembling running through the fabric betrays his position.

Closing the door behind her, Mikya moves up to sit beside Gilden on the floor, her gaze falling to his intent face. "What's wrong? You looked like you'd sensed something big when we first came in," Mikya whispers. "The scent has been masked by charms, but the entire place smells of blood. The Sisters are dangerous, and we had to leave Vachel in their care," Gilden replies, guilt slipping into his words.

"Dangerous doesn't even come close to cutting it," Ven replies in a whimper, letting the hood drop so his brown hair stands out against the black. "What do you mean?" Mikya asks, gazing over at him. He slips the cloak completely from his back before hugging himself and shaking his head.

Standing, Mikya makes her way over to him, kneeling at his back in silence. Sobs slip from him as he trembles, but they are partly masked. "If she comes for me just because she can...I don't know what I'll do," he forces out, curling up all the more. At this, Gilden even moves from his position to join the huddle: "We'll not let her take you without a fight. If I'd thought Vachel would have let me, I'd have fought for him, as well."

Shaking his head furiously, Ven protests, "No. It's her right to have me because of her deal with Master. Trying to keep her at bay will only succeed in getting you killed." "You can't expect us to just sit by and let her take you against your will," Mikya counters. Leaning into the corner, Ven whispers, "Yes...yes I can. If you won't help the person who's supposed to be keeping you safe here...then there's no reason for me to believe you'd help me."

"You deserve to be helped, especially against the High Sister."

"And Vachel doesn't?"

Both are silent for a moment.

"See? You won't help him because he's a demon. I'm even lower..."

"'Lower'?"

"On the list of those mortals would aid. Hybrids are rare for a reason."

"What?"

"Hybrids are naturally hunted because of their unique beginnings."

Mikya falls silent at this, her eyes going wide as she stares at his back. Reaching forward, Gilden places a hand on Ven's shoulder as he replies, "The Shiku Hara keeps you safe from mortals...so let the mortals keep you safe from those who use the Shiku Hara." "Do you realize how ridiculous that sounds?" Ven asks, leaning back up, "I'm the slave of a Halfling and a demon sorceress...no mortal could ever keep me safe from them."

"Wait...the High Sister is a demon?" Mikya asks, a small smile coming to her face as an idea seeps into her mind. "Yes," Ven whispers. He keeps it from his face, but has to wonder how she could ask such a stupid question. Darkhaven is the realm of demons. It would be more appropriate to ask who isn't a demon, not who is.

Getting to her feet, Mikya explains, "I know a spell that can ward off demons. If we all stay in here tonight, there should be no problems keeping the High Sister out." "Princess, that spell requires blood," Gilden cautions, standing as well. "I know that, but we're out of options presently. Ven, do you have a knife?" Mikya replies, her smile brightening. "In my room," he whispers, fear still in his voice. "I've got one with me," Gilden offers, moving over to the bed to retrieve his things, "But, I'm performing the spell."

Mikya does not argue with him. Personally, she does not want to have to slice her palm open to perform magic, even if it is to protect them. It seems Gilden has no such qualms and steps before the door without a word. He slips off the gloves and lets them drop to the floor, all his attention on the door.

Gently sliding the blade along his palm, he presses it firmly against the door: "With blood and power I declare this place forbidden." Then, he pulls his hand back to open a wound on his finger, drawing the symbol for demon[2] beside the line of blood from his palm. Dropping the knife, he raises his other hand and sends the final spark of green light into the surface. For a moment the marks glow green, and then the light slowly fades.

"That should do it," he adds, gazing at his handy work. "Yeah... *should*," Ven whispers to himself. Turning to him, Gilden gives a smile suggesting it is not really the expression he wants to use: "If my power can't keep her out of here then nothing can." "I still really want to go home," Ven whimpers, sniffing against new tears.

Panting against the pain, Vachel jerks as Niko forces the blade into his side again. He is in too much pain to keep it and the fear from creeping out any more. Of course, with Sherri still on top of him, that is definitely not in his favor. They had to shackle him to the bed frame to keep him from trying to push her away when she forced him up inside her. They also decided shortly after the first blood it would be more fun to have him together. Niko being more into the pain and Sherri more into the sex made it an even match.

Suddenly, Niko grinds the blade in as far as it will go and continues pressing against the skin. Vachel cannot help but cry out against the pain this time. "Just a little more, Trinket, you haven't given either of us what we want yet,"

---

[2] This symbol consists of a set of fangs with claws on either side.

Sherri answers, breathlessly. "You won't get it, either," Vachel growls, "I'll not scream, and I can't give into you." "We'll just have to change that," Niko challenges, jerking on the blade so that it tears the skin rather than actually cutting. Vachel grinds his teeth down against the cry of pain threatening to burst from his throat.

"Why don't you dig into it," Sherri suggests, gazing over at Niko with a smile. Nodding, Niko slips the blade from his flesh, so she can force three of her fingers into the wound.

He arches his back against the pain, letting loose a cry closer to the scream they want. In response, Niko forces a fourth finger into the wound, pulling harder at the already torn skin. This cry is even closer, but he manages to keep it just shy of a scream. "One...more," she whispers, forcing her thumb inside as well. This time, the skin does tear, pulling an ear-splitting shriek from him just as Sherri releases. She collapses against his chest and the blood welling up from the wounds in it.

"Get-your-hand-out-of-me!" Vachel growls, blood seeping from the corner of his mouth now. He bites back hard on the tears that seek to spill form the corners of his eyes. With a jerk that causes him to slam his head back against the pillows in pain, Niko does as he demands. Once she does, she grips his side, running her tongue across the blood now spilling from his side. It burns because of the magic she is using to heal the wound, and Vachel grinds his teeth together to keep from screaming again.

"Come on, Trinket, what could one more hurt?" Sherri taunts breathlessly. "Go to hell!" Vachel yells in place of the scream against the pain. Smiling at him, she leans forward and kisses him again, forcing her tongue into his mouth to get at the blood. He has the urge to bite down, but knows Niko would waste no time in causing him enough pain to make it not worth the effort.

Finally, Sherri releases him, slipping away to lie down at his side and drape her arm across his chest: "See, Trinket? The curse hasn't completely ruined you." Vachel remains silent, all his attention focused on catching his breath. At this, Niko climbs over their legs to settle in a sitting position at Sherri's back. "Forgive me," Sherri whispers, repositioning herself so that only her arm and head are touching him. Smiling as if thoroughly pleased with their work, Niko lays her head down on his stomach, closing her eyes. Sherri shifts once more, so her arm and head rest on his chest before they both go still.

For a moment, Vachel continues to stare up at the ceiling, his breathing less labored now that he has his pulse under control. Finally, he turns his gaze to them and spies the crystal still resting innocently on his skin; although, now it is nearly touching Sherri's blood covered fingertips. The chain is smeared with blood, but the crystal is untouched, as if it kept the blood away from itself. Vachel would like nothing more than to be able to clutch it in his hand until the sharp edges dig into his palm, but the shackles around his wrists keep him from it.

It suddenly strikes him as terrible that he kept it around his neck throughout the entire ordeal. Somehow it feels almost as bad as it would have if they had made Sister Crystal watch the performance. He lets his head fall back again as tears well up in his eyes. He can't keep them back anymore.

His gaze is fixed firmly on the ceiling above, but he is not actually seeing it. Instead he is seeing the look of mingled shock, hurt, and fury that would be on her face if she had seen this. She would revoke her love entirely if she saw what he let them do to him for the sake of a stupid mission. It brings a burning rush of tears spilling from his eyes despite his efforts to stop them: "Crystal...I'm so sorry."

Mikya wakes suddenly, clutching the blanket to her chest as a final tear slips away from her eye. She cannot remember dreaming of anything that should have made her cry. Sitting up, she gazes around the room to find Gilden stretched out in the center of the floor and Ven curled up in the corner. The Hybrid's eyes are open, and he stares back at her as if afraid she will jump at him for being awake.

"What's the matter, child?" she asks. If at all possible, Ven's eyes grow wider. Mikya is about to ask about this when she thinks about what she just said. "Did I just call you 'child'?" she asks, concern springing to her face. Still staring at her, Ven gives a shallow, shaking nod. Sighing, she lets the edge of the blanket drop, revealing the top of the white nightgown she managed to claim enough energy to put on before climbing into the bed.

"I didn't mean it, Ven. It just slipped out...I'm sorry," Mikya whispers, folding her hands in her lap. "There's nothing to apologize for," Ven whispers so low she has to strain to hear, "It just shocked me is all." "You seem more afraid now that Vachel isn't here...does he make you feel safe?" Mikya asks, bringing her knees up to her chest.

"Yes...is that strange?"

"Considering that he attacked you with the Shiku Hara, yes."

"He was making a point. I was being disrespectful; that's dangerous."

"To him or you?"

"Yes. Disobedience is seen as a weakness of the master."

"But, he's not your master."

"Not by agreement, no. But he's stronger than I am. Since we're traveling together, that makes him my master in Darkhaven," Ven explains, pressing his forehead into the corner. "Doesn't that make you upset. To know you're almost everyone's servant for one reason or another?" Mikya asks. Shaking his head slowly, Ven replies, "No. I've never lived without a master. I don't know how to live without one. Having a master isn't all bad...you might have to listen to them all the time and follow orders, but you gain their protection, too." "I've never had a master, so I can't really relate," Mikya observes with another sigh.

"Can I sleep at your feet?" Ven asks abruptly, gazing back up with his frightened look. Mikya gives him a searching look in response: "What?" "Can I sleep on the bed at your feet?" Ven asks again, "Master lets me do it at home...if I've been good." "Will he let you if you bring Gilden and me to him?" Mikya asks, doing her best to keep the frown from her face. Hugging himself, Ven whispers, "I hope so...he hasn't for a long time because he's found himself a woman." *Women is closer to it. He's got a freakin' harem.* "Will it really make you feel better?" Mikya asks skeptically. "Yes," Ven replies. "Alright, but on one condition," Mikya explains, "You have to stay at my feet...no cuddling, alright?"

"I'm too scared to be interested, princess, but I promise to keep my hands to myself," Ven whispers, casting a glance over at Gilden, "What will *he* think?" "It doesn't matter. I outrank him," Mikya replies in the same whisper. Nodding, Ven gets to his feet, dropping the cloak in the corner as he makes his way over to the end of the bed.

He pulls the boots off before she has to ask and tentatively climbs up onto the bed. It is as if he is waiting for her to strike him and cast him back out, laughing. She merely stares, watching him feel along the mattress, apparently looking for a comfortable spot. Once he finds it, he lays his head down first, in an almost submissive posture, before curling up into a ball. It is not until he has snuggled into the mattress on his side that Mikya realizes he is still wearing the gloves.

"Don't you want to take those off?" she asks, giving a gesture to indicate she is referring to the gloves. Shaking his head, Ven explains, "Without them, if I accidentally brush you with my fingertips when I can't control the power, it could kill you, and I doubt you want to endure a true trust sign to prevent that." "Is it that you think it would be tedious for me, or is it that you don't trust me enough to give one?" Mikya asks, leaning forward onto her knees. "Yes," Ven whispers. His voice sounds suddenly tired. "So, if I told you it would probably just make me blush, you still wouldn't consider doing it?" Mikya presses. "I don't know...is that what you're saying?" Ven asks, gazing at her over his interlaced fingers. "Yes," Mikya replies, giving him a small smile.

Ven brings his hands to his arms again and rubs them furiously as if a sudden chill has fallen over him. Silent and waiting, Mikya just sits watching him. "I...I don't see the harm in it...all right, I'll give the sign if you want it," Ven replies, turning his gaze back to the princess. Still smiling, Mikya nods and is about to push away the covers and move over to him when he gets up on his hands and knees.

She pauses, watching him creep over like a puppy afraid of being reprimanded. She gives a small move again, and he freezes in motion, gazing up into her eyes in fear again. "Am I not supposed to move?" she asks, gazing steadily back into his eyes, the smile gone. "Not in a true trust sign...the one you saw me give those girls was only temporary. To move during a true trust sign means you are rejecting the sign," Ven explains, looking downcast, "Are you rejecting it?" "No. I just didn't understand the implication. Go ahead," Mikya replies, the smile slipping back to her face.

Nodding, Ven begins to creep forward again, hesitating before her left knee. He takes a deep breath before brushing the side of his face against it, like a cat this time. He follows the same procedure with his entire side, running it against her knee before following the path of his head along her side. She grows as still as possible to keep from giggling and pushing him away as a flush spills to her cheeks.

Ven does the same to her back and right side before coming to sit before her, legs tucked beneath him and palms flat against the mattress before her feet. Giving a deep sigh, he allows his body to collapse, causing his head to rest on her feet before he begins to run his cheek along her leg. Now, she has to swallow hard to keep from striking out at him just to make the embarrassing blushing stop. He makes it up to rest the side of his face against her knees before holding up his hand and whispering: "Now I need your hand."

Mikya slips it up into his open palm, glad his eyes are closed. Turning it over so that the palm is up, Ven runs his tongue from the tip of her middle finger to her wrist, pausing at her wrist. As Mikya watches, a small spark of violet light slips into her skin. At this Ven slips back to a sitting position and opens his eyes. A smirk slips to his face at the sight of the flush on Mikya's cheeks.

"I've never had someone brush against me that way," Mikya protests in a whisper. Nodding, Ven explains, "That's why a true sign is usually only given to someone a Hybrid is intimate with. I don't have anyone like that other than my sisters, but they're safe because they're siblings." "Explain how you mean intimate," Mikya whispers, uncomfortable with his statement if it means what she thinks it does.

"You know...close enough to share a bed. Nothing has to happen, but close enough to let them touch you when you're upset," Ven explains, "Why? What did you think it meant?" "That something has to happen for it to be considered intimate," Mikya explains, feeling embarrassed now because of the partial accusation. "I never said that something didn't happen. It's more acceptable to show affections to a sibling that way in Darkhaven," Ven replies, spying the embarrassment in her eyes. Mikya's eyes go wide, but she prevents herself from expressing her disgust more openly.

Smiling at her, Ven explains, "You've nothing to worry about, princess. I've already given my word that I'll keep to the end of the bed...'no cuddling', remember." "That isn't a problem for you, is it?" Mikya asks, spying a small glint of bitterness in his eyes at being confined. Gazing down at his hands, Ven replies, "If I didn't think you'd reject my presence completely, I'd ask permission to curl up against your back."

"Contact makes you feel safe, doesn't it?"

"Yes. It's probably because my father is half wolf demon."

"Why would that make a difference?"

"The wolf packs gain power and structure through touching."

"Order makes them feel safe."

"Yes...I'm sorry if it makes you uncomfortable. I can sleep here."

"I don't mind...it just seemed odd at first...the request, I mean."

"You would let me?"

"I've just given you permission."

Smiling, Ven slips off the gloves and tosses them back in the corner before settling down to wait for her. Mikya stretches slightly before lying back down and rolling over onto her side. Tentatively again, Ven creeps up to her back to search for a comfortable spot and curls up. Once his weight is pressed against her back Mikya realizes it is his head that is actually resting against her. Pulling the blanket around her in a sudden chill, Mikya is suddenly and oddly glad to have him close enough to feel the warmth of his body.

The door crashes open, startling both Niko and Sherri out of sleep. Vachel opens his eyes, having not been asleep, but does not bother to turn his gaze to the doorway. He already knows who is standing there, furious. However, when she yells in her fury, it is not at the Sisters: "Trinket! You knew those peons could shield against demons, did you not?!"

"No, Selene, I didn't know about any such ability," Vachel replies in a bland tone. Storming into the room and slamming the door, the High Sister cries, "I have been denied because of those fools, and you cannot even be the least sympathetic?!" "I've been stabbed and raped all night, Selene. So, no, I can't be sympathetic just because you couldn't get someone in your bed," Vachel replies, closing his eyes against the memory.

"As you wish, Trinket," she growls, "It is you who will pay for my suffering. Sherri, Niko, untie him. He will be joining me this day." Sherri opens the shackles without a word and sits back beside Niko, not apparently awake enough to be aware she is not wearing anything. Vachel, however, notices his lack of cover immediately and forces his aching frame up to get dressed.

He barely has the final boot pulled on when the High Sister demands, "Hurry up, Trinket, I do not have all day!" "You have as much time as you see fit, Selene," Vachel whispers, slowly standing. The High Sister slaps him around the face before yelling, "You will address me by title, Trinket. You have already lost the privilege of calling me by my name."

"As you wish, High Sister," Vachel replies in a hollow voice, not even bothering to touch the stinging flesh of his face. Nodding abruptly, she turns on her heel and stalks away, expecting Vachel to follow without any protest. He does, but only because he has no desire to spend another minute in the same room as Sherri and Niko. Apart they are bad enough, but together is the worst experience he has ever had.

Even the sound of her heels against the stone floor sounds angry as she leads him back to her expansive, crystal room. She is silent as she makes it over to her throne and drops ungracefully onto the cushion. However, once she realizes the break in grace, she smoothly slips down to lie on her side, watching him walk toward her.

The grace of *his* movements does not go unnoticed, and she brings a hand to her lips as if remembering a time long past. Still, it is not until he has climbed up onto the platform and stopped before her that she remarks on it: "It has been some time, Trinket. But, I see you have not lost your ability to glide into a room." "You didn't bring me in here to watch me walk around the room, High Sister. Can't we just get this over with for once?" Vachel replies, a hint of pleading in his voice. "'Get this over with'? You act as if being with me is some form of torture, Trinket," the High Sister remarks, a small twinge of hurt coming to her face.

"It is as you are," Vachel whispers, "You can't have lived this long without aging, High Sister." "I am not nearly so beautiful as I should be, Trinket. My face has been ruined," the High Sister explains, turning her face away. Sighing, Vachel protests, "I have already explained to you that our ideals of beauty are on opposite ends of the spectrum, High Sister." "Even *you* could not find my face beautiful now, Trinket," the High Sister whispers dismally. "Why don't you let *me* be the judge of that?" Vachel offers, staring at her despite her stubborn unwillingness to look at him.

He is fighting back the urge to take her anyway, for the old lust has slipped to the surface again. He has no idea what it is about this woman that breaks down every barrier he has, but it's already annoying. Sister Crystal should be the only object of his desire, and yet here sits a she-demon who wipes his mind of the faerie he loves.

Sighing, she sits up as if something in his words forced her to make the decision. She closes her eyes, allowing this form to melt away and reveal her true self. Her curves fill out, making her look more the twenty-two-year-old woman that she should. The smooth line of her jaw has less of the child-like look to it. However, destroying the picture is a group of scars marring the left side of her face. It appears as though something first tried to claw its way into her face and then was forced to burn away some of the incriminating marks. It leaves her face only half the perfection she wishes it were.

"Do you see, Trinket? I am no longer even pretty," she whispers dismally. Silence fills the space, but before she can speak again, Vachel moves forward, wrapping his arms around her waist and pushing her back down with a kiss. His head hurts from the silent struggle to keep away that he is losing. The sight of those scars, scars she deserves for what she did to him, tosses him over the edge. *Sweet crimson...I've always loved scars. Sweet crimson...I have to get a hold of myself...but I just don't want to.*

She does not protest other than to force him up enough to allow her to speak: "What is this? I am not the perfection you once knew, Trinket." "I know...I don't care...I...I shouldn't be doing this," Vachel whispers, pushing hurriedly away after he says it. "Why not, Trinket?" the High Sister asks, not bothering to right herself. Gripping his arms as if to hold himself back, Vachel forces out, "I belong to Sister Crystal!" *Dammit! I need some help here...she's invaded my mind again.*

"Giving into old lusts will not make it any less so, Trinket," the High Sister purrs, flashing a small hint of her fangs at him. Vachel drops to the floor and laces his fingers on the top of his head, shaking it vigorously: "No, no, no. I can't do it...not knowing what it would do to her." "Then let me erase your fears, love, and it can be as it was for a time," the High Sister purrs, slipping down from the cushion. "I...I just--" *No! I can't let her do it! Someone stop her!* "Shhhh, love, I will make it all better," she replies, lifting his head and placing her fingertip on his lips. The guilt and worry leave his eyes, seeping away as he removes his hands from the top of his head.

I...I've given in. I've done it all over again.

She guides him to a standing position, watching the old lust flare up in his eyes as he follows her willingly back up to the throne. Carefully blocking just enough of the love he feels for this Sister Crystal has made the power she held over him flash back to life. To keep him when he was Death, she placed just enough of her power in him to act as a leash. He has no idea what causes his compulsion to reach out for her, and she knows she will have to take her power back once this is done. He can't belong to her anymore, not after her revenge. Lying down on her back, she allows him to straddle her with his legs on either side of her waist. "I have not been had as a queen in some time, love, be gentle with me," she whispers, closing her eyes with a smile.

Leaning down so that their foreheads touch, Vachel responds, "You don't like it gentle, pet. Don't ask for something you don't want." "You have caught me. Fine, love, I will admit it...I want to be ravaged this day...I want it to hurt," she replies with a small, feigned sigh. Smiling furtively, he whispers, "As the lady wishes."

Mikya wakes to find there is an odd warmth seeping into her hands. Slowly, she slips her eyes open to find she has somehow become pressed against Ven's chest. His arm is carefully draped over her, as if what ever put her here decided this would add to her shock. It does, and she pushes against him, demanding: "Ven, what do you think you're doing?"

His eyes snap open, and he immediately recognizes what it wrong. Fear leaping through him, he quickly withdraws his hand and scrambles away to the end of the bed. His chest heaves against the sudden, racing pulse as he stares wide-eyed at her. He somehow broke his promise, and he does not remember doing it.

"I'm sorry, princess...I-I didn't mean it...I-I don't even know how it happened," Ven apologizes quickly, his eyes racing over the room almost as if in search of a way to escape her wrath. "I don't understand what you're so afraid of," Gilden remarks, smiling up at the ceiling, "I for one wouldn't mind waking up with a woman in my arms." "But...but I--" "He promised he wouldn't do any of the cuddling," Mikya protests, pulling the blanket up all the higher.

"If you didn't want it to happen, you shouldn't have let him curl up at your back," Gilden responds, turning his gaze to the princess, "Especially with the strange link you seem to have formed with the demon quarter of our little group." "What are you talking about?" Mikya asks, confusion evident in her face.

"You were crying in your sleep last night about the time I could no longer hear the horrible screams coming from down the hall," Gilden replies, gazing down at the floor. "So?" Ven interjects, still pressed firmly against the wall. Shaking his head, Gilden answers, "So, someone wanted us to be able to know what Vachel is feeling, so they set up a link with the princess." "But, wouldn't we have sensed it if that were the case?" Mikya protests.

She is not at all comfortable with the fact Vachel could have been crying the night before.

Sighing, Ven whispers, "Not necessarily...some of the more powerful demons of Darkhaven can mask their power well enough to fool even Master. Still, if you *did* sense it, you wouldn't have recognized it as magic because you're not familiar with it." "True...but I haven't been able to feel anything since we first arrived," Gilden answers, turning his gaze back to Ven. The Hybrid has peeled himself away from the wall, but still stays pressed into the corner created between it and the foot of the bed. "Could it have been done accidentally?" Mikya asks, letting the blanket drop finally.

"How do you mean?"

"I mean, could one of us have created the link because of fear?"

Ven's eyes grow wide again, and he plasters himself back against the wall, his entire frame trembling. Gilden takes the time to stand and move over to the edge of the bed before he asks, "Could you have done this?" Swallowing hard and pressing himself even farther into the wall, Ven gives a shallow nod. "Why didn't you warn us against it? I might have been able to prevent some of this embarrassment," Gilden replies, crossing his arms.

"I-I...I said I was sorry," Ven responds, a hint of anger in his voice. However, once he realizes that the disrespect is there, he tosses himself forward on the bed and wraps his fingers over the back of his head: "I didn't mean that, I swear. Please forgive me." "I've dealt with worse before, Ven. What did you think I was going to do, bite your head off?" Gilden responds with a small smile.

Taking a deep breath, Ven nods slowly, as if afraid this truth will get him in worse trouble. Silence fills the space for a moment, and Mikya pushes her way out from under the blanket. Carefully, so as not to frighten him further, she wraps her arms around his shoulders in a light embrace. He tenses for a moment, as if expecting to be jerked up and struck. Instead, Mikya rests her head on his back and whispers, "It's alright...we understand...we're scared too."

⚡

She reaches over to gently brush his hair from his face as he lies panting at her side. "Did you exhaust yourself, love?" she asks. Trailing his fingers up her arm, he replies, "Not enough." "You will hurt yourself if you try to keep this pace," she cautions with a small laugh. Shaking his head so that his hair falls back in his face, Vachel whispers, "Since when have you been worried about my hurting myself?" "It is all for me...so it would bother me to know you have hurt yourself," she replies, sighing deeply.

With a bit of effort, he pulls himself over to lay the side of his face on her chest, and look up at her face. "What is it? Does that surprise you so very much?" the High Sister asks, gazing down into his eyes. Running his tongue along her collarbone, Vachel replies, "I'll know when I've enough thinking capacity to understand what this really means."

"This means I have at last gotten Death back in my clutches. It might only be for a time, but I have what I have wanted for so very long," the High Sister responds, placing a hand on his shoulder. "Do I mean that much to you? Or is it the thought that you have seduced Death again?" Vachel asks, bringing up a hand to drape over her waist. Even having asked it, he finds himself thinking he doesn't really want to know.

She quickly takes his head in her hands, forcing him to a position requiring him to use his hands to support himself: "You are the master of asking dangerous questions...to answer either of the two alone in the affirmative is asking for trouble...yet to answer both as yes is even worse. If I told you both were false, I would be a liar, love. Why do you put me in such a situation?"

"Just habit, I guess."

"Habit, bah! You enjoy watching me squirm under your stake."

"You enjoy the squirming, pet. Don't even try to say you don't."

"Perhaps...but like it or not...it does get bothersome."

"Do you really mean that, pet?" Feigned hurt slips to his voice.

"You are confusing your stakes, love. I will never tire of the one you have been using thus far," she counters with a small smile.

Leaning into her hands so that she has to support more of his weight, Vachel whispers, "I still don't understand how you could think of yourself as unattractive." "I have been turned away for these, love. That makes one think less of herself," she explains, sorrow filling her eyes again as she runs her fingers over the rough edges of the scars. Vachel leans forward, breaking the hold she has on his face.

Gently, he brushes his cheek against the rough scars, letting his hair fall in her face. "What are you doing, love?" she asks, pushing his hair back away from her face. It is not until he has his mouth next to her ear that he whispers, "I like battle scars, pet...you should know that by now." "Death likes his loves with such imperfections as scars...you still confuse me sometimes, love," she replies, letting his hair drop back and closing her eyes, "Where then are the scars on your Crystal?"

"She has none that I've found...but I didn't get a feel inside," Vachel answers, smiling bitterly because she cannot see it. "Death did not have his way with a woman? Now you are just teasing with me, love," she responds, pushing him back over onto his side. "Am I such a bad liar that no one will believe me when I'm telling the truth?" Vachel asks, rolling over on his stomach and burying his face in the cushion.

Her eyes go wide as she asks, "Then, you are not teasing? Why ever did you hold back?" "I didn't want her to know about one of the side effects of the curse...I *still* don't understand what she sees in me, so I was being cautious. I didn't want to give her a reason to pull away so soon," Vachel replies, his voice muffled by the cushion.

"Am I not worthy enough of the same concerns, Death?"

"*You're* the one who seduced *me*, High Sister, and you knew already."

"They are not so noticeable unless one holds them." *But*, she considers, *it was very noticeable when he would not rouse, no matter what I did. Perhaps this is more the reason he did not take what he wished...he did not completely wish it.*

"And you really enjoyed making me feel bad about it."

"Tad self-conscious are you not, love?"

"I don't have anything else but that to give."

"Nonsense! That is merely the clincher, love."

"You always were a bad liar, pet," Vachel replies, sitting up.

"Now who is not giving the other enough credit?"

"How did we even come across this topic of conversation?"

"It was most likely a bad group of tangents, love. I am not entirely certain which ones led where," she answers, sitting up to face him. Sighing, he stretches his arms and back, somehow managing to make it look graceful. He knows that is a lie. She did it on purpose. "Perhaps I could use a rest...just not up to par," he whispers, seeming to be disappointed in himself. In truth, he's just tired of giving where he can't receive anymore. Not even the look on her face at the end could bring him happiness as it had when he'd done the same to Crystal.

Smiling, she replies, "I think I can content myself with being held, love." "That reminds me of what Crystal said when I kept her away from the serious stuff...I just can't please anyone anymore," Vachel whispers dismally, his head drooping. Even when he gives he can't please. What hope is there for something that requires more of a group effort? *None...that's what.* He bites back hard to keep the tears from his face at that thought. Slipping forward with the same liquid grace he exhibited earlier, the High Sister rests herself neatly in his lap, her back to his chest so that his cheek rests against her scars again: "I can assure you that no such thing is true."

They spend the next day in much the same manner. Mikya and Gilden comfort Ven, while Vachel rekindles old lusts. At one point Gilden has to reapply the spell to the door to keep Ven from whimpering all night. Eventually they all end up curled together on the bed, all in an effort to make him feel safe. In the mean time, Vachel finds that the High Sister is not quite as secure as she wants him to believe, and he has to push his own fears and discomforts aside to comfort her. Still, she releases him just as promised.

Port of Under

Ven opens his eyes to the sound of pounding. Even sandwiched between the sorcerer and the princess, fear slips readily to the surface. He is about to wake them himself when a voice joins the pounding: "You better open this door or I will keep your demon!" It is now that he remembers the spell on the door. *It seems Gilden wasn't exaggerating when he said it would keep out the demons.*

Still, he springs over Mikya, landing carefully on the floor before scrambling to open the door. The instant he touches it a wave of demon aura smacks him forcefully in the chest, throwing him to the floor as the door slams open. *Or perhaps he didn't know what he was talking about.*

He gazes up into the face of the High Sister from his position on his back on the floor, fear creeping back into him. She is now her fifteen-year-old guise, all raven hair and smooth skin. Smiling as if pleased with herself, the High Sister steps easily into the room, towering over him in her heels. "Took you long enough, Messenger. I was afraid I might have to break my promise and keep our Trinket," she taunts, walking around him like a shark circles prey.

Finally, she sits gracefully on his chest, smoothing her skirt so it does not cover his face. She spies the wide eyes and look of pure terror on his face and laughs. It is deep throated, and she adds the traditional flick of her head.

If Gilden and Mikya were not awake before, they are now. The sorcerer climbs from the bed to stand before the princess. "Good morning, little ones. I have brought Trinket back just as promised. Bring him in, boys," she calls, smiling sweetly.

At her command, two large, muscled demons toss Vachel headfirst into the room. He lies still for a moment on his stomach before taking a deep breath and pulling himself to a sitting position. The High Sister giggles softly at the half-hidden wince. "I hope to see you within the next millennia, Trinket," she adds as she stands, making her way out. Ven cannot help but stare at the over-exaggerated sway of her hips as she leaves.

However, his focus quickly turns to Vachel when the demon gives a small moan before collapsing back onto his stomach. "Vachel!" all three cry, scrambling to his side, but afraid to touch him. Moaning again, he demands, "Someone help me up." Ven is the first to comply, easily finding a place to brace the demon that does not run the risk of his fingers touching Vachel's bare skin. Once he is sitting up, however, it is Gilden who has to keep him from slipping back down.

"What happened to you?" Gilden demands, watching the slight tremble to the demon's arms. Smiling weakly, Vachel forces out, "At least they didn't put me back in the coffin." "Please don't toy with me this morning," Gilden pleads quickly. Before Vachel can answer, however, he pushes away from Gilden in a rush, and heaves blood onto the carpet.

"Are there any of those eggs in here?" Ven asks, gazing around the room, but keeping his head low. "Not from the curse..." Vachel whispers before bringing up more blood. Placing a hand on his back, Gilden asks, "Then, what is it?" "I've had someone tear open a hole in my side, and then heal the outer wound...my body's still trying to heal the damage inside," Vachel explains breathlessly, trembling running along the line of his body.

"Will it hurt you to continue on?" Mikya asks, hugging herself against the sight. "Just let me finish this," Vachel replies, taking a deep breath. Another rush of blood bursts from him before he collapses to the floor, breathing in air like he has been holding his breath for some time. He lies panting for a few minutes before a jerking begins in his back.

It is only a small part of his back, and no other part moves with it; however, it is moving slowly up his back, seeking escape by the way it pushes against the skin. Gilden, Mikya, and Ven all stare wide-eyed as it forces its way up to the line of his shoulders and slowly slides around to the front of his neck. It is only then that he takes any interest in the throbbing form just below the skin.

Jerking to his hands and knees, Vachel gives a gentle swallow, as if afraid to push the mass back down inside. He breathes in like there is something wedged deep in his throat. The thing trembles for a moment, as if considering whether to stay put or not. Eventually it decides to make a break for it.

Vachel coughs like a cat trying to rid itself of a hairball. Liquid the thickness of blood but the color of the carpet beneath him begins to spill diligently from the corners of his mouth. A shudder passes through him and he coughs again, bringing the lump up into his mouth and casting it to the floor below. It lands with a sickening splat in the wet spot on the carpet. As they all watch, the thing, black and shining like the strange liquid, begins to pulse, as if it has decided to be a heart. However, it soon decides that is not worth the effort and takes a deep, shuddering breath.

"Is that thing breathing?" Ven whispers, horror and disgust evident in his voice. Vachel shakes his head slowly: "No...but it thinks it is. Just don't touch it, and it will die. If you touch it, it can feed off life forces." Just as the words escape him, the thing takes a deep breath and lets loose a shriek that makes even Vachel cringe. "This one's more powerful because of the amount of damage," he explains in a whisper. Another shriek erupts from the thing, and it begins to writhe in the damp spot, trying desperately to move closer to them.

"Does it have to do that?" Mikya asks, her hands hovering over her ears. Sitting up, Vachel whispers, "It's trying to get my sympathy...if I was still a full demon, I could give it a small amount of demon aura, and it would be able to grow to maturity." "What do you mean 'grow to maturity'?" Gilden asks, his gaze flicking from Vachel to the writhing lump and back again.

"This thing is a Gristle. Sorcerers who want to create demons without the need for a ritualistic sacrifice use it. You have but to supply it with a full amount of life force for it to grow into a demon. However, if the demon that it stems from gives it even a small amount of demon aura, the Gristle will grow into an obedient slave that would give its life in service of the demon. The thought of having even one such servant sickens me," Vachel explains, his distaste obvious on his face.

Wide-eyed, Mikya asks, "Do you mean there are demons who have more than one of these things?" "Master has close to twenty...they're all female," Ven replies with a sigh. "He's certainly been doing some heavy duty work since I left. He only had two the last time I checked, and they were both male. What did he do with them?" Vachel adds, turning his attention to Ven. "He didn't have perfect control over them because they came from other demons. They would die for him, but they refused to be part of his tortures, so he killed them. He actually has a hold on the new servants because he can give them something he could not give the others," Ven explains, giving a small shudder this time.

Nodding, Vachel gets to his feet, still shaky, but steady enough to keep from falling back to the ground. As he turns on his heel and moves across the room from it, the Gristle makes steadily more piteous noises. Finally, Vachel has had enough and commands, "Silence, wretch! You'll get nothing from me, so die already!"

None of the others understand the language he is speaking, but the Gristle immediately ceases to shriek. However, it continues that labored, shaky breathing. Vachel collapses on the bed on his back, suggesting: "You might want to do something to keep your minds off of that thing for a while. A dying Gristle is not a pretty sight...or smell...or pretty anything for that matter."

Shuddering again, Ven rushes away from the thing to gather up his gloves and boots. He stares down at them for a moment, as if unsure what to do with them, before dropping to the floor and pulling them on with shaking hands. Gilden turns his back abruptly and seizes Mikya by the wrist to pull her along behind him, toward the bed and away from the Gristle. Still, her eyes are fixed on the trembling form, and she has a sudden desire to touch it, to help ease its misery.

Without realizing she is doing it, Mikya pulls against Gilden's hold on her arm, seeking to get back to it. "Princess? What are you doing?" Gilden asks, gripping her arm tighter. She continues to pull as if he has not said anything. Turning his gaze to Vachel, Gilden asks, "What's wrong with her?"

"Release her mind, or I will see you peeling away layer by layer...or perhaps a flaming rock on the carpet," Vachel hisses in that strange language. The Gristle issues a whimper of protest, but Mikya soon blinks hard, asking: "What just happened?"

"Pathetic wretch was trying to get you to provide life force since I refused to feed it demon aura," Vachel explains, kicking off his boots and curling up on his side so he can gaze out at the room. "How did you get it to stop?" she asks, turning to face him. Giving a small yawn, Vachel replies, "Old fashioned method, really...I threatened it with a painful death."

"Slowly fading away isn't a painful death?"

"Long and frightening, but it isn't in any real pain."

"What about those awful shrieks?"

"It was trying to get sympathy, so it tried for the dramatic..."

"How do you know it doesn't really hurt?"

"I had a servant from one once...I ordered him to tell me the truth."

"I thought you said the thought of having one sickens you."

"It does. I didn't realize what its life would be like, but now I know."

I didn't realize what I would mean to him...

"I don't understand?"

"That kind of loyalty is stomach churning for those of us who can't exhibit it," Vachel explains, sighing and closing his eyes, "I'm really tired at the moment, so could you tone the questions down to those I can answer with a yes or no?" To be perfectly honest, he's ready to just tell her to stop asking questions at all. At first, he could understand because she was curious about him, but he's becoming annoyed with having to explain everything he says to her.

"If you were a full demon, would you have helped this one?" she asks, giving it a small glance over her shoulder. "No," Vachel answers, slipping up to the top of the bed. "Why not?" she asks before she can stop herself. Sighing, Vachel manages to slip beneath the top blanket and pull it up to his chin before repeating, "No." "Would you answer that question later if I asked it?" she presses, crossing her arms in frustration. "Perhaps," Vachel whispers. Throwing up her hands, Mikya declares, "I'm not learning anything like this."

"I think that's the point," Ven offers quietly, huddling in the corner again. Before anyone else can speak, Vachel observes, "It's really cold in here." Gilden and Mikya give each other a look but do not speak. Neither one is willing to point out that this observation is far from the truth. However, Ven understands the meaning completely and pulls the boots off again, a small hint of a smile on his face.

Climbing carefully over Vachel's legs without touching him, just as he'd been taught, Ven takes up a position at Vachel's back and curls up against the demon. His lips allowed a small smile to slip to his face. A small sigh of relief slips from Ven almost immediately.

⚡

Just as promised, the Gristle soon dies, giving a final, shuddering breath before ceasing to even tremble. Of course, Vachel's other promises come true, as well. Shortly after death, the Gristle's "skin" turns a dark, sickly green color before more of the black liquid bursts forth. It is as if the outer layer can no longer hold in the substance, and has burst to bleed into the carpet. It seems the interior is quite the advantageous bit of decorating. Still, as the liquid seeps into the carpet, a rank odor begins to drift up from the dead Gristle. It has the scent of decaying meat, an outhouse, and liberal amounts of blood all worked into one sickening smell.

Vachel has already slipped deep into sleep by the time this occurs, so Ven comments, "They're going to have quite a time getting that smell out of here. It seems the perfect departing gift." Neither Gilden nor Mikya argue with him, but both consider it a rather monstrous way to die. Ven wastes no time in explaining there are far worse ways, with an abundance of gruesome details before Gilden and Mikya tell him to stop. Still, they can't argue with Vachel's point now. Even with the smell hanging in the air, Vachel manages to get roughly four hours of sleep before waking with a stretch to his back and shoulders.

"I take it the little wretch decided to call it quits," he comments, giving the greenish lump a small, casual glance after sniffing the air. Shivering, Mikya asks, "How can you not be bothered by that smell?" "I've smelled much worse, princess, and that was coming from a living thing," Vachel replies, not even a hint of distaste to his voice. *Hell, I remember smelling worse than that over the last five hundred years.* She falls silent at this, her hands, instinctively by now, slipping up to clutch her arms in a makeshift hug.

As Vachel slips his boots back on, Gilden asks, "Does this mean you are well enough again to travel?" There is a twinge of something like guilt in Gilden's "Yep. It's amazing what even a Halfling's body can do with the proper amount of sleep," Vachel replies, intending for the last to weigh heavily. Gilden has to give an involuntary swallow, but he does not show his discomfort otherwise.

Vachel leaves it, making his way back toward the dead Gristle and the door. He has half a mind to move the "body" into a corner somewhere where the Sisters will be forced to find it. The High Sister deserves a room that stinks just for her actions this time around. However, before he can make up his mind or get to the door, Ven suggests, "We should head to the Port of Under next. That was where the crystal was last seen. If it isn't there, then we might have to force someone to hand it over." "'Port of Under'?" Gilden and Mikya ask together.

Knowing that, too, is most likely a lie, Vachel explains, "That is short for Portal of the Underworld. If one sails out from the port, legend says they will eventually be cast into the Underworld to spend all of eternity trying to find a way to escape." "But, all maps show that there are other continents beyond our borders," Mikya protests. "True, but no map has been created that shows any to the east, past the Port of Under," Ven counters, his gaze flicking to Vachel for a moment.

Shaking his head, Vachel replies, "No map that has ever been released to the people shows anything past the port. There's at least another island out there...but the magic around it prevents any from being able to sail back from it once they arrive. The seas become too treacherous, making it impossible to get back by boat." "Does that mean there are other ways to get there?" Mikya asks tentatively. "Yes," Vachel explains, "I have personally flown. Of course, those who are forced to take boats out that way do not have the luxury of that ability, so they are lost out there."

"Why did you have to go out there?" Mikya asks. "Personal questions, princess," Vachel warns, "I'm tired of having to explain everything that comes out of my mouth having anything to do with my past." Finally, he gets to say what he's wanted to for so long. Having done what he has in the past is enough without having to explain why he did every little thing. "I'm sorry," she apologizes, gazing down at the toes of her boots. Shaking his head again, Vachel opens the door and steps out.

Vachel and Gilden have to wait for both Ven and Mikya to gather their things from the other two rooms the High Sister allowed them to use. However, it is Mikya, Ven, and Gilden who must wait for Vachel as they make their way out of the castle. Just as they reach the front door, the High Sister rushes forward, her heels making a hurried clicking against the floor.

"I almost forgot, Trinket! Will you forgive me for not remembering to give you a proper goodbye until now?" she calls, as she catches up to them. Straightening his posture just slightly, Vachel replies, "Just as long as you keep the replacement simple...*High Sister* Selene." He places too much emphasis on the title, telling the others he is anything but comfortable with the idea of having the High Sister give him any kind of goodbye.

"You are going to have to bend down here. You are too much taller than I am at the moment," the High Sister replies as if he has not said a word. Vachel does as she asks, bending down so they can stare into each other's eyes, but the frown remains on his face. Giving him a sly smile, the High Sister leans forward for a kiss only to have him pull away and respond, "Not like this...it's all a lie like this." Gilden gives Ven a questioning glance, but the Hybrid can only offer a shrug; he has no idea what Vachel is talking about either.

Glaring at him, the High Sister protests, "I will not in front of these people. In private is one thing, but I will not have my reputation soiled for the likes of you. You only came to me because you were forced to." "Then I will say my goodbye and leave you to the rest of your day," Vachel replies, standing up and turning away.

"What is it that makes you hate this form so much?" she calls after him. Vachel crosses his arms but does not turn around as he answers, "It isn't the real you. It's just some copy you made to hide from the real sorceress

185

beneath." "What about you?" she accuses, "You use this more calculating, aloof little man to hide from the true demon. You hide from the demon that used to walk into a room and send tendrils of fear through all of the inhabitants. You hide from the demon that used to appreciate time spent with me. You hide from the demon who could send even Rust into a quaking fear with a mere glare. That was true power, and true feelings. What makes you hide from yourself, yet be upset because I do the same?"

"I never said I was perfect, Selene. I just said that I wished you would be closer to it than I could be," Vachel answers, a glare slipping to his face even though he still refuses to face her. "If wishes were horses, Trinket," the High Sister counters, crossing her own arms. Shrugging, Vachel makes his way toward the door again as he finishes, "We still have to ride, High Sister." "Fine, but if any of my girls find out, I will personally see you just as maimed. We will see if your Crystal enjoys your company then," the High Sister threatens.

Crossing her arms over her chest, she commits herself to changing form again. Once she is finished, she makes certain to keep the scarred side of her face partially hidden behind her hair. Vachel turns to face her finally, but the glare is still on his face as he observes, "You're still hiding, Selene." "You will get no more than this from me, Death," she replies shortly, frowning at him. Shrugging, Vachel moves up to her, and wraps an arm around her waist to pull her close. She rests both hands on his chest to give her that small amount of space.

Using his free hand, Vachel runs his fingers along the line of scars as he holds her face steady. "When will you learn that these don't steal anything from you?" he asks in the strange language. "When will you come back to me again?" she replies. Shaking his head, Vachel answers, "I can't do that, and you know it." "Then you know the answer to your question, Death," the High Sister responds, closing her eyes.

Vachel stands silent for a moment, during which time, Mikya leans over to Ven and asks, "Can you understand what they're saying?" "Yes," he replies simply. Turning to look at him, she whispers, "Then what are they talking about?" "I can't tell you that," Ven replies, averting his gaze, "They chose this tongue to keep you from knowing...it's personal." "Then why are *you* listening?" Mikya demands quietly. "I already know about their previous time together. You don't, so it's not for you to hear," Ven answers.

"I'm sorry that I make you feel that way," Vachel apologizes finally. The High Sister opens her eyes again as she whispers, "No...it is nothing you can help...love. I am far too afraid of what I will have to do to control my girls if they found out." "That's not true, and we both know it. You fear no one except Rust, because he is the only being in all of Yossa who has more authority than you," Vachel counters, running his fingers lightly over the scars again, "What is it that you are truly afraid of, pet?"

"All right...you have caught me again, love...I am fearful of being alone for the long millennia ahead," she confesses, shaking her head as if disgusted with herself. In response, Vachel pulls her forward into the kiss she was trying earlier to get. *No, you will find someone. You just have to look harder than this.* In it he pushes a small burst of power through his lips into hers.

The power shoots through her, causing her to grip the front of his shirt in an effort to keep her feet, despite the arm wrapped around her waist. He holds the kiss in place, letting the power rage through as much of her as it can. Once he is satisfied with the tension of her hands, he slowly slips away, feeling the sigh escape against his lips. "That's just ours, pet," he whispers, slipping his arm and hand away.

She is silent as she lets her arms fall to her sides, staring wide-eyed at him with no thought to hiding her scars from view. Mikya has to clamp a hand to her mouth to prevent the gasp of surprise from escaping. Gilden's eyes narrow even though he keeps control of his breathing. Ven, meanwhile, is the only one to gaze at her face with a blank look that suggests he has just seen something he sees every day.

Smiling as if pleased with himself, Vachel turns away and starts toward the others again. His posture has returned to its straight-backed state, and the grace has filled his movements again. There is even a small hint of a smirk to his face. He has passed Gilden, Mikya, and Ven before the

High Sister regains her voice: "You must remember to see me at least once more in the future, Death. I do not mind if I have to wait, but I will be very upset should you forget." "I understand, Selene," Vachel replies, placing a flat palm against the doors. The smirk turns to a smile for a moment before he forces it back at the memory of Sister Crystal's face.

He can't believe he forgot her, even for a moment. And yet, he can't recall having thought of her once since High Sister Selene drew him to her in her chamber. It takes him only a moment to realize it had to have been the High Sister's doing, but he holds tight on the anger. His molars grind into each other as the hand at his side squeezes itself into a fist. The High Sister is going to have to answer for this. It might not be now or even soon, but she can't be allowed to do this without consequences.

The doors open slowly enough Vachel has to stand waiting for a moment before there is enough room for him to exit. In that time, he has to feel the sharp gaze of the others on his back. It is an irritating feeling against his spine, but he ignores it as much as possible. There are more important things to think about at the moment. He continues the silence as they follow him away from the glittering, white structure out into the sea of black sand.

Despite his discomfort, he is the first to speak once he is satisfied that they are far enough away: "I don't want any questions about what happened until after we complete this mission. I feel shitty enough as it is." *Especially after what happened with my mind. Crystal...forgive me.*

Ven and Gilden give Mikya a small glance, as if waiting for her to ask anyway. Shaking her head defiantly, she replies, "If he doesn't want to talk about it, I don't want to hear about it." "How long will this frame of mind last, princess?" Vachel asks, turning around to look at them. "If it's something so horrible you don't want to tell us about it, I don't want to know what it entails...I don't think I could handle it," Mikya confesses, glaring down at the sand.

Vachel gives a weak smile as he remarks, "It seems you're learning after all." "Can we just get away from here...*please*?!" Ven interjects, trembling slipping to his hands again. "Sure thing, child," Vachel replies, "Just get over here and we can all leave." Ven is the first to make it over to Vachel and stands as close as he can without touching the demon. Of course, if he could have, he would have wrapped his arms around Vachel's waist in thanks, most likely dissolving into tears of gratitude.

Gilden and Mikya are not far behind him, though, and take their positions in the tight circle around Vachel. Again, Vachel focuses to gain his concentration, causing the black sand to spill up around them in a rush. The magic feels stronger when it takes hold of them this time. Still, they are left with the feeling of holding their breaths before their feet touch down. However, what they find when they open their eyes is not at all what they expect.

He steps out of the room with a smile and blood splattered across his chest and face. His fangs show against the smile as he takes a towel to the blood. It is not proper to return home covered in the blood of a soldier of Dehurst, especially if that soldier was killed in the heat of passion. The master gave him permission to have one last go around with her, as long as she died before he left for Darkhaven. This quick reprieve from the mundane has made him eager to get home. After all, once he's done with this stupid thing concerning Ven and Vachel, he can spend some time with his mate. He misses her. *Yep, nothing like a she-demon. Nothing at all.*

Running his tongue over his lips, Reno makes his way to the hanging hiding half of his second room from view. If she took a gaze behind this cover, she made no hint of it throughout the time they spent together. And if she didn't, he has to wonder just how she managed to claim her spot amongst the warriors, unless Dehurst is as lacking in training and guidance as it is in royalty. The princess is just pathetic.

Hidden in this space is his proper armor. It has the appearance of a scaled coating, but can stand up to most weapons and magic. The color is black, and a violet dragon is spread out over the chest. He slips the armor on over a black, sleeveless shirt and black pants so the metal does not rub against his skin. Black boots are slipped on to his shins, meeting the metal. The plates at his shoulders hold a row of silver spikes, and the gloves are adorned with similar spikes that rest over his knuckles.

A sword complete with a silver hilt rests in a black sheath at his left hip, held in place by the thick belt around his waist. The gold buckle of this belt holds the symbol for beast[3] in the language of Darkhaven. He pulls his hair back tight against the back of his neck before taking a deep breath. Finally, he will get to see some real action. Lin was just a diversion until the real fun starts. "I'm coming for you both," he declares, tapping his chest three times. The smile is still perched on his face when the blue light engulfs him and he disappears.

"What is this stuff?" Mikya asks, wiping a glob of thick, white, gritty slime from her face.

Gazing around she finds that the boys are covered in a thick layer of the slop, as well. A large glob falls right next to her, splattering the slime all over her again. This makes Ven and Vachel gaze up. There is a white cloth stretched out over their heads on poles. In the center of this cloth is a hole large enough for someone to fall through, which is most likely what they did.

Framing the cloth is a black sky, suggesting, somehow, night has fallen this early in the day. Vachel turns his gaze to the surroundings and finds them inside a hole carved out of stone. They stand atop a platform edged with more stone in an attempt to keep this slime from slipping

---

[3] This symbol consists of a wolf head. Quite appropriate, no?

down to the stone floor below. "This is feed for a high level guardian," Ven explains, tasting some of the slime from his arm.

"'Guardian?'" Gilden asks with a raised eyebrow as he flings some of the slime from his arms. Nodding, Ven explains, "A guardian is responsible for keeping any unwanted demons from entering a particular territory. This one just happens to be a demon with a beast form instead of only a human form like Vachel or the Sisters." "Is that why they called you Death? Because you killed any demons who threatened to venture into territory they should not have?" Mikya asks, gazing over at Vachel. "I was wondering when you would pick up on that...but yes, that is the reason," he replies, giving himself a shake that flings slime in all directions and rids him of most of the layer that was clinging to him.

Mikya takes to slipping the goop from her, taking special care to get off as much as she can. "This stuff is really gross!" she exclaims, spitting after getting some of it in her mouth. "I disagree...I find it to be so much better than some of the other things I could feed on," a voice responds from the edge of the hole.

Rust

All eyes snap up to watch the form slip over the edge and drop to the stone floor beside the platform. He stays in the shadows, flashing his bright eyes at them as his smile shows glittering fangs. They stare at each other for a few silent moments before he steps out of the shadow and into the moonlight. A glare slips to Vachel's face as he catches sight of the figure's face, while Mikya and Gilden both gasp. "Traitor!" Gilden yells at the sight of Reno dressed in his Darkhaven armor. Shaking his head, Reno replies, "Not so, sorcerer. I have been quite loyal to my master throughout these last few centuries. I have done everything he has asked of me."

"You know what he was talking about, demon," Vachel growls, only now spying the wolf ears perched atop Reno's head. *How could I have been so stupid? He didn't even change his name, dammit! Was I so absorbed as to be blinded by this fool?* Smiling as he inhales deeply, Reno counters, "It seems you are the one who has been unfaithful, Death. What will you tell Sister Crystal when she smells this other woman on you?" "Faerie noses cannot detect the presence of such things, Beast," Ven interjects, stepping forward. Fear thrills through him, but he keeps his gaze steady into Reno's piercing blues.

Just as the words escape his mouth, Reno leaps up onto the platform, landing with a heavy crash suggesting he weighs more than he should have with the current form: "And you...you have not given your mistress her dues, Messenger. Master will be most displeased with your performance. He might use the collar on you. I just love listening to the screams. They're so frightened, and sound so much like food." Anticipatory saliva makes his fangs shine under the beams of the moon. With pure fear in his eyes, Ven stares back at that fanged smile.

"Enough, Beast. He's got the point," Vachel growls, taking a step forward. This fight is between him and Rust. There's no sense in bringing any of the others in on it just to get them hurt. "Oh no, not yet he doesn't, Death," Reno replies, swinging his arm back. "No!" Vachel snarls in warning as the spikes glint against the black supporting them. Ven has just enough time to close his eyes before Reno's spike-covered knuckles collide with the side of his face.

The impact tears through the skin of his cheek, shredding it as he spins around with the force. His blood tastes metallic on his tongue and the tears burn in his eyes. Not only is his throbbing in pain, but he is completely ashamed at having to be reprimanded like this. He should have been able to keep himself out of trouble after all the pains Nera went through to teach him how to be a proper servant. *It seems I still haven't learned.* As the ground reaches up to catch him, Ven only has time to think that hitting the ground will hurt until his forehead crashes into the platform.

Vachel rushes forward, but it is not Ven's side he rushes to. Instead, he crashes full force with Reno's nose, his fangs flashing as they both go over the edge. Snarling into the face of his attacker, Reno throws his own punch. Vachel misses the spikes, but the rest of Reno's strike catches his cheek, tossing him backwards. Angry, he leaps at Reno who dodges his assault by inches. Swinging around again, Vachel finds Reno hasn't moved and his right side is open for an attack. However, when he goes for it, there is a smile on Reno's face. Vachel feels the magic building beneath his feet a moment later. His eyes widen when he recognizes the aura behind it.

Mikya and Gilden manage to reach Ven's side just as a cry rings through the air. They turn their gazes to where Vachel and Reno fell to the floor to find Vachel caught in a ring of violet light.

Blood forces its way from his mouth in a rush, splattering him and the ground, and his arms are wrapped firmly around his waist, as if bracing against some terrible pain. Reno stands watching, a smile on his face. Suddenly, Vachel's back bows backwards, jerking him into a rigid posture that not even he could balance with unless he had support. His hands have jerked to a rigid, claw-like position before his face, his arms pinned against his sides. A ragged cry escapes, and his gaze jerks to Ven who has forced his way to a sitting position and stares over his shoulder in horror.

"This is your doing!" Vachel accuses in a yell.

Ven begins to tremble again, tears slipping into his eyes as he gives a slow nod. It is his magic, but he did not know for what his master intended it to be used. He hates to admit it now that he has been admitting to himself how well Vachel has treated him. It hurts even more to know he has done this to the one demon who knows him for what he is: a person.

Red rays of light burst from the ground and air above Vachel. One shoots through his back, another through each of his legs and arms, and finally, the last forces its way through his head, spilling out of his forehead. Both of his eyes shine bright with it, and he takes a shuddering breath. His body gives a sudden jerk before the violet light releases him, dumping him to the stone floor. He lies still, even his chest refuses to rise and fall, with eyes glazed over with a hint of that red light.

"It's killed him!" Mikya cries, her hands finding their way to her mouth. After all they've done to him, he has to die like this. It isn't fair! It isn't! At her side, Gilden bows his head in shame, remembering what his magic did to the demon. Vachel doesn't deserve this. Shaking his head, appearing to feel sorrow as well, Ven whispers dismally, "He isn't dead...this is worse. It has frozen him. This way he will be much easier to get back to Master." "How could you do it?" Gilden demands, catching two fistfuls of Ven's shirt and jerking him up.

Tears streaming from his eyes, Ven bursts, "I didn't want Master to hurt my sisters! He promised me if I brought

Death back then they would be free." He has to believe the Master. There has been no reason to doubt him, even with the extensive amount of pain the Master has caused him. After all, his own father wouldn't lie about returning his half sisters back to him. *He has to do it. He promised me. He's bound by his promise, right? Right?!* "Are you stupid?!" Gilden demands angrily, his eyes flashing as readily as any demon's, "Rust has no intention of letting them go! They were most likely dead by the time he forced you to wear the Shiku Hara!"

He shakes Ven hard enough to jerk the Hybrid's neck and make him whimper in fear. Silently, Ven has to consider the possibility in the face of Gilden's certainty. Why else would Rust be so insistent he bring Death back quickly? Sure, the Halfling hated waiting, but there was no reason for that much haste. And the sight of Gilden's pure fury in the face of his reason for betraying Vachel makes him feel worse about doing it. Maybe he's been lying to himself for so long, he can't tell when someone else is doing the same.

"Alright, sorcerer, release my pack member!" Reno growls, interrupting Ven's thoughts and tossing Vachel over his shoulder like a sack. Watching him, Mikya winces at the way Vachel's head snaps around on his neck. Gilden jerks his own head in the demon's direction, but continues to shake Ven as if he is daring the demon to make him leave Ven alone now that he knows the truth. There is an anger and hatred in his red eyes that has not been there before.

Leaping back up onto the platform, Reno growls again, "*I'm* alpha and I'll not tolerate being disobeyed, especially by a human! Now, unhand that pup or I will pull your arms off." Ven whimpers to him, but remains silently crying other than that. It is partially a plead to Gilden to do as Reno says in order to keep his limbs and partially a plead to Reno not to attack Gilden as he threatens.

His gaze still on Reno, Gilden releases Ven, dropping the Hybrid in a heap at his feet: "There, you can have your pup, alpha. But, this will not go unpunished, of that you can be assured." "You haven't the power to do anything against my pack. Master will see you and your princess in chains, sorcerer...and then it will be *you* in *my* grasp crying like a bitch," Reno threatens, his ears flattening back on his head and his fangs bared like the angry wolf he is. Sniffing almost inaudibly, Ven cringes at being compared to a female.

I'm powerful for what I am...
Pain has said so.

Still, Ven gives a small, involuntary whimper, just like the frightened pup he has been compared to. At this, Reno's gaze falls to the Hybrid furiously wiping tears from his eyes, even though they slip down his cheeks just as quickly as he can get rid of them. He is getting frustrated and is about to just give up on it when Reno reaches down and takes one of his arms. Sniffing loudly against his whimpers, Ven gazes up. Without a word, Reno pulls him to his feet. Gilden steps back but only after Mikya pulls hard on his arm. She isn't comfortable with him being near the alpha wolf anymore.

"I'm sorry for disobeying, Beast," Ven apologizes, sniffing again as he wipes at his eye with his free hand. He gives a small sound of pain as the rubbing bites into the torn wounds on his face. Bending down without a word, Reno runs his tongue gently along the wounds, gaining as much blood as he does salt from the tears. This will speed the healing process a little. Just before he pulls completely away, Ven gives him a small flick of the tongue on his chin in thanks.

"There, child. Now we must go see Master."

He leans back against the rigid back of the gold throne. Patience has never been his strong suit, but the amount of time being spent on this mission is getting longer and more ridiculous by the minute. The court is all present except for Beast and Death. Just because they will be arriving shortly does not mean their absence has no effect on the meeting. It is about Death's punishment, and Beast must be here to help make the decision. True, he has the final say, but they are the ones who will be deciding what is appropriate for Death's desertion of not only his duties, but his people, as well.

Even as a Halfling he was powerful enough to play Death for me.

Shaking his head at the thought, he runs a hand through his hair, causing the wavy, golden strands to spill forward over his broad shoulders again. The black robe strains against the muscles of his shoulders and does its best to hide the ones running up and down his arms. Only his hands peak out from the gold-rimmed sleeves. His black shirt has no sleeves and is slipped neatly into the equally black pants. The gold of his belt buckle can be seen clearly because the cloth is kept from the front by his pants, and engraved into the metal is the symbol for master[4].

At his shins, the black boots slip over the pants. He gazes around the expansive room with his violet eyes as a small frown slips to his face. His mind has been so busy with other things he just now noticed Ven is not here, either. The Hybrid has to be here, too, if things are going to proceed in the timely manner they should. Of course, as soon as this thought springs to his mind, he remembers it was Ven he sent after Death in the first place. It seems Beast will have to collect the boy to be punished, as well. There is no excuse for this taking so long.

He already had permission to travel Darkhaven the moment he returned from Dehurst, so there is no reason for him to have had to visit the Sisters. Of course, Ven would not have willingly gone to see his other master. He fears the High Sister of Darkhaven much more than the King. Of course, this might have something to do with the fact that Rust hurts him while he still has some semblance of dignity. High Sister Selene strips him of his pride and barriers before

---

[4] This symbol consists of a crown and staff.

she spills his blood. It is why Rust only allows her to have Ven only every so often. The boy has to be able to walk in order to serve as Messenger.

Perhaps the plan went more smoothly than it should have, and the boy got caught up in his ruse. This is why one does not send his children to take care of important things for him Rust muses, fighting the urge to shake his head in pure frustration. He should have known better than to allow someone as pitiful as that mongrel to take on something this important. Still, the Hybrid was good for one thing: his sisters made excellent additions to Rust's little gaggle of girls. *Well, excellent until they started trying to rebel. I can't have any more rebellious women than I already have. The Sisters are bad enough.*

The four present members of the court stand around the room, their eyes narrowed in thought. He has to wonder what sort of things go on inside the minds of ruthless demons when they are not killing. Perhaps they think of what to do about their deserter. Or perhaps they are more closely focused on the needs of their king. He considers this latter possibility only because of how silent they are. No one dares to even tap his foot for fear the resulting sound against the stone floor would get on Rust's nerves. It is not a good idea to make the king angry with you. He's certainly glad they have all learned this lesson with time to spare.

The red rug running to the wood door divides the room in half, each side having two members of the court. On the right stand Pain and Violence, the perfect pair really, especially since they have chosen each other as their lover. It has to be a mutual decision between them because neither will stand to be with someone who is not sure of their decisions.

Pain is the only woman of the court, but then she has to earn every small scrap of respect the king gives her. He just does not see women as powerful enough for any kind of recognition, well any that does not include a horizontal surface. Considering she does little more than torture those he has no desire to send to the Sisters, he has to wonder why he gives her any respect at all. Maybe it has something to do with the cold killer he can see in her eyes.

She glares out at the room in general, her arms crossed as if daring anyone to come close. The black robe over her slim shoulders falls to her ankles. Only a leather band manages to cover her chest. At her slim waist is a black belt complete with a gold buckle that has the symbol for pain[5] worked into the metal. Black leather pants that are tight enough to be an extra skin slip into a pair of black boots at the knees. The heels are two inches high and made of gold blades that make every step a balancing act.

Her black hair falls to her shoulders, but has been pulled back as tight as she can get it. The blue of her eyes is piercing and cold enough to freeze most demons in their tracks. They appear as circles of ice formed into the pale skin of her face. Perhaps that is one of the reasons Violence

---

[5] This symbol consists of a chain and whip intertwined with each other.

was attracted to her in the first place. It has given Rust pause, at least for the moment. He will be tired of her in a moment's time. He can feel it.

Violence is almost her opposite, making them seem to fit together. The muscles of his chest and shoulders strain against the cloth of the black robe and are so large he cannot properly cross his arms. His gaze on the room is more neutral as if he is bored rather than challenging anything that moves as having a reason to attack. The black shirt is sleeveless and tucked into his black leather pants. His gold belt buckle bears the symbol for violence[6].

At his shins, the pants slip smoothly into a pair of black, military style boots. Only his hair tries to take away from the image of huge and imposing. It falls to his knees naturally, but he has it pulled back in a braid that is tight enough to make the hair slip just below his waist.

Of course, he has a perfect way to keep the hair from being anything but dangerous. Worked into the strands beneath the tie are four small blades, and he has learned enough control of the braid using only his neck that he can attack most things with just the braid. The green of his eyes is not quite so piercing as Pain's, but there is still a hint of danger flowing through them. Standing next to Pain and her pale skin makes his tan seem all the darker.

However, when compared to the darkness of Frenzy's skin across the room, Violence looks almost pale. He has a

---

[6] This symbol consists of a sword.

small amount of muscle, but it is only enough to keep him from looking frail. Of course, the black of the robe over his shoulders is loose enough to make him seem smaller, not bigger. He wears a black, collared shirt, the top two buttons left open. The shirt is slipped neatly into his tight black pants that are in turn tucked into black boots at his knees.

Slipped through the belt loops of his pants is a red cloth tied just over the left pocket so the end falls to his knee. Attached to this cloth against the knot is a metal circle bearing the symbol for frenzy[7]. At the base of his neck, his blood red hair is held in place by a black tie. The hair has been slipped forward over his shoulder so it rests in contrast to the black. A smooth, almost feminine face hides the dangerous demon within, and every member of the court knows he does it on purpose. His eyes are purely black and reflect the room around him as if he should be unable to see past that reflection.

There is only one small thing that keeps him from seeming too feminine and helpless: a tight scar worked over his face, which slides from just above the right eye to the middle of his left cheek. A small frown is spared for the room, but no true emotions show yet. Just because he acts like a person with a nasty case of bipolar disorder in battle and when provoked does not mean he does not have moments where he is as unreadable as the best trained.

---

[7] This symbol consists of six star bursts of varying sizes.

To his left is his partner in crime, Chaos. This demon is actually much younger than his counterpart, but he is truly the brains behind the partnership. Just because one feeds off chaos and brings more of it than one stops does not mean one is mindless. He is only slightly more muscular than Frenzy, but it his extra height over the elder demon that makes him appear more dangerous. The black robe falls to the floor around him even with the extra height.

He wears a tight, black, short-sleeved shirt. It has been given free reign of his waist. However, the medallion bearing the symbol for chaos[8] is secured on a loose chain around his waist, only the belt loops keeping it from slipping off his hips and down to the floor. The black pants are baggy and shoved sloppily into a pair of wide-rimmed, black boots at his shins. His hair is a bright, florescent green. It is shaved short on the sides, but there is enough hair on top to be pulled up into jagged, uneven spikes atop his head. The eyes in his slightly tan face are just as brightly green as his hair.

Nothing human could ever have eyes like that. The eyes of a predator are softer than the look of Chaos's eyes. Of course, very few demons have eyes like that, either. Only those with powers that enable them to feed off such things as chaos, fear, or anything that is not completely physical have eyes like that, which explains why the High Sister and Rust have bright eyes that shine even without the aid of

---

[8] This symbol consists of a scribble with jagged edges.

light. Both are masters of feeding off things without ever really touching the person off whom they are feeding. The High Sister can feed from fear and panic, while Rust feeds directly off pain. Thus the reason why each brings so much of it into their presence.

Rust is about to speak and break the silence when a shouting voice slips into the air: "Put me down, demon! I'll not be carried in there like a helpless child!" All five stare intently at the door and immediately understand whom it is that is doing the yelling. No one but Death would make such a fuss over something so trivial. But then, Death is also the only one who has a pride-laden temper that refuses to quit even under the most dire of circumstances. There is the sound of rattling chains and something being dropped to the floor as Beast's voice counters, "There! If you want to be stubborn about it, I'll just let you carry yourself through the damn doorway!"

"Must you yell like that?" a female voice none recognize asks. "Silence!" Beast growls, "I'll deal with your problem once this pathetic sack of flesh makes up his mind!" "Don't go all bitch on me, Beast. Just because you can't handle a little opposition doesn't mean you have to shrink away with your tail between your legs like Nera," Vachel's voice adds angrily. Reno immediately comes to Nera's defense: "Leave my mate out of this, demon! Hah! I can't even call you that anymore...I guess *Halfling* will have to do!"

"I wouldn't have called you a demon even at the pinnacle of your power," Vachel growls as the door is flung open, "Now you're just a lap dog for his high-and-mightiness." Even from across the room, the crimson running down his chin and splattered across his arms is visible. Reno shoves him through the door as he yells, "I am no dog!" As Reno makes his way into the room, Ven scrambles to his position in the corner as if afraid to be found out of it with the court assembled.

The last to enter the room is a pair the court has never seen before. One is a sorcerer it is obvious, and, from the look of his robe, he is an Elder of Dehurst. However, the woman is not quite so easy to place. It is obvious she has power, but she is not quite powerful enough to be even a low-level sorceress.

"Who are these others?" Rust demands, forcing his way into the argument. Both Reno and Vachel cease to speak, but neither offers to tell the king who Mikya and Gilden are. The king grinds his molars together in rage. There can be nothing more infuriating than these two. If there is, he pities the poor creatures forced to be in the presence of such a nuisance. Rust is about to ask again, a whole lot less nicely this time, when Ven explains, "This is Princess Mikya of Dehurst, and Elder Sorcerer Gilden. They followed me home." His voice is small, and there is something closer to panic than fear in it. Turning his gaze on Ven, Rust asks, "And just why did it take you so long to return?"

"We had...uh...a few bumps along the way," Ven offers, swallowing hard. His heart is stuck in the way, making even breathing difficult for him. If he had the ears of his third of demon, they would no doubt be forced so hard against his head that they would appear to be trying to slip beneath the skin and hide. He finds himself wishing he could sink through the wall and hide from what he knows is coming "Bumps? What sort of bumps, Messenger?" Rust presses, his eyes narrowing. Swallowing hard enough to hurt, Ven explains, "Once I got them here...I didn't know how to break the ruse and force them to the castle."

"That sounds like only one bump to me, child," Rust observes, his eyes narrowing further. "It kind of snow-balled from there...until Beast came," Ven replies, his voice now having a slightly higher pitch to it. "It seems the Messenger has been overestimated," Frenzy observes in a whisper. Compared to the yelling between Reno and Vachel, he has barely even spoken. His voice is deep and measured, as if he is trying as hard as possible to keep it even and calm, but Rust and the rest of the court know the observation was not made idly. "At least he can control himself...Frenzy," Vachel replies, dropping the opened shackles to the floor and adding at the looks from the other demons, "It seems the lot of you have lost a bit of edge if you didn't notice."

Pain turns her gaze to him with a deep glare as she corrects, "You are not threat enough to need them, Death. It is *you* who has lost your edge." "If you think I'm going to

209

believe that, you're even slower than I thought, Pain," Vachel replies, crossing his arms. The look is condescending, letting her know he thinks she is just as worthless as she thinks him to be. He has hated her since the moment she first spoke to him all those centuries ago. It was she who announced his first assignment as Death to him. Reno jabs him in the back with his fist, growling: "Stop insulting my comrades, Halfling."

"Your only true comrades are your pack members, Reno, but I don't see you aiding them," Vachel replies, giving him the same stare he gave Pain. Ven stands silent in the corner, but his head is slowly moving from side to side, as if silently pleading with Vachel to stop poking at Reno. There is nothing to be gained from a fight with this many demons to jump into it. Pain gives Rust a small glance, asking for permission to retaliate. With an anticipatory smile, Rust nods at her. Unlike her, he knows she cannot win this. A smile slipping to her own lips, Pain makes her way to the red carpet, stalking toward Vachel with her piercing gaze on his eyes.

Reno watches her move forward and slips to the side next to Violence, evening out the room again. She steps up before Vachel, her eyes narrowing. To any other demon, that look would have meant torture was eminent. Vachel's only response is to flash her a smile that exposes his fangs. The fist seems to come out of nowhere, but Vachel easily avoids it by simply tilting his head to one side.

"You're going to have to do much better than that," he whispers, the smile never wavering. Stepping back slightly, Pain jerks her hand up, sending fire shooting into his face. His smile grows all the wider, and the fire begins to slowly disappear, having never touched him. Shock spread out on Pain's face for just a moment. Violence has enough time to warn, "Look out!" before Vachel sends her own fire back at her with his own added to it. Pain is not fast enough to keep from being hit with the flame, and because she cannot control it, she receives a large burn to the right side of her face.

Spying this, Mikya gasps, pointing out what Vachel already knows, has known since he saw the wounds on Selene's face: "She's the one who attacked the High Sister!" "Exactly, princess. She's the only person I know who would stoop so low to get rid of her competition," Vachel explains, his eyes narrowing. This declaration makes the anger flare all the worse. Pain glares at him in her fury and is about to attack again when Chaos steps in, placing a hand on her wrist: "You are outmatched...continuing would serve no purpose."

Gritting her teeth, Pain turns her furious gaze on Chaos. "Do not be angry with me for your inability, Pain. It seems your brand of talents lie with those who cannot defend themselves," Chaos counters, his face calm. Off to the side, Frenzy's shoulders have tightened minutely as he nods in agreement with his partner. Shaking his head, Vachel replies, "It is not her inability that is holding her back. It is that the type of ability she possesses makes stealing from her so much easier. Given any other type of opponent with my strength as a Halfling, and she would not be having this much trouble." "Perhaps," Chaos agrees, letting the barest hint of a smile touch his lips.

"I don't need you to defend me, Death," Pain growls, her pride hurting just as much as her face. "Enough. We have other issues to see to," Rust commands, getting to his feet. Vachel flashes Pain a triumphant smile that flashes fang as she turns away. When Pain takes her place along the wall, Reno steps away to stand behind Vachel again.

"Messenger, front and center," Rust demands, stepping away from the throne. Ven does as he is told, having already abandoned his pack to the floor in the corner. The sound of his steps across the floor pound in his ears as he steps up before his father. He has to concentrate to keep from trembling and crying at being in the face of this furious Halfling. Gazing down at Ven, Rust directs, "You know what you are to do." Ven takes a deep breath before slipping the gloves from his hands and letting them fall to the floor.

He clasps his hands behind his back before gazing up at Rust. It was he who made Ven use this trust sign in the first place. The king presents his wrist, and Ven gently runs his tongue over the wrist. Once this is done, Ven drops his hands to his sides and stands silent, waiting to be reprimanded for what he has done. Just because Beast tore open his face for denying the High Sister does not mean

Rust was the one who told him to do it. It was most likely about pack law instead of Rust's rules, so Rust will want his own punishment. At the thought of his wound, it throbs painfully in protest to his elevated heart rate.

For a moment, Rust just stands silent, gazing down at the boy, that is, until he catches the lack of the scent he is looking for. There is blood, yes, but not a trace of the High Sister's scent is on him despite what he said about being unable to end the ruse at an early enough stage. At this, his eyes narrow and he demands, "Why did you not serve your mistress? She expects payment for our agreement."

"She...she took Death," Ven whispers, fear raging through him all the worse now that he has Rust standing over him. "I don't care what she did," Rust replies, his voice a dangerous whisper, "I want to know why you did not willingly do what I told you to do." "I-I was...frightened, and then there was a spell put on the door," Ven explains, his fingers tightening into rigid claws at his sides. It is just part of being of the wolves: when one is frightened or his safety is threatened, his body reacts in a defensive manner no matter how inappropriate.

Rust takes hold of the chain of the Shiku Hara in response. He uses it to pull Ven up off of the floor so he can stare into the Hybrid's eyes: "You disobeyed a direct order, Messenger. I will not stand for this."

"Mikya, you might want to cover your ears and close your eyes," Vachel warns, his fists tightening at his sides. "What? Why?" she asks, fear slipping into her voice. "This is what it looks like to have the true master of the Shiku Hara wield its power," he explains in a whisper. Before she does as he cautions, Mikya gives Reno a small glance with no real thought to why she is doing it. The demon's ears are flat against his head, telling her he does not like what is going to be happening in the least. This thought alone frightens her more than Vachel's warning.

Hybrid's Bloodletting

Mikya manages to get her ears covered and her eyes clamped tightly closed just as Vachel suggested when Rust whispers the words of the spell: "Pain...violence...frenzy... chaos...beast...death. Teach this child what it means to be mine."

Violet light bursts from around the collar, immediately engulfing Ven's entire frame. No one has to see his eyes to know fear is thrilling through his veins. He has just enough time to grit his teeth before the violet turns black and rushes inside in one scalding wave. The first sound from his mouth is a shriek that even Vachel's use of the Shiku Hara did not bring forth.

His head jerks back in as close to an arch as he can get it while hanging in mid-air. Both hands jerk up automatically to the collar, gripping it against the pain as if that one hold makes so much of it go away. As Vachel watches, the color of Rust's eyes changes. They are now a violet dark enough to be just this side of black; he is feeding from the pain. A growl forces its way from his throat as tension speeds across his shoulders. The sound of Ven's cries makes even his fingers thirst for Rust's blood. Tears stream down Ven's face in scalding lines, their very presence causing lines of pain to run along his face.

With every breath he takes, a shriek of pain issues forth. His muscles are all tense, as if trying to shield themselves from the pain that racks them. Soon, the shrieks turn into wet, strangled sounds, meaning the spell has spilled into his throat and torn the flesh apart again.

Blood spills up and out of the corners of his mouth, running back over his cheeks to slide through his hair and drip to the red carpet. Fear rushes into his eyes along with the pain at the thought that this time the damage might be permanent. He closes his eyes tightly against the pain, so he does not realize until he is dropped to the floor that anyone in the room moved. The feeling of the floor catching his shoulders brings a painful gasp from his chest and leaves him trembling in a heap against the aching in every inch of skin, bone, and muscle. He forces his eyes open enough to realize it was Vachel who stopped Rust before they drop back down.

He's saved me again. I don't deserve it.

Vachel stands before Rust, his fist raised to strike again while the king is glaring up from his kneeling position on the floor. The blow to his face surprised him more than it actually hurt, but he still released Ven and the source from which he was feeding. The rage in his eyes is a mirror of the same fire burning off of Vachel's skin.

"How dare you," he demands, jerking to his feet so he towers over Vachel again. The smaller demon stares back into those rage-filled eyes and growls, "You went too far, arrogant bastard. Just because you can inflict that kind of pain on someone doesn't mean you should. You'd have killed him, and then you'd be without your favorite means of feeding." "You have no authority to speak to me in such a manner," Rust replies, his voice a dangerous whisper. Growling, Vachel counters, "Someone's got to tell you you're being a stupid jackass!"

At this, Reno reaches forward and jerks Vachel back by his hair, threatening: "You'll not get away with talking to the master like that, Halfling. I'll personally see you bleeding." His rage is flaming out of control, and Vachel seizes the opportunity to retaliate when Reno redirects his attention. Vachel spins around faster than Reno can follow and sinks his fangs deep into the demon's hand. The teeth pass straight through the leather, and he has positioned his mouth, so the spikes do not touch him.

"Let go of me!" Reno demands jerking his hand into the air. This only serves to make Vachel wrap his hands around the demon's arm in an effort to keep from having to support his entire weight by his teeth alone. Just for spite, he grinds harder into the wounds under his fangs. In response, Reno takes a fistful of Vachel's hair and yanks him off of his arm. He growls out a curse as Vachel's fangs are jerked out of his flesh.

Vachel might not be hanging on to him anymore, but the torn skin of his hand still throbs as Vachel pulls from his grasp. "What the hell did you bite me for?" Reno demands, his anger obvious. Growling at him, Vachel yells, "He's your pack! You should have been the one to help him! Instead, you attack me for doing it!"

"You don't have any business lecturing me on responsibility, Death!" Reno counters angrily, "Besides, it's none of my concern how a wolf chooses to discipline his young." The room goes silent at this declaration. Even Ven bites down against the whimpers of pain he so wishes he could make. "Excuse me?" Vachel demands, a new fury seeping into his face. He knew Ven is a wolf from all the time he was spending with the pack, but he had no idea Rust was the one to spawn the Hybrid.

"It's just like I said it, Halfling. I'm not responsible for patrolling how wolves discipline a pup that has disobeyed a direct order," Reno repeats, holding his hand firmly in an attempt to ease the bleeding. "What kind of monster would do such a thing to his own child?" Mikya demands, fury, horror, and concern flowing steadily over her face. It has taken her this long to work up the anger and nerve to speak. That Rust is Ven's father has pushed her over the edge, just as it has Vachel. Turning his glare to Rust, Vachel responds, "The worthless sack of flesh that calls himself the King of Darkhaven."

"The boy understands the consequences of disobeying me, yet he did it anyway. What would you have had me do? Break my word for some accident too weak to even defend himself?" Rust demands, his voice still a low whisper. Surprisingly enough, it is again Mikya who steps forward to answer his question, "A king is responsible for helping those who are too weak to defend themselves. You are nothing but a bully who has decided to wear a crown and either frightened or killed any challenger."

"None but cowards rule over anything in this manner. You, sir, are a coward in the deepest sense of the word," Gilden adds, making his way forward to stand at Mikya's side. Finally, seeing her stand up to this Halfling has put charge to his own courage. His eyes narrowing, Rust replies, "It does not matter what you think of me, princess. I will rule over Darkhaven as I see fit until someone rises up who has power enough to defeat me. Until that time, my word is law and no one may question my actions. Beast, see to our rebellion! Pain, you can deal with the Hybrid!"

With this, Rust turns his back on them and makes his way back up to the throne. Reno catches Vachel's arm before he can go after the king's exposed back, dragging the angry, struggling demon from the room and pushing Gilden and Mikya out before them. It is not until they are out the door and partly down the hallway that Pain moves forward and jerks Ven to his feet.

The moment she releases him, Ven collapses back to the floor, unable to support his own weight. Rolling her eyes, she takes hold of the back of his cloak and drags him from the room. Tears well up in his eyes anew at the thought of what she will do to him now, but he has no way of keeping her from it. She drags him down a twisted path of stone turns and stairs before jerking him around in front of her and locking a wood door behind. By this time, he has regained enough of his muscle function to curl up defensively.

❧

Once Reno has locked him in his cell, Vachel continues to growl. He can't believe he was blind enough to miss Ven being Rust's child. No matter how unimportant it seemed at the time, he should have been able to at least guess the family resemblance. *They have the same eyes, for crimson's sake. That should have been the first clue!* Still, even as he snarls at himself, he can't help but wonder how Ven is holding up with Pain leaning over him with her weapons of torment. Even the Sisters have some finesse when they beat one near to death.

Slamming his fist down into the stone floor, Vachel leans against the wall. As his eyes fall closed he reaches into his shirt and pulls the crystal out. The surface is warm from being against his skin, and the sharp edges dig imprints into his skin. Sighing heavily, he wishes he would have just spoken to Selene about getting the Crystal of Yossa. However, at that thought, he realizes the crystal in his palm is warmer than it should have been just being up against his chest.

He opens his hand to look down at it balanced in his palm.

There is now a blue light in the center, and heat radiates from that point. He stares at it with a curious look on his face before he realizes what it means. Sister Crystal has been protecting something he and all the demons of

Darkhaven had long decided no longer exists. He holds that very thing in his hand right now. A smile spreads out on his face, and he has to admit that the crystal *has* been speaking to him.

"Crystal...I love you so much," he whispers.

Pressing the crystal to his forehead, he adds, "Tell me how to free myself." He waits only a moment for the crystal to grow hot against his skin before he sees it all flash into his mind. A smile befitting his species appears on Vachel's face as he opens his eyes. All he needs now is a certain Hybrid.

She does not bother to tell him to do it; instead, Pain just jerks the cloak from his shoulders and rolls him over onto his stomach with a swift kick in the ribs. Securing his wrists and ankles to the floor with the shackles embedded for just this purpose, she moves away to the far wall and asks, "Which do you prefer, Messenger? Leather, steel, or both?" Ven can only whimper in answer because his throat will not work for him.

Again, the thought that it might be permanent without Vachel's magic spikes through his mind, bringing fear along with it. The thought of what Pain might be planning for him takes a backseat under the fear he will never be able to talk again.

"I know. I always have a hard time deciding between them, too," Pain remarks as if she were discussing a favorite food, "Still, I like the way the steel looks most of all, so we'll just go with it." And that comment just brought her back to the front of his mind. He can still remember limping for a week after the last time Rust gave him over to her tender care.

The tears have now evolved into a batch of sobs, as he lies pinned and helpless. The sound of rattling chains can be heard as Pain makes her way back over to him. "Oh, don't cry so much, Messenger. It feels good if you'll just let it," Pain taunts like one would a hesitant lover.

Ven shakes his head, the tears streaming all the faster now that his heart is racing with them. He expects the chain to come crashing down on his back only to have her whisper, "You know, I don't want to have to explain to the master why you are running around in rags. So, we're going to change the rules just a little bit."

Ven does not like the sound of this at all and lets her know it with a series of whimpers as he shakes his head even more furiously. His earrings snap painfully against his face as they jerk against his ears. Pain completely ignores him as she reaches down and jerks his shirt up, so it pins his wrists even further. She goes on to do the same to his pants, so there is an open area of completely exposed skin for her to work with: "There now. We can have our fun, and the master will not be angry about another set of ruined clothing. It's not a good idea to make him angry right now, don't you think?" Ven presses his forehead against the stone as hard as he can from this position, but does not even whimper this time. There is no use in it now.

Taking up the chain again, Pain stands far enough away from him that she can manipulate the end against his back without wasted effort hitting the surrounding floor. "This might sting a little, Messenger," she warns with a laugh as she raises her arm for the first strike. Ven grits his teeth and takes a deep breath just as the metal comes crashing down against his back. He coughs out the cry of pain as the barbs along the links tear into his flesh when she pulls it back up. The next sound is more pronounced as his throat clears of the blood.

Her pattern is random, but she makes certain to get every inch of skin she can with the chain before deciding to move on to the whip. Blood and sweat make him feel sticky, and the latter burns in the solid wound she has made of his back. For her round with the whip, she stands behind him, so she can strike the wounds from a different angle. This causes the cries to intensify into screams of pain, and Ven digs his fingertips into the floor against it. Finally, once she is finished with the whip, Pain kneels beside him and bends down to run her tongue along the wounds between his shoulder blades.

Ven tries to jerk away only to have her press harder with her tongue when she catches him again. "No! Stop it, please!" he begs before he realizes he is doing it. However, once he understands the begging is coming from him, Ven swallows hard. The pain in his throat is no longer there, even when he tries to get it to hurt. Laying her palm flat on his wounded back, Pain asks, "And just why do you want me to stop, Messenger?" "It hurts...r-really bad," he whispers, tensing up against her hand on his back.

At this, Pain slips her hand from his torn skin and gets to her feet. She reaches to his wrists and forces the shirt down, scraping against the injured skin as she does so. Ven bites down on the cries in an effort to keep from sounding ungrateful for release. She is just as forceful with his pants, but she does not release his wrists and ankles once she has him fully clothed again. Instead, she slips back into a corner and replies, "I think we should both get some rest before I let Death tear into you for your betrayal. I really want to have all eyes for *that* performance."

This thought makes the fear spike back up into Ven's brain. He understands that Vachel will be angry, and has every right to be, because it was his magic used to trap the demon and allow Beast to bring him to the castle in the first place. He also doubts, no matter how the demon saved him from the Shiku Hara, Vachel wouldn't be itching to claim his revenge for the betrayal. As he has often in the recent past, Ven wishes he could be anywhere at anytime other than here. He would even settle for having to spend the night with the High Sister to having to face Vachel tomorrow.

It is the sound of a knock on the wood door that wakes Ven the next morning. He is still aching and tired, but he knows it does not matter to these people. To be honest, next to what he fears will be coming from Vachel, he doesn't either. Pain makes her way over to the door, opening it to reveal Reno standing in the doorway.

"What is it, Beast?" she demands with a raised eyebrow. Giving her a small shrug, Reno explains, "The master has told me to come get the boy and take him down to one of the cells. He says Death will really want to see him." "I thought I was supposed to see to him," Pain protests, a small hint of anger in her voice. She has a strong feeling this punishment is for failing to hurt Death the night before. Shrugging again, Reno replies, "I've no idea what made him change his mind, but he told me so himself." "Fine. He's right there if you want him," Pain answers, turning away with a jerk.

Reno moves forward and opens the restraints before gathering up Ven's cloak. The Hybrid forces his steady way to his feet, wincing all the while, as the muscles strain against the wounds. As soon as Ven is on his feet, Reno carefully drapes the cloak over his shoulders before ushering him out the door. Because he is so tired, Ven's eyes refuse to open more than halfway for him, so he just lets Reno lead him down the corridor. However, once they are out of sight and earshot, the demon bends down to gaze into Ven's face with concern in his eyes.

"What is it, Beast?" Ven asks, his voice hollow and tired. He isn't certain he cares what his alpha has to say about his punishment. Without a word, Reno turns the boy around and pulls off the cloak. Ven is about to question him again when he gently peels the shirt away from his back. It hurts enough to pull a whimper from Ven, but it is Reno who gives the loudest whimper.

"What's wrong?" Ven asks, gazing over his shoulder. He regrets it, as the movement of the muscle tugs at the injured skin. Instead of explaining, Reno leans forward and runs his tongue gently over the wounds, immediately making the pain ease somewhat. He does not cease until he has gotten to all the wounds on Ven's back. Not willing to undress any further, Ven does not mention the ones running up and down the back of his legs.

Letting the shirt fall back into place, Reno whispers, "It's the least I can do for abandoning you yesterday. I'm sorry, little one." "But, you have to take me to see Death," Ven replies, tears springing to his eyes as the fear takes hold of him again. Nodding even though Ven cannot see it, Reno answers, "Yes. But you'll find that he is not as angry with you as they want you to believe. I think he spent all his anger on two other wolves so you won't get the brunt of it."

"I'm not a real wolf...I've proven that with this performance," Ven whispers bitterly, "I wasn't fit to be a wolf from the moment I was born. I'm just pathetic and will be until I die." "Being weak doesn't make you pathetic, little one. Giving up because you're weak does. Before this you always kept the determination that this was all to help your sisters. Don't let that go just because of me and my squeamishness."

"I can't do it anymore...I just don't have enough of the wolf in me to be worth anything to the pack, and I'll never be worth anything to anyone else. I can't keep that hope and determination anymore," Ven protests, the tears streaming now. He isn't going to admit to Reno that part of his hopelessness comes from the fear Gilden was right and his sisters are already dead. Shaking his head, Reno replies, "Just wait until you see Death. He'll show you that you're wrong."

Ven falls silent as Reno replaces the cloak and leads the way again. The tears still fall, but he keeps the sobs silent as he makes the long trek down into the dungeon. When they arrive, Ven can hear angry voices drifting up the stairs; however, once Reno opens the door to the corridor of cells, everyone falls silent. As they pass, Ven takes a small peek inside each of the cells.

It is not long until he spies Mikya and Gilden. Both are huddled in corners opposite from each other, anger evident in each of their eyes. The rage passes over him as he moves by, and it makes the hair on the back of his neck stand on end. Still, it is the cell Reno actually opens that sends a true thrill of terror up his spine. Ven recognizes this cell as the last place he saw his sisters alive, but he cannot see them now. Instead, he sees a wash of blood covering the floor.

Gilden was right! Sweet crimson, he's already killed them!

Reno seeks to push Ven gently inside when the Hybrid rounds on him, clutching desperately to the demon's leg. "Where are they? Where are my sisters?" he demands, a pleading to his voice. He already knows the answer, but he can't bring himself to completely believe it yet. There has to be some slim chance they are still alive. Reno looks down cast, but remains silent.

"Tell me, Beast. Tell me what happened to my sisters!" Ven nearly screams, the tears spilling out even faster now. Reno seeks to push him away only to have Ven latch onto his fingertips, immediately burning a partial imprint onto the demon's skin. "Let me go!" Reno commands, kicking Ven hard in the stomach. He hates to do it, but he can't look the little one in the eyes anymore. The Hybrid releases him, but continues to cry, "Where are they?! What happened to my sisters?! Tell me what he did to them! Tell me!"

In response, Reno slams the door closed and stalks away.

Ven finally just breaks down, his knees tucked underneath him and his forehead pressed against the floor. He pounds his fists repeatedly against the stone surface, crying miserably. Gilden was right, and he betrayed them all on a lie he believed just because he wanted to. In his misery, Ven does not realize the other inhabitant of the cell has moved until he kneels beside him and whispers, "That never solved anything, child. You're going to have to make Rust pay for what he has done to all of Darkhaven."

"I don't know how," Ven bursts in frustration, still crying. Pulling him to a sitting position, Vachel gazes into his eyes and replies, "Let me have some of your blood."

"What?" Ven demands, confusion setting in. His eyes narrowing, Vachel responds, "You heard me, child. I need some of your blood." "I heard that part, but why?" he asks. Pulling the crystal out from under his shirt, Vachel explains, "I've come up with a way to cure the curse and get all of my demon powers back at once. I just need the crystal and your blood."

"How will that crystal help you?"

"This crystal is the faerie's equivalent to the Crystal of Yossa."

"How do you know that?"

"I know the signs. This isn't *the* crystal but it has the same power."

"Where does my blood come into it?"

"It requires the blood of all three to be used. Ven, you're a Hybrid."

"...a melding of all three."

"Meaning your blood has all of the ingredients I need."

"But, I..."

"What's wrong?"

"I don't want to be tied to anyone else."

"You won't be tied to me," Vachel responds, a small hint of anger in his voice now. Everything is in his grasp, and now Ven decides to turn bitch-demon. Sliding away slowly, Ven whispers, "No...I-I'm scared." "Fine then, give me a trust sign, and I'll just do it myself," Vachel replies. Ven is quick to point out, "But, it'll only be temporary, and it means I have to do it again." "I'm not asking you to mark me as trustworthy until all of time using them. I just need enough time to get the blood," Vachel explains impatiently.

Shaking his head, Ven presses himself against the wall. At this, Vachel seizes both of Ven's wrists in one hand, jerking the boy so he is leaning over him. "Just lick my wrist and get it over with," Vachel growls, his fingers digging into Ven's skin. Ven still refuses, shaking his head furiously. Purely angry now, Vachel squeezes Ven's wrists as hard as he can without breaking the bones. He still needs the Hybrid functioning to get the rest of the plan underway. Ven gives a small whimper of pain, and Vachel replies, "Just do what I told you to, and I'll let go."

Finally, Ven leans up and does as Vachel commands, running his tongue gently over the demon's wrist. As promised, Vachel releases his wrists, but only long enough to pull off the cloak and jerk his shirt up to find the wounds on his back, which the scent of blood drew him toward. Slipping the crystal from around his neck, Vachel gives it a small kiss before plunging the red surface deep into one of the still-bleeding wounds.

Ven gives a small cry of pain and protest as Vachel slips the crystal out and sits back. He gazes at the blood-coated crystal as Ven rights himself with a flush of pain and humiliation on his face. Then, he takes a deep breath before stabbing himself in the forearm with the sharp end. The pain makes him grit his teeth, but Vachel gives no other hint he is in any kind of pain.

As they watch silently, the part of the crystal still visible over Vachel's skin slowly bleeds to blue. The color is backed by an inner light that grows brighter until both are bathed in blue light. Vachel's eyes are narrowed as he gazes down at his arm, while Ven's are wide with fear. Soon, a burning sensation begins around the crystal. The only indication this bothers Vachel is how his eyes narrow all the more.

Along with the burning, the blue light flashes brighter, turning nearly white in their eyes before a red light begins to spread out along Vachel's skin. It travels along the lines of blood vessels, but makes his entire arm seem to light up with the red. As the light seeps up his arm to reach any available blood vessel, the burning is carried with it. This time, it causes him to grimace against the pain. Ven can tell when the light seeps up into his face, but the only indication it has passed over his chest or legs is the way Vachel hunches over.

He gives a small moan before whispering: "It's everywhere...it burns like fire in my veins." Just as the words escape, the light flashes as bright as it can beneath Vachel's skin. He takes in a shuddering breath against the burning before the light changes to blue. All the pain drains away from his face, only to be replaced by a confused expression. Ven is about to ask if he is all right when the demon pitches forward, trembling with his eyes now closed.

"What's wrong?" Ven asks, reaching a tentative hand out to Vachel. In response, Vachel shakes his head slowly, but does not open his mouth to speak. Because of this silence, Ven hesitates instead of touching Vachel as he had planned. Instead of words, a rush of blood mixed with that black liquid forces him to open his mouth and expel it all with a splattering noise against the stone.

If he was not already pressed tight against the wall, Ven might have backed away from the sight. But, because he is essentially trapped, all he can do is hold still and silent as small flecks of black and red slap him in the face. However, a fear that the rush will not stop slowly spills up into his brain, as if put there by someone who understands the magic they are using. Before he can think about doing it, Ven reaches forward and touches Vachel's bare shoulder gently, as if expecting the trust sign to fail. As soon as their skin comes in contact, Ven feels a burst of power crash into him.

It slams him back against the wall hard enough to make him slump back to the floor. Of course, now that he has slipped down, his open palm rests in the perfect position to receive a rush of blood and two small, heavy objects. They are small spheres, but they weigh enough to feel like solid metal. Ven gazes at them for some time, but still cannot decide what they are. When he raises his gaze to Vachel, there is a smile on the demon's face.

"Do you know what these things are?" Ven asks, still staring up at Vachel. Nodding his head, Vachel whispers, "They're lead." "You mean they're..." Ven replies, gazing at them with a spark of realization that soon turns to disgust.

Of course, when Vachel nods his agreement, Ven drops them like they have burned him: "Gross! Get them away from me." He sits back up in a huddled position against the wall, making certain not to touch himself with the blood-coated hand.

"Oh, they're not all that bad, child," Vachel remarks, picking them up and slipping them in one of his pockets, blood and all. Sitting back up, Vachel takes hold of the crystal and slowly slips it out of his arm. He is about to slip it back around his neck when the new wound on his arm catches his attention. As he gazes down at it the skin is already reknitting itself. "Look at this. Do the wolves do that?" Vachel says, jerking Ven back over to gaze at the wound, as well.

Nodding, Ven explains, "Yeah, the more dominant members of the pack can do that...but why are you doing it?" "I could be drawing on the pack's powers now that I have some of your blood," Vachel offers, looking over at the crystal. It has bleed back to red and sits twinkling innocently, as if to say it has nothing to do with any of this. Vachel finds that hard to believe, but he slips it back around his neck anyway.

Demon's Fire

"Now what do we do?" Ven asks, diligently wiping his hand on the wall in an attempt to get the blood off of it. Getting to his feet, Vachel replies, "Get off your ass, and I'll show you." Ven does as he is told, moving up to the demon's right. "This is where it gets fun," Vachel whispers, raising his arm up. Ven has a moment to think about it before he latches onto Vachel's arm, and the magic bursts forth in a roar. He does not realize until the cell door crashes to the ground and everything goes quiet that he is screaming.

Of course, once he realizes he is doing it, he immediately stops, a small flush coming to his face. He gazes at the fallen cell door and realizes the only things on it that are even damaged are the hinges and lock. If the master had tried the same thing, the entire metal structure would have been reduced to a deformed mass. Keeping it intact like this with that much power being thrown around takes quite a bit of control.

"How did you do that?" Ven asks in amazement, his fingers still tightly curled around Vachel's arm. Smiling as if pleased with himself, Vachel replies, "Practice? Alright...no teasing. It was easy after I got my power back." "So, the crystal really gave you back your demon power?" Ven asks, gazing up at Vachel's face to see the smile is now directed at him.

"Yep, and all I needed was your help."

"What?"

"I had to have your blood and a release for the excess power."

Ven falls silent, frowning at the floor.

"See? You're good for helping people after all."

Releasing Vachel's arm, Ven gives the floor an embarrassed smile. "Now, let's go take care of our tag-alongs and serve Rust his ass on a platter," Vachel declares, making his way out of the cell. Ven follows close behind, his eyes darting around now that the shock of the magic is over. He knows someone has to have heard all the noise they were making, and it is only a matter of time until they come bursting through the door. Vachel skips the amazing magic and just jerks the cell door open, breaking the lock like a cracker.

"Were you the one who made that horrendous crash?" Gilden asks, getting to his feet. Vachel just smiles triumphantly at him. Just as Mikya and Gilden make it out of the cell, both Frenzy and Chaos burst through the door. The tension of their muscles tell how ready they are to do battle. However, when they feel the demon aura rolling off Vachel's skin, their eyes go wide, and they drop to the floor on their knees, pressing their foreheads to the stone.

"The Great Fire has been returned to her master. We are no match," Chaos whispers, shaking his head. Smiling, Vachel replies, "So glad you feel that way, boys." "Are you going to kill the king?" Frenzy asks, lifting his head to gaze at Vachel. "Of course I am. No better revenge than to take his throne, now is there?" Vachel responds, making his way around them. Both jerk to their feet as he passes, his grace returned to its full glory. "We ask to give our aid to the cause," Chaos offers, gazing at Vachel's back, "I'm tired of being forced to do his bidding…it's no fun."

Mikya and Gilden give each other a small look at this, only to have Ven explain a demon's idea of fun entails many different things, and he might be referring to not having all of his needs met. Mikya decides she doesn't want to ask any more questions while on this mission. Shaking his head, Gilden moves ahead to stand right behind Vachel. Just as he does, Vachel whispers, "The only way you could help me is to stay out of our way until Rust is just a fading victim of Death. You can relay the message to Beast if you wish."

"He has already seen to Pain and Violence. He might be going after Rust himself," Frenzy explains, fidgeting slightly, as if he is trying desperately to keep himself in check and it is not working well. "Idiot!" Vachel growls, taking the stairs at a run. Ven pushes his way past Gilden to catch up with Vachel, fear thrilling through him again.

"He could get himself killed," Ven whispers once he is on line with Vachel. Nodding, Vachel replies, "I might not like him, but that doesn't mean he isn't the best demon for alpha of the pack."

As they make it closer to the throne room, Ven trips over something in the hallway and lands face first into the bloody remains of Violence's chest. His eyes go wide as he scrambles out from between the torn and shattered ribs. The body lies sprawled across the expanse of the hallway. The eyes are glazed with death, and the mouth hangs open with blood in a long line down the cheek from the edge of the mouth. It is untouched except for a few splatters of blood until one gazes at the chest. All the ribs are cracked and broken, leaving an open path down to the mush that used to be the lungs and heart. Ven shields his eyes from the sight, but he whispers, "Oh crimson...it smells so good."

"I think it reeks, but that's just personal preference. I'd rather it be alive if I was going to eat out the internal organs," Vachel remarks, shaking his head and stepping over the body. Ven scrambles after him, nearly slipping again on the blood strewn all over the floor around the body. When they reach the second body, just outside the throne room door, Ven has to bury his face in Vachel's side to keep himself from going after it.

Pain's body is sprawled out like the first, but she lies on her stomach. The skin has been only partially stripped off, leaving small flaps that obscure the view inside. Still, the muscles of her back have been ripped away, leaving the cracked spine visible. It takes them both only a moment to realize that the pulpy mass that has been left on the floor to her right is all that remains of her heart.

"That smell...makes me want to...no, we have to help Beast...Vachel, we really need to get in there," Ven whispers, fighting against his urge to finish the job and eat the remaining meat. Grasping Ven's hand firmly, Vachel pulls him along (he doesn't have to speak to let Ven know now is not the time for feeding, even if the meat is just going to sit there) as he pushes the door open to an equally bloody scene.

Still, at least both parties are still alive.

Reno stands with his back to them. His ears are flat against his head, and the growl can be heard rumbling into the room. The top half of his armor has been abandoned to the floor in a twisted lump. Both gloves are shredded on his hands because he has allowed them to slip into a rigid form, complete with the actual claws. Blood is splattered along the walls and floor, but scent alone tells Ven none of it belongs to Rust.

Bleeding wounds run along Reno's bare back, chasing each other around his sides and over his shoulders to expose bone in some places. "I'll not stand for this, Beast," Rust replies, his hand raised, "No one attacks my people or me and gets away with it." "No one nearly cripples one of my pack and goes unpunished, Halfling!" Reno roars, crouching slightly to get a better shot, "I don't care if they *are* part of the pack!" He charges forward just as the words are out of his mouth, catching Rust in the side with one of his claws. In response, Rust brings his hand down in a swipe that brings more bleeding wounds to the surface.

"Coward! Fight me like a real wolf! Don't hide behind your pathetic magic!" Reno roars again, snapping at Rust with his fangs. They are both too absorbed in their fight to even notice the two witnesses to the struggle. "We're going to have to get between them," Vachel whispers, taking a step forward, "You got any ideas?" "I know how to get *me* between them...but it's gonna really hurt," Ven replies, slipping the cloak from his shoulders again. "What do you mean?" Vachel demands. Ven steps forward, creeping to about the center of the room: "Just watch me."

As soon as the words are out of his mouth, Rust forces Reno stumbling back, and Ven dashes forward. Rust and Reno charge back at each other, each ready to slice into the other. Ven manages to make it in between them just as Reno's claws and Rust's magic come down. A scream rings through the room, and Vachel forces his way to Ven's side.

"I told you it was gonna hurt," Ven explains weakly, holding his sides as gently as he can. Both are split open and bleeding, the left from Reno's claws and the right from Rust's magic. Shaking his head with a small smile, Vachel replies, "You didn't have to do it this well, child." "Little one...I'm so sorry," Reno adds, bending down to scoop Ven up in his arms. His hands have reverted back to their human form at the shock of having hurt a pack member again, and he gives Vachel a pleading glance as if begging to be told what to do now.

"Tend to the pup, alpha. I can handle this Halfling from here," Vachel replies, glaring into Rusts eyes. As Reno slips away, Rust demands, "Are you here to challenge me again, Death?" "No," Vachel replies with a scheming smile,

"I'm here to kill you." "You don't have the power…Vachel," Rust responds, narrowing his eyes. Rust knows the insult will not be allowed to pass. The demon standing before him is too pride-ridden for that. Vachel's eyes flash red before Rust is thrown back against the throne, the impact opening a wound on his forehead.

Rust rounds on him, fangs bared as he sends a burst of fire after Vachel. "I thought we established yesterday that this tactic doesn't work," Vachel remarks, holding out his hand to catch the flame. It stops just before it reaches his fingers, reforming back into a swirling sphere of energy. Rust's eyes go wide in his fury as Vachel feeds his own flames into the sphere, causing it to nearly triple in size. He sends it jetting toward Rust who has only enough time to drop rather ungracefully to the floor. The fire reduces the throne to a mass of cracked fragments, as if it was caught in the middle of a small, contained explosion.

In response, Rust sends a massive tangle of black chain, shooting in Vachel's direction. Most of them find a place to wrap tightly around the demon's body, but the smile on Vachel's face never wavers. "Now who has the upper hand, Vachel?" Rust demands, climbing to his feet. There is now a smile on his face, and it does not even flicker when he spies the one perched on Vachel's face.

"Well? Where's the great power of Death?" Rust demands again, closing his fist so that the chains tighten, "Who's going to claim power now, Vachel?" "Me," Vachel replies simply, his smile growing. "I am your master…come forth in service of me...bring the fury of my soul in retribution for all wrongs this being has committed...come to me, and be my power!" Vachel commands, throwing his head back.

As soon as the words slip from his mouth, the chains melt away as if touched by some extreme heat. Rust stares wide-eyed as a green flame slips up around Vachel and takes control of his eyes, so they are two balls of burning green. "You have crossed a line not meant to be crossed, Halfling. Now feel the wrath of a true demon!" Vachel declares, the flames intensifying around him.

Rust slips down into a crouch and slowly begins to back away on all fours. His eyes are too wide for his face as he gazes up into the fiery depths of Vachel's. He knows the power behind that fire all too well. "Come forth, my servant, and show this creature what it means to defy us," Vachel commands in that strange language. At this, the flame surrounds him in a huge ball of energy before slipping before him. It wavers there for a moment, as if taking in its surroundings, before dipping down to the floor.

Vachel takes a deep breath, and the flame arches its back, taking on the shape of a large wolf nearly as tall as he. At the sight of the Great Beast, Ven and Reno both throw their heads back and howl. The wolf of flame joins in their chorus before taking a heavy step toward Rust. He gazes up into the black, flaming eyes with fear coursing along his skin.

"That's not a good idea...fear makes us hungry," Vachel warns, his voice deeper with a small growl to it. The wolf growls in agreement, baring its fangs at him. "You would attack me with the Great Fire? The Great Beast?" Rust demands in a whisper, still trying to keep the fear back.

"No, we are going to eat you...because you deserve it. Your head should be tasty," Vachel replies, his voice still that growl. Ven tugs at Reno's arm as he points and observes, "She's talking through him. I thought Vachel was the master." "He is...but he allows her to take possession of his body while she uses her powers. He can call her back at any time. I never thought I'd see the Great Beast unleashed for the likes of us," Reno explains, shaking his head.

Rust jerks away just in time to avoid being snapped up in her jaws. "Be still! You only delay your punishment!" Vachel yells, the growl becoming more pronounced. The wolf catches the edge of Rust's robe in her mouth, and he pulls out of it, running back the way he came. "Fine. I like my food scared," Vachel whispers as the wolf stalks toward Rust, her fangs bared.

Vachel, Ven, and Reno all move forward, making certain to block all of Rust's available escape routes. Still, he decides to try and squeeze past Vachel. He takes hold of Vachel's arm in an attempt to jerk him out of the way only to have the demon rake newly formed claws across his face and growl, "Don't you dare touch us! You have no right!" Rust decides to abruptly change tactics and rushes toward Ven.

The Hybrid wastes no time in catching hold of Rust's forearm with both his hands and fangs. He tries desperately to push Ven away only to have the Hybrid dig his fangs deeper into the muscle. Worrying at the arm like a dog with a bone, Ven takes all of Rust's focus. "Release me!" he commands in a near scream, his eyes wide with fright.

"He is our wolf...he will not heed your commands."

"Just get him off of me!"

"But...it smells so good...like fresh meat," Reno whispers.

Rust falls silent in fright.

"You cannot win against us...surrender and you will know little pain."

"No! I'll never give in to you!"

"As you wish...Reno!"

Rust screams as Reno latches onto his other arm, jerking against the muscle. "Get them off of me!" Rust cries, still trying to fling Ven off his arm. The wolf moves up behind Ven and Reno as Vachel replies, "Heed our demands of surrender, and they will release you." "No!" Rust yells, jerking his arm hard enough to tear Ven from it. Of course, Ven takes a mouthful of the arm with him.

He grinds at it with his teeth for a moment before throwing back his head and swallowing the bite whole. His tongue slips along his lips as he gazes longingly at the arm again. However, before Ven can latch onto the arm, Reno pulls away with the sound of tearing flesh, bringing a shriek from Rust. Hanging from Reno's mouth when he sits back on the balls of his feet is a long strip of skin and part of the top layer of muscle.

Ven scrambles over to him, giving a small whimper as if asking to share. Reno does not growl or shoo him away, so Ven latches on to the tip of the meat and begins tugging. In response, Reno tugs back until they are in a small tug-of-war over it. In the end, after a few playful snarls and a final pull, Reno ends up with the majority, but Ven still gets a sizeable piece.

"They are feasting on your flesh...they will want more," Vachel remarks in the deep, growling voice, "We will not stop them, and you will be in for a long and painful death unless you surrender to us." Bleeding and helpless without the use of his arms, Rust still refuses to give in.

However, Vachel pulls through and whispers, "Enough of this playing. Just get rid of him...he isn't even worth the meat." Nodding, the wolf gets to her feet and begins stalking toward Rust again. In response, their chins covered in his blood, Reno and Ven both fall in line just behind her, their fangs bared. All three growl in unison just as Rust comes into contact with the wall. He opens his mouth to scream, but never makes it that far.

She snaps his head up in her jaws before he can make a sound. Ven and Reno throw their heads back again and howl, but this time, Vachel joins into the chorus instead of the wolf. Rust's now headless body pitches forward to the floor as she turns around to sit before Ven and Reno to stare down at them. Immediately, all three boys cease to howl and merely stare back at her.

King of Darkhaven

They all stare silently for another moment before she bends down and runs her tongue gently along the side of Ven's face. To his surprise, her touch does not burn; instead, it feels cool against his skin. It is not wet enough to feel like the caress of a real tongue, but it is still cool. If he had known it would not hurt, he might have returned the gesture of affection. She goes on to do the same to Reno before taking up a position beside Vachel: "Go, children. The spoils of this battle belong to you. You have certainly earned it."

Both Ven and Reno immediately rush over to the fallen body at her permission, tearing away the cloth to sink teeth into the flesh. Just as the Great Fire predicted, they want more after having tasted him. Nodding, she slips back to the form of the sphere of fire and takes her place around Vachel again flickering there as if waiting for him. "**Well done. I am thankful to have you on my side**," Vachel whispers, closing his eyes. The flames give a final pulse around him before slipping back within, taking the fire of his eyes with them.

Sighing, Vachel slips to the floor and lies down on his back, crossing his legs at the ankles and cradling his head in the palms of his hands. It isn't fatigue as much as contentment wriggling around in his chest. He might have smiled had the boys been doing something else with their time. With his eyes closed, all he can hear are the sounds of Ven and Reno feeding, and they are not exactly pleasant if one is not joining in on the act. "You guys are really loud eaters, do you know that?" he remarks in a whisper. Could they not sense the power floating along his skin, they might have thought the sigh in his voice meant he was tired from using the Great Fire. "You're supposed to be over here, too," Reno counters, "She told her children to eat. You are a wolf now."

"What makes you say that?"

"It's in your aura."

"I can't be a wolf…I have no link to the pack."

"Then you couldn't have called the Great Beast."

"The Great Fire chooses her own form…I don't dictate her preference."

"She chose it because you are now pack."

"You don't know what you're talking about."

"Come on. At least eat the heart in declaration," Ven protests.

"'Declaration?'"

"Of your victory…you're the new king."

"Again, what makes you say that?"

"He said he'd be king until, and I quote, 'someone rises up who has power enough to defeat me', end quote," Ven explains sitting up to gaze back at him, "You've defeated him, so that makes you king." "So now, my word is law…blah, blah, blah, blah, blah. Is that about right?" Vachel replies, opening his eyes. Suddenly, having killed

Rust doesn't sound like a good thing. Being king has never been high on his priority list, and he has to wonder how Crystal will take to being thrust into the life of a queen.

"That is exactly right, your highness," a voice replies from the doorway. Vachel tilts his head enough to spy the High Sister making her way into the room, a smile on her face. The frown remains on his as he watches her move across the room. He still has yet to take his vengeance for her making him forget Crystal, and now he has to wonder why she cares who the king is. No matter who sits on the throne, she holds the real power of Darkhaven. It's something he's always known.

"I knew you would at least try to do it, your highness," she adds, stepping up as close to the mass of meat that once was Rust as she can get without getting blood on her shoes, "Still, I will admit that I had my doubts."

"Did you just come here to poke at me?" Vachel asks, closing his eyes again. *Because I'm not in the mood for it, especially not from you.* "Not at all, your highness," she replies, the smile in her voice now despite the thoughts she heard dancing around in his head, "I came to give my wolf a farewell, considering I do not have an agreement with the current king and the Shiku Hara is bound to the position of king, not to me."

"The 'position' of king?" Vachel asks, sitting up abruptly. He can't have heard right. *What idiot binds a Shiku Hara to a position? He could potentially...oh, shit! That's just hilarious!* Smiling at him, she replies, "Why yes...stupid

Halfling had no idea that I was just giving him a form when I told him how to bind someone to the collar. I said bind it to the King of Darkhaven...and he did...to the letter."

Reno and Vachel burst out laughing, but Ven is still confused as to what difference it would make, and the High Sister has already used up her laughter for the moment. "He was *so* not meant to be a wolf," Reno remarks, breaking from his laughter first. Vachel, however, seems to have found something even worse than stupidity that kicks Rust in the teeth, allowing him to keep the laughter rolling a little longer. Eventually, he gets enough control of himself to explain, "You know...this means our little guy could potentially live for all eternity."

"What?" Ven asks in shock, his eyes widening. Getting shakily to his feet, as he is just now beginning to feel the strain from calling on the Great Fire for so long, Vachel replies, "The wearer of the Shiku Hara does not die until his master does. And since the Shiku Hara's tied to the position, you'll live until the position is no longer a valid one." Ven's eyes go wider as he thinks about it, gazing up at the ceiling. Even he can't keep the smile from his face for long at this news.

"So then, would you permit me a small kiss?" the High Sister asks, gazing over at Vachel. With a raised eyebrow and crossed arms, Vachel responds, "Who? Me or him?" "Would 'yes' make you say 'no'?" the High Sister replies, crossing her own arms. Shaking his head to add emphasis, Vachel answers, "No it wouldn't, but you'll have to ask Ven about kissing him."

"But...you are his master, your highness," the High Sister protests a frown slipping to her lips. "First, don't call me that. I've always hated that stupid phrase. Second, it's Ven's body you're going to be touching, not mine, so he should get to say," Vachel explains, sighing because he has to explain this to her. He would have expected this sort of confusion from Rust, but he thought she was at least capable of higher thought. Blinking slowly, she asks, "Does this mean you do not want a kiss?" Even the blink lets him know she is not sure she wants to hear the answer. "I didn't say that," Vachel replies, his voice falling to a low whisper as he gazes away.

He hates to admit it, but the desire is still there.

And he doesn't think it's her magic this time.

Son of a bitch!

Smiling again, the High Sister turns to Ven and asks, "So, little wolf, will you permit me a kiss?" "What happened to the 'small' part?" Ven asks tentatively. Even being told he is practically immortal doesn't lessen the fear of this she-demon. He has been her servant for much too long to quell it. However, with only one master to please now, he has to consider whether it would be terrible to be under her attention more often. He barely suppresses the flush before it makes it to his face.

Giving a small laugh, High Sister Selene replies, "Stalling makes one want more. I thought you knew that, little wolf." "Oh..." Ven answers, staring up at her, "Well...I guess...it can't hurt that bad, can it?" He has to work to get the words to come out, and he can't figure out why. Had it been any other time, he would have jumped to answer her in the affirmative just to escape pain. "He does not know me well at all, does he?" she asks, placing two fingers against her bottom lip and gazing over at Vachel again. Frowning, he replies, "If it hurts him, all bets are off."

"Fine, fine, love. I will make sure you get the pain, hmm?" she suggests. Vachel just gives her a small shrug, not trusting his voice or the words that will go with it. With this, she holds out her hand to Ven who takes it along with a deep breath. Just thinking about touching her hand sends a thrill of something completely foreign into his brain. It holds much more fear than the thought of her touch. The High Sister gives him a small frown as she asks, "Is this such a horrible experience for you?" Ven's eyes go wide again, but he does not speak. He didn't realize until she spoke that he had appeared to hesitate. That brings the fear of her back into his mind.

Her frown becomes a glare, and she drops his hand: "Fine. I will leave you to yourself, and you will get a goodbye. Good riddance!" She turns on her heel and stalks away, nearly passing Vachel by until he grasps her wrist and pulls her back. Behind her, Ven's hand reaches for the hand that has been jerked away from his grasp. He can't believe how stupid he was being. The glare is still perched on her face when Vachel brings his hand up to cradle the left side of her face, but it does not last long against the kiss.

"They look like they're trying to eat each other," Ven remarks quietly, a look of disgust on his face. He won't admit it anyone, barely even himself, but the disgust hides a much stranger emotion. He can almost feel his gaze turn green with jealousy. Now that Rust is through messing with everything, he should be the one to whom she is paying attention. Shaking his head, Reno replies, "I think they are."

Ven gives a small shudder but keeps silent.

He can almost feel her mouth on his again.

The torture...

"Still, why didn't you let her give you the kiss?" Reno asks. Ven grapples with the desire not to answer him, but, in the end, he decides on a lie that would make sense to the wolf. Hugging himself for a moment, Ven replies, "I remember what it was like when the kiss was just the beginning of something else." And that is precisely the reason why he is struggling now. Every instinct the wolf in him possesses wants him to jerk into motion and tear Vachel and Selene away from each other. Reno does not press further, but keeps his gaze on Vachel and the High Sister. It takes them a minute or two more to decide to let the other breathe.

When they pull away, the High Sister is the first to speak: "So, when do I get to meet the previous owner of your little trinket?" Her finger curls around the chain, absentmindedly playing with the links. "Should have known you wouldn't let that go," Vachel sighs, shaking his head. "Oh, why can you not just give me an answer this once?" she demands, a partial frown forming on her face.

Sighing again, Vachel replies, "All right, I give. I have to take Gilden and the princess back to Dehurst, and then I'm going to get Crystal to bring her back." "Ooh! You will come see us then?" the High Sister asks, "It will be wonderful, your hi...no...hmm...there are not many pet names left in my arsenal, love. I will have to think on some for a while. Do you have any preferences?" "When I bring Crystal? My name will do just fine," Vachel replies pointedly. Shaking her head, the High Sister protests, "You are just being difficult. I could always just call you 'love'. I would like to see how she reacts."

"Don't torment her, Selene. And my name will work."

"Fine. Then, I shall just have to give her a kiss in greeting."

"Why?"

"The greeting must be special, love. First impressions, you know."

"Why can't you just behave yourself? She's sensitive."

"Ooh. Sensitive enough to use to get you back to me, hmm?"

"If you scare her off, I'll never forgive you."

"I doubt that much, love. Besides, you do not use *my* real name."

"Wait, Selene isn't your real name?" Ven interjects. He suddenly feels extremely stupid. *How could I have not known her name? She doesn't go by any other, duh! But still...I should...no, I just want to know.*

"No. My true name is sacred enough to start a war over, little wolf."

"See? That's why it's off limits, and I use this one for her."

"I will still give her a run for her money, love. It is just my way."

"Just don't expect me to call you 'pet' in return."

Sighing, the High Sister replies, "I will remember that, love. I did not have high hopes for it, anyway." Still watching them, Ven has the urge to call her "pet" just to get her attention away from the demon holding her. Vachel is about to tell her not to take it so badly when she brightens and adds, "Still, I will be able to have my fun and not have to clean blood off my walls. What a happy time!" At this, she makes her way out of the room, a small laugh escaping. Ven and Vachel follow her movements with raised eyebrows, while Reno shakes his head.

"I'll never understand what you saw in her," Reno remarks, looking up. Vachel turns his gaze to Reno and replies, "Simple. She had power. And her position actually helped me in the past. Rust so happily forgot that she was in line to be High Sister when he sent me to them for punishment." "Yeah...there was only *one thing* aching when you got home," Reno replies with a sly smile. Vachel gives a sly smile of his own as he steps up beside the others: "So…all you want me to eat is the heart, right?" He has to push Selene from his mind. She is the past, and Crystal is the future. No matter what Reno thinks on the subject, he prefers his faerie to the she-demon.

At this, Reno digs out the heart and stands, holding it over the demon's head. "Just open your mouth…it's part of the ritual," Ven whispers to Vachel's raised eyebrow. Narrowing his eyes, Vachel tilts his head back slightly and opens his mouth as directed. Reno slips the heart into Vachel's mouth, and the demon immediately bites down, causing blood to trickle from the sides of his mouth, before gulping it down in one swallow. Reno shakes his head as if to criticize the way he ate it, but does not make any other comments. There is a small smile on Ven's face as he suggests, "Why don't we go see to Gilden and Mikya?"

They find the two in question right where they left them.

"Why are you guys out here?" Vachel asks with a raised eyebrow. "I don't want to be in that place any longer than I have to be, and you were too fast for us to follow," Gilden answers, heat in his voice, "You didn't have to leave us behind." "Geez! You think after living for a century, you'd know how to speak to royalty," Vachel remarks, frowning. At his side, Ven has the urge to snicker. Gilden gives him a raised eyebrow in return. "What, you didn't know, sorcerer? I swear…you seem to know everything

else, I just assumed you'd be on the ball with this one, too,"
Vachel replies, crossing his arms as if disgusted by Gilden's
neglect of information. Gilden's frown seeps into a glare at
this.

Smiling as if pleased with himself, Vachel adds,
"You're looking at the new King of Darkhaven. How does
that make you feel?" Both Mikya and Gilden's eyes go wide
at this news, and they give each other a small look before
turning their attentions back to Vachel. "You mean...you
killed Rust?" Mikya asks, shock evident in her voice.
"You're confidence overwhelms me, princess," Vachel
replies, his eyes narrowing.

This gets both Ven and Reno to burst out laughing.
"You could always just go get Sister Crystal and leave them
to fend for themselves," Ven offers, through his laughter.
Reno manages to burst, "Yeah...I'm sure me and the boys
could find some use for them. Ha!" "Nera might like
someone to play with!" Ven adds, wrapping his arms
around his waist. Reno has to try three times to finally say,
"We could hook the sorcerer up with some of the rough
ones...see how good he is in a fistfight." Finally, they just
dissolve into a ceaseless string of laughter. Both Mikya and
Gilden give Vachel a look, as if asking him whether he will
take this advice.

A smirk on his face, Vachel replies, "I was
considering it until the boys let the cat...excuse me, wolf out
of the bag...but now there's just no point. It wouldn't be a
surprise, so I guess I'll just have to take you back with me."

They glare at him, but do not speak. "Ok. Ven, you're with me. I want you to stay here for the time being, Reno," Vachel adds, gazing up at the ceiling as if he is still deciding what to do.

"Is this going to be a quick trip?" Reno asks slowly. Ven gazes up at him, understanding immediately why he wants to know. "Chaos and Frenzy have declared their loyalty, Reno. But yes, it is going to be a short trip," Vachel explains. Shaking his head, Reno replies, "I know that...I just wanted to know if I had enough time to bring the pack in closer to the castle again." "Just make sure they don't have a moonlight howling session every night," Vachel responds with a smile, realizing he jumped the gun.

Reno gives a shallow nod before turning away and slipping down the corridor, his shoulders straight as if he doesn't want them to see some of the excitement in his posture. Smiling now, Ven gazes at Gilden and Mikya to find that their glares have softened, but they are still angry. "What's wrong?" he asks, "Shouldn't you be happy to be going home?" "Yes...but we're still in this castle presently, now aren't we," Gilden replies, his voice still containing that heat. Taking Ven's wrist and pulling him to his side, Vachel growls, "Don't take your anger out on the pup, sorcerer. You won't like what happens." With his wrist in Vachel's grasp, Ven can't understand what would make the demon think he cares how Gilden speaks to him.

Gilden does not answer, but keeps his gaze fixed firmly on Vachel. In response, Vachel turns away, pushing

Ven ahead of him. It takes only a moment for Mikya to follow them, but Gilden refuses to move until she glances back at him, a mix of pleading and anger in her look. Grudgingly, he follows her, his anger still burning. Something about Vachel's new found confidence and position is getting on his nerves, and he just can't get the burning to leave him alone.

Once outside Kigotsu, Ven runs ahead to stand in the midst of an expanse of the black sand, staring up into the violet sky. "Is this where you want to take off from?" Vachel asks him once he has caught up. Ven turns his gaze to the demon before giving a grin and nodding his head. "What's so special about this place?" Vachel asks, gazing out at the horizon with a raised eyebrow. It doesn't seem like anything special compared to what looks exactly like it everywhere else.

Giving a small blush, Ven whispers, "This is where the pack comes when one of the females is getting ready to have a pup." A knowing smile creeps up to Vachel's face as he whispers, "Who is it this time?" "Nera," Ven answers simply, his face flushing all the worse. "What's with the red glow, child?" Vachel asks, "What is it about her?" "She's the one who took care of me after my mother died," Ven replies, his grin widening. Vachel knew that, but he also saw how she treated him, and he can't help but wonder if Ven isn't the type of servant to fall in love with his masters, if only a little bit.

Shaking his head, Vachel replies, "I'll never understand you wolves." "You're one, too, don't forget. You ate the heart of a pack member and you have some of my blood in you. That's your link. So, you're pack whether you want to be or not," Ven explains, his features caught in a determined frown. Sighing, Vachel replies, "Fine. You can have it your way."

Just as the words escape his mouth, Gilden and Mikya make their way forward. "Ready to go?" Vachel asks with a small smile at Gilden's frown. Mikya answers before Gilden has the chance to make a crack, "Yes. Can we please hurry?" "Sure thing, princess," Vachel replies, his smile never wavering.

At this, Ven, Mikya, and Gilden all slip into their circle around Vachel. Gazing up in recognition, Vachel observes, "You know...I might be able to get us inside the castle in one shot now that I've got my power back." Mikya gazes over at Gilden as if asking if this feat is possible, but the only response she gets is a glare into the horizon.

Nodding as if deciding to try it, Vachel closes his eyes again. This time, instead of sand flowing up around them, a wall of green flames surrounds them in a protective barrier, casting a green glow to their skin. Mikya has enough time to wonder about this before the feeling of flight takes hold of her stomach and the air is swept from her lungs in one solid burst.

The impact of coming back to the ground shoves her off balance, so she topples to the floor on her face. As she collides with the surface, she hears another grunt of protest and realizes immediately Gilden has been forced to the floor as well.

"Not quite the graceful entrance I was hoping for, but it did the trick," Vachel observes, taking a step away from her. Slowly pushing herself to a sitting position, Mikya asks, "What do you mean 'it did the trick'?" "We're in the castle," Ven answers, holding out his hand to help her to her feet. Mikya takes the offering, watching Gilden sit up beside her. "What's with the impact?" he demands, rubbing the back of his head. Ven offers him a hand as well as he explains, "A lot of demon energy was used, so the landing wasn't quite as soft as it could have been." Gilden refuses the offered hand as he gets to his feet. Ven returns to his full height, paying Gilden's refusal of his help no mind.

"We should probably go tell the others we've returned," Mikya whispers, placing a hand on Gilden's arm as she senses the anger just beneath the surface waiting to lash out at anything. He agrees only by nodding his head and following her as she leads the way from the room. Something tells him he will feel better once he has some space. There has to be something about the trip to Darkhaven that has rattled the control he usually has on his temper. Maybe it's just the result of everything that happened. At Gilden's side, Mikya gazes back at Ven and Vachel and mouths the words, "I'll see you later."

Once they are out of sight, Vachel replies, "I guess the time is now for us to go find Crystal." "But she could be anywhere," Ven points out, "It would take us hours to search the entire castle." "That's why we should see Riko, first. She'll know exactly where to find Crystal," Vachel explains. Giving Vachel a sly smile, Ven asks, "Will I actually get to talk with her this time?" "She snuck away the first time, that's why she had to hurry," Vachel counters before making his way toward the corridor.

Silence falls over them as they make their trek to find Riko, broken only by the sound of their boots on the floor. Both find this a little odd, especially since there are usually a number of servants and Sisters roaming the hallways, that is, until they hear to high-pitched scream ring down the corridor. Surprisingly enough, Ven is the first to take off running, but Vachel is faster than he, easily catching up and passing him as the sound of the scream leads them to the kitchen doorway. Bursting inside, Vachel immediately spies Riko backed into a corner on the opposite side of the room. A large knife is poised in her hands as she stares wide-eyed into the face of an armor-clad soldier.

"Put down the knife!" he commands, moving forward, "You've been charged with treason, and I'll take you out of here no matter what I have to do to do it." "Stay away from me! I've done nothing wrong!" Riko shrieks at him, her hands trembling around the handle of the knife. Before Vachel can make his way over to her, a group of five women, all armed with knives, rushes up behind the soldier and begins slamming their blades against the armor. "He'll beat them senseless," Ven whispers, his eyes narrowing at the scene.

Vachel nods, but does not make a move to intervene. He cannot get much of a shot at the man with the women around him. The soldier rounds on them, knocking one to the floor. This only serves to make them all the more determined, and they all rush at him again. As Vachel and Ven watch, the soldier manages to knock the knives from their hands and send them crashing to the floor before turning back to Riko. Two of the girls cry her name in warning as fear charges their looks.

"Get away!" Riko screams, tears sliding down her face now. In response, the soldier lunges forward, catching her arm and jerking it over her head. Riko lets out a cry of pain and protest as the blade spills from her grasp to the floor. The girls yell her name again, calling the soldier names not fit for a lady to utter. "Now, you're coming with me!" the soldier growls angrily, jerking her behind him as he turns.

When he does, he comes face to face with Vachel, fury flowing steadily through the demon's eyes. "You're the demon," he observes anger spilling farther into his face, "Did you think you could hide the fact that this little wench was your sister forever?" Vachel's fist collides with the soldier's jaw with enough force to topple him. However, the soldier manages to keep his firm grip on Riko's arm, so he brings her down with him.

"Release her, damn you! Or I'll beat your face in!" Vachel threatens, the fury rolling off him like demon aura. Jerking to his feet, blood blossoming at the corner of his mouth, the soldier yells, "Never! The High Sister has given me an order, and you're not going to stop me from fulfilling it! I'm not about to live under the same roof as a Halfling wench!"

At this, Ven launches himself at the man's arm, easily tearing loose the metal and gripping the bare flesh as hard as possible. Immediately, the flesh begins to burn under his fingers. The soldier gives an angry roar, trying to jerk him off with his other hand.

In response, Ven sinks his teeth into the man's flesh, forcing him to work against the fangs' hold, as well. Still, the soldier jerks against Ven's collar, making the wound give under the fangs. With his attention all on Ven and keeping his tight hold, the soldier does not spy Vachel setting up for his punch until it is too late for him to do anything about.

The punch connects with his jaw, easily cracking the bone and snapping his neck all in one movement. Immediately, his grip goes slack as he falls to the floor, Ven still pinned to his arm. At the sight of Vachel's raging anger, Riko drops to the floor herself, her hands coming up to hide her face. Other than a ripped shirt and a few hairs slipping from the tight bun, she looks none the worse for the wear, except for the bitter tears and sobbing.

At the sight, Vachel makes his way over to her and wraps his arms around her in a gentle embrace. She shakes her head furiously, mumbling rapidly under her breath. "I can't understand a word you're saying," Vachel replies, brushing some of the stray hair from her face with a gentle thumb. "I'm so sorry...I couldn't stop them," she bursts, tears streaming all the worse. Confusion springing to his face, Vachel asks, "What are you talking about?" "The new High Sister has taken it upon herself to rid the castle of anyone who sympathized with you!" Riko bursts in frustration, "She found out about Sister Crystal! She's already been taken!"

The color drains from Vachel's face, as the fury burns brighter.

"Vachel?" Ven asks tentatively, slipping up to Riko's other side, fear on his face. "I'll kill them..." Vachel whispers, his hands shaking as he releases Riko and gets to his feet. "I'll kill them all! Do you hear me?! They're dead! The lot of them are dead!" he bellows, his fangs flashing as he grits his teeth. Ven has just enough time to yell, "Vachel, wait!" before the demon bolts out of the room. Giving Riko a small glance, Ven takes off after him, the fear growing all the worse.

Demon's Fury

Ven spies Vachel's blurred form streak around the corner just as he rushes from the room. He knows there is no way for him to keep up with that kind of speed, but he also knows it is not a good idea to leave Vachel and his fury to their own devices. Innocent people could be killed. Even as he mulls it all over in his mind, his feet are taking him on a desperate trek to keep Vachel in sight. Every door that has the misfortune to be in the demon's way is either shoved forcefully into the wall or pulled off of its hinges.

"Vachel, wait for me!" Ven yells, in an attempt to get the demon to slow his pace. He does, but only enough to keep Ven from having to work at keeping him in sight. When he finally hits the outer doors, they slam open with a crash and the sound of screaming metal, as the hinges and latch twist and snap under the force. Gritting his teeth against the sound, Ven rushes after him. There is another crash as Vachel forces his way through a portion of the outer wall, leaving a hole through which Ven easily follows. He hates to think of who's going to have to clean that.

Jagged imprints appear in the ground as though something purposely shoved its foot deep into the soil as it moved. Ven knows this is from the force Vachel has to exert on the ground in order to keep his speed. Over the flat expanse of ground, Ven can easily keep track of Vachel;

however, he is forced to admit to himself that he will never be able to catch up unless Vachel stops for him.

Finally, after struggling along for a few more minutes, Ven yells again, "Vachel! Wait for me! You're too fast!" At this, the black streak ahead stops moving. Ven breathes a sigh of relief, but continues his forced trek forward, his breath already coming in short bursts. Of course, once he makes it to Vachel's side, he instantly regrets the sigh. There can be no relief had from the sight of the rage boiling just under the surface of Vachel's skin.

A slight tremor to his hands, Ven asks tentatively, "What are you going to do?" "Kill them...they won't just lock her away for what she has done," Vachel answers in a dangerous whisper. It is worse than if he would have yelled it. Taking a deep breath to steady himself for the next question, Ven asks, "Will you let me help with Crystal?" "I assumed you'd rather help in the killing, child," Vachel whispers, his voice still holding the threat of an angry burst. Shaking his head slowly, Ven replies, "No...I'll leave the revenge to you. It wouldn't be right for me to interfere in that." Nodding, Vachel takes hold of Ven's wrist and begins moving again.

The pace is still the same, but this time Ven can keep up with it. It is as if, just by touching Vachel, he is gaining a small portion of the demon's abilities. With this pace going, it is not long until they arrive at the Sisters' gathering place. What should have taken days to walk has taken less than an hour to run at demonic speed. Just as in Darkhaven, the structure is made up of glittering, white towers. Vachel wastes no time in shoving his way through the doors, Ven right at his heels. At the sight of him and the fury he is emanating, the Sisters gathered in the corridor scramble against the walls, some screaming in fear.

"Where is she?!" he demands of the hallway in general. Not a noise can be heard. Even the frightened whimpers are being stifled in an effort to keep his attention away. "I asked you lot a question, and I expect an answer!" Vachel bellows, his voice magnified, so even Ven has to cringe. When no one answers this time, Vachel moves to the first one and drags her to her feet by her collar. "Where is she?" he demands in a growl, "Where is Crystal?" Even with her eyes and voice quivering, the Sister replies, "I-I'll tell you n-nothing, demon." Vachel's eyes flash red, and she falls limp from his hands. Ven does not even have to touch her to know she is dead.

Moving up to the next, Vachel uses her hair to pull her to her feet. She simply refuses to speak in the face of his growling tone and furious eyes. Of course, she is also dead as soon as Vachel's patience for her wears out. He continues on down the line until one of them gets the bright idea to try and escape. Tears spilling from her eyes, she races down the corridor. Her blonde hair trails out behind her as she runs. From the look of her dress it is evident that she is one of the lower ranking Sisters. Both it and the heels she is wearing hinder her in keeping away from Vachel's notice.

Dropping the dead Sister in his hands, Vachel sends black chains after her. She screams in fear as they pin her hands up on either side of her head and keep her from moving even enough to strike out at him when he pulls her back to him. "Sister Cea!" several of the Sisters cry from their positions against the walls.

Vachel pulls her close enough that a hard thought would make their noses touch. Glaring into her blue eyes, he whispers, "So, child, are you ready to tell me what I want to know?" She stares at him in fear, tears streaming down her face. Vachel is about to release his power into her when Ven tugs at his arm.

Letting his gaze fall on the Hybrid, Vachel asks in a whisper, "What?" "She's afraid. Even if she was willing to tell, she's too afraid of what they'd do to her if she did," Ven explains, casting his gaze over the other shaking Sisters. Turning his gaze back to the Sister, Vachel asks, "Is this true, child?" Slowly, she gives a shaking nod, her eyes flicking out to those around her as she does. Those of her rank huddle down farther as if afraid her actions will bring punishment down on their heads, as well. However, those of higher rank than she glare up at her as if to say she is already in more trouble than she's worth.

Spying this reaction, Vachel whispers, "How's this, child? If you tell me what you know, I'll keep them away from you." "I c-can't take the help of a d-d-demon," she forces out, her eyes wide enough to be far too big for her face. Gripping Vachel's arm in pleading, Ven whispers,

"Then don't. Take *my* help, and give *me* the information. I just want to help save Sister Crystal."

"C-can I g-get down?" she asks, fear still thrilling through her face. "Do you promise not to run?" Ven replies simply. Swallowing hard, she gives him a shallow, shaking nod. At this, Ven gazes up at Vachel, waiting for him to release her. Vachel has the urge to ask him if he is out of his mind, but keeps the thought to himself and lets the Sister go.

She stands shivering from fear, hugging herself, but she does not try to escape; she understands it is futile. "Now," Ven presses, "Where is Sister Crystal?" "She...she's--" "No! Don't tell them anything!" several of the Sisters yell, interrupting her, "You mustn't give anything to them! They're demons!" "Shut the fuck up!" Vachel commands, his voice ringing through the corridor in a loud boom. Immediately, the voices stop, but the glares on the faces of some of the Sisters remain. Vachel glares back at them, as if daring any of them to speak up again. He is vaguely surprised his fangs aren't showing by now. Then again, once the snarl registers, he guesses they actually are.

Finally, the Sister gets the courage to speak again: "She...Sister Crystal that is...is in the dungeon...they've already...already started her punishment." She cringes at the word "punishment", and the other Sisters take it as their cue to start screaming at her: "Blasphemer! Demon's wench! You'll die a terrible death for this! You'll never be forgiven! Wench! Bitch!"

The stream of insults continues for close to a minute more before Vachel decides to put a stop to it: "I told you lot to shut your mouths! If I hear another word out of you, you're all dead! And I'll make certain it's the painful one you've been threatening!" Ven takes hold of the Sister's arm, careful to keep his fingers away from her bare hand.

"They can't hurt you now," he whispers, "I'll make sure of it." She gives him a shallow nod, but cannot find her voice enough to speak. Without a word to indicate he is moving, Vachel begins his trek toward the dungeon. "Come on," Ven whispers, pulling her along behind him as he makes his way after Vachel. Once they are at Vachel's back, Ven releases Sister Cea and asks, "What kind of punishment do Sisters of Dehurst participate in?" "Sister Crystal is delicate. They will have probably sent some of the prison guards after her," Sister Cea replies slowly, as if afraid of Vachel's reaction to the news.

"I knew as much when I was told she was brought here. It's custom to punish a Sister by twisting something she enjoys and making it painful or frightening...or both," Vachel whispers, the anger still a knife-edge in his words, "That's the one way the Sisters of Dehurst are like the Sisters of Darkhaven." Rubbing his arms furiously as if he has been stricken by a sudden chill, Ven asks, "How are we going to help her?" "You'll see, child," Vachel replies, his voice giving the hint he is not in the mood to talk. Falling silent, Ven continues to rub his arms as if he is cold.

When they make it down to the dungeon, Ven and Vachel immediately smell the scent of blood drifting up to meet them. But it is tainted with a smell Vachel would be more familiar with. "Bad things have happened down here...it reeks," Ven whispers, slipping closer to Vachel. His gaze forward, Vachel whispers, "Like blood and old lust." "Like the High Sister's room," Ven adds, a shiver running through him. Fear for that memory lasts only a moment before the shiver turns to one of excitement. *What's wrong with me? We're here to save Sister Crystal.* Merely nodding, Vachel takes the stairs all the way down, letting the scent wash over him in a continuous wave. It is strengthening his desire for vengeance by the moment.

"I won't go down there," Sister Cea protests, stopping in her tracks on the stairs. Not even bothering to slow down, Vachel replies, "Fine. Stay there." Just as the words are out of his mouth, Vachel hears the sound of her scrambling back up the stairs, and he shakes his head. *She would have been better off to follow us down into the dungeon.* Still, he and Ven continue their trek down the stairs, their boots echoing against the stone. On the final step, Ven grasps Vachel's arm tightly, whispering: "We can't wait any longer."

At this, he releases Vachel to tear off into the dim light of the corridor lined with cells. Chains rattle in each as the demon passes, the only sign there is anything alive down here. Vachel does not have to use much of his speed to keep pace with the Hybrid, and he easily passes him again. This time, the pit of his stomach wishes he had not.

The room at the end of the corridor is expansive enough to house the entire court of Dehurst with enough room for the personal guards of each member of royalty. Splattered along the floor is drying blood and larger pieces, no doubt belonging to the rotting bodies. Eyes glare out of crushed sockets, forever frozen in that look of fear. Streaks of blood trail from the stumps of fingers, the victims of a furious but fruitless struggle to escape.

Again, Ven has to bury his face in Vachel's side, but this time it is to help block out the horror of what he is seeing. Each body has been sprawled out, suggesting each was still being assaulted when she died. Dried blood trails from their open mouths and between their legs. Vachel has the urge to scream in his fury as he spies the bloody knives and other sharp instruments that were no doubt used in the process. Not only were they taken advantage of, but their skin is riddled with bruises and bloody teeth marks, as well. In some places it appears as though the skin was bitten off. The ones who did this enjoyed themselves while they were doing it.

"And demons are considered impure," Vachel whispers bitterly, his disgust tightening like a fist in his chest. *At least a demon would let you live after suffering like this. If you are meant to die, it is done quickly, efficiently so the next kill can be seen to.* It is only a moment after he says it that he hears the muffled cries of fear and pain. His eyes going wide in his anger, he pulls away from Ven to make a trek toward the sound. Every vein within him is on fire with fury. If he could, he would have been glowing red. He has to make quite a journey across to the far side of the room, but it serves to strengthen his resolve for what he has decided to do, not stifle it.

The sight that unfolds before him sends his limbs in a raging flurry of motion his mind is too fury locked to comprehend or stop. One man is taking his turn with their latest victim, shoving a freshly sharpened dagger up inside. Another is kneeling at her head, holding both hands over her mouth in an attempt to keep all the noise back. Two others have a tight grip on her arms, their fingers bringing bruises to the surface. Vachel's hand takes a fistful of the first man's hair before his brain even realizes he recognizes their victim.

As the man is jerked back, the knife is forcefully pulled away. As soon as Vachel has his fangs sank deep into the man's shoulder to protesting screams and flailing arms, the others realize what is happening and decide to join in on the fight. One takes a hold of Vachel's hair, only to have him sink newly formed claws deep into the first man's chest, tearing into the flesh. The other two seek to pull him away from the wounds, but he is holding on too tightly for that.

Finally, a chunk of flesh is ripped away as the one with a hold on his hair gives a mighty jerk. A snarl escapes Vachel's lips as he lunges forward, digging his claws deep into the man's gut and jerking shredded bowels from the wound. The issuing shriek rings off the walls as the three manage to get enough leverage to pull Vachel away from the wound, succeeding in ripping it open all the worse in the process.

Now satisfied that the first man is going to stay down, Vachel rounds on the one holding onto his hair. His fangs sink deep into the side of the man's neck as his claws tear open the chest. He can feel ribs cracking as he digs his way inside, sending blood pouring down his front as it spills up around his teeth and chin. Again, the remaining fighters yank on his shoulders, jerking his fangs from the wound and ripping open the man's throat in the process. He falls to the ground in a heap as Vachel attacks the man clinging to his right.

Managing to force him to the floor, Vachel shoves his claws deep into the man's sides. He tears through the flesh enough to force some of the organs out the openings. At this, the final man jumps up onto Vachel's back, forcing him down and his claws deep into the man's gut. In an effort to get his claws free, Vachel rakes them upwards, spilling the man open until he has to break through bone to pull his claws free. Vachel forces his way to his feet before taking hold of the man on his back's face, claws slipping just beneath the surface of the skin.

With a grunt and a scream from the man, Vachel forces the man over his shoulder and onto the floor. His claws find their way deep into his back, tearing muscle away in a single swipe until he reaches the spine. Taking it in one hand, Vachel jerks upwards, cracking it in half as he lifts the man up from the floor slightly.

Growling, he proceeds to take the man's head in his hand and slam it against the stone floor. He does not stop when the claws return to hands, meaning his rage has been taken over by fatigue. He does not stop when he feels the skull crack beneath his fingers. He does not stop when he can feel blood seep through the torn places in the man's head. It is only the feeling of two arms wrapping firmly around his waist that gets him to stop and release the man's crushed head.

"Vachel, they are dead. Please, just stop," she begs, sobbing against his back and smearing the blood over her face. Vachel's chest heaves as his eyes narrow at his handy work. To know he would be willing to go to such lengths for revenge does not settle well in his stomach. He did not just kill them; he destroyed them.

Slowly, she slips away to cover her face with her hands as she sobs. In an attempt to make up for his display, he spins around, taking her gently in his arms as he whispers, "I'm sorry, Crystal...so, so sorry." "No...I am sorry. I did not mean to get caught," she replies through her sobs.

Shaking his head as a steady stream of tears begins to slip down his face, Vachel counters, "I've failed you, little one...I don't know how to be more sorry than I am for that." She gently pulls away to gaze at his face through her tears. Biting his lower lip, Vachel tries to turn his head to keep her from seeing the tears sliding through the blood spatter on his face. "Why are you crying?" she asks, forcing him to acknowledge that he is. He gazes at her in silence for a moment before flinging himself down on the floor before her: "Please...please forgive me for this. I couldn't bear it knowing you hated me for this."

"But...I do not hate you."

"I've been terrible...you shouldn't have had to see that."

"You were angry and let it get the best of you."

"I should have had more control than that..."

"Not if you really love her," Ven interjects.

"What are you talking about?" Vachel asks, sitting up.

"I would have done the same for my...my sisters."

They all fall silent, and Ven slips the cloak from his shoulders, handing it to Crystal while keeping his gaze firmly on the floor. Giving him a small smile even though he isn't looking, she slips it on, making certain to adjust it to cover herself properly. "Why didn't you join in earlier?" Vachel asks, slowly getting to his feet. Ven gazes down at the floor in shame as he whispers, "I would have just been in your way...I didn't realize helping her meant all that killing."

"It is alright, little one," Crystal replies, standing and pulling him into a gentle embrace. The top of his head fits easily beneath her chin. She feels him tense in an effort to keep his fingers away from her skin, so she releases him to take hold of one of his hands.

His eyes go wide, and he is about to jerk his hand away when he realizes not even a spark of the power is slipping through his skin. "I am safe from your power, little one," she explains, interlacing their fingers. Shaking his head slowly, Ven replies, "No...it's not at all possible. I haven't given any kind of sign." "Might she be family, child?" Vachel suggests, moving up behind him. He shakes his head more furiously as he protests, "No...they killed all my sisters, and my mother died shortly after I was born." "How do you know all your sisters were killed, little one?" Crystal asks. He starts having trouble stringing words together: "No...I don't even...I don't know...I-I-I've never seen...you can't be."

"I was no longer in Darkhaven when you were born, little one," she explains, "But our mother is the same." "How do you know that?" Ven demands, a slight squeak to his voice suggesting he is about to burst into tears. Lifting his hand still clutched tightly to hers, she replies, "This proves our relationship, and your father was not a faerie." This finally does it for him, and the tears stream from his eyes in a warm rush. He flings himself forward, wrapping his arms tightly around her waist and burying his face in her chest.

"What is so wrong, little one?" Crystal asks, running her hand through his hair. Crying all the more, he bursts, "You're family...and I didn't even lift a finger to help. I let Vachel do all the work. What kind of brother does that make me?" "Consider it payback for helping save my sister," Vachel replies quickly, clapping a hand on Ven's shoulder. Turning his head so as to get a better look at Vachel, Ven asks, "Do you really mean that?" His voice still has the high squeak of one on the verge of bursting into tears.

Nodding, Vachel answers, "I wouldn't have said it if I didn't mean it, child." "Thank you," Ven responds, spinning around to cling to the demon's waist now. He lets the tears spill forth again, but he manages to keep the sobbing silent as he buries his face in Vachel's chest.

As Ven cries, Crystal moves forward to wrap her arms around Vachel's neck, pinning the Hybrid between them, but careful not to press too tightly against him. Oddly enough, this makes the tears and sobs ease somewhat, as if being trapped between them makes him feel more secure. In response, Vachel eases his own arms around Crystal's waist, careful not to squeeze hard enough to bother Ven. As if he understands what they really want to do, Ven squeezes himself in tighter against Vachel. A smile slips to both Vachel and Crystal's faces as they lean forward for the kiss. At this, Ven smiles in the darkness of his haven, glad to have at least made them happy.

They stand silent for a few minutes more before Ven whispers, "You know…you two smell really good together." There is not even a hint of the tears in his voice now. Giving a small laugh, Vachel replies, "Coming from a wolf, I'll take that as a compliment." "The smells just fit together…like each is the perfect perfume for the other," Ven explains quickly, as if afraid the statement will eventually start to make Vachel angry. "I know what you meant, child," Vachel replies slowly, "I was just messing with you."

"I do not mean to break up our little circle, but would you mind if we went back to the castle…and in search of something I could wear," Crystal interjects. "The princess probably has something," Vachel observes, stepping back as he does. As he pulls away, Vachel realizes immediately that, while Crystal lets her arms slip free, Ven keeps his tight grip on his waist.

"Would you mind letting me go so I can perform the magic, child?" Vachel requests, gazing down at the top of Ven's head. Reluctantly, Ven slips his arms away and takes a step back, the threat of tears evident in his face again. "Don't be like that, child. I just need some space to perform the spell," Vachel responds, running a hand through his hair.

Ven nods, but he cannot keep the edge of tears from his face.

Moving forward, Crystal places a kiss on Ven's head before taking one of his hands, making certain to keep the cloak closed over her in the process. "Is this better, little one?" she asks, gazing down at him. Giving a small sniff, he nods, squeezing her hand. Closing his eyes in concentration, Vachel calls up the flames to surround them again. A small look of wonder slips to Crystals face as she watches them, but Ven keeps his gaze on his feet.

Despite what Vachel said, he is still a little ashamed for not helping Crystal, and he is having some problems dealing with the news that he has a sister alive. Still, he does not have the time to dwell when the magic steals away the air from his lungs as it lifts them from the floor.

Healing Hands

Ven braces himself in anticipation of the hard impact from earlier, but he is not rewarded with what he expects. When they make it inside the castle, the impact is not quite so bone jarring. Still, Crystal has to take only one step to realize it was still too much for her. As her legs give out and dump her to the floor, she gives a little yelp of pain, wincing against it. Vachel makes it to her side first, gently wrapping and arm around her shoulders.

"I am sorry...it did not hurt so much before," she explains in a whisper. With a small, crooked smile, Vachel replies, "Why are you apologizing to us? We're not the ones who are hurt." She gives him a confused look as if he has just spoken in another language. "What is it, little one?" he asks, gazing down at the blood covering him with the knowledge that none of it is his. Crystal places one finger just under his collarbone and gently presses. Only now does Vachel feel the twinge of pain that should go with the wound she is seeing.

"What does it look like?" he asks, straining to see it properly with no luck. Removing her finger, Crystal explains, "It looks like a blade wound, but I only saw the one blade." "His back was to you when the guy pulled the knife, trying to get him off of the third man," Ven explains, shaking his head as if reliving the experience. Vachel frowns at the floor as he replies, "But, I didn't even feel it go in."

"You were crazed with fury," Ven replies, "I doubt anyone with that much anger and hatred in their eyes would have felt the blade. They might have felt the wound before now, but not when they received it."

"I guess being a demon has its perks every now and then …'cause it hurts like a bitch now," Vachel replies, his frown hardening. Giving the room a sweeping glance, Ven observes, "Maybe we should find a place where we can take care of the wounds." As soon as the words are out of his mouth and he considers where Crystal's wounds are located, a bright flush slips to his face. Vachel gives him a knowing smile as he asks, "What say you let me take care of them, child?"

Ven nods furiously, unable to trust his voice at the moment. Crystal giggles softly before the pain cuts her off, and she is forced to wince again. In response, Ven's face is red until he hears her tight breath and concern appears on his face instead. Vachel is about to speak again when he hears a voice call his name. He has just enough time to look up before Riko crashes into him, knocking him over on his back with her embrace.

"Ouch!" Vachel protests as he returns it. "You left in such an angry rush, I was afraid you might do something stupid and get yourself hurt," Riko explains, burying her face in his chest. Shaking his head, Vachel replies, "It's the elder sibling that's supposed to worry about everything…quit stealing my job."

"You're the only one who gives any reason to worry."

"So, soldiers chasing you around your kitchen is commonplace?"

"Vachel!"

"I can be a pain in the ass, too, you know. It's like my right."

"Sorry..." Riko replies, climbing off of him.

"Now, don't go getting all upset."

"How am I supposed to act? I was worried about you!"

"Well, stop it. I can take care of myself."

"Sure you can! That's why you ended up cursed and imprisoned!"

"Riko..." Vachel warns, getting to his feet.

"No! I'm tired of you trying to make something small out of a monstrous tragedy! You could have been hurt worse than just a little knife wound! One of them could have been hurt!"

"But they weren't, and that's the whole point."

"What about you? Do you mean that little to yourself?"

"Yes, if you must know."

Riko is about to argue further when Ven steps up in front of her, separating her from Vachel as he whispers, "Can we do this another time? We've got an injured party, or have you two forgotten?" Riko glares off at the wall as Vachel moves over to Crystal, scooping her up in his arms. "So, where do you suggest we go, child?" Vachel asks, gazing over at Ven. Giving a small yawn, Ven whispers, "Somewhere where I can take a nap."

"I have a place in mind, but you might want to get cleaned up, first," Mikya interjects, making her way into the room. She is back in one of her usual black, flowing dresses, her heels making a small click against the floor. Gazing down at his blood-covered chest, Vachel replies, "Yeah, I think a good scrubbing is way over-due."

Shortly after peeling off his blood soaked clothing and climbing into the full tub, Vachel decides not to bother with the ritual scrubbing for a while. Just being able to sit back and think for a time has more merit than he thought it would.

"I've killed so many people today in the name of revenge," he observes, closing his eyes, "And I got more blood on me from the human kills than when I killed Rust." *That's just too wrong for words.* He sinks down farther into the water, so only his head is above the water line and rests it against the side of the tub.

"I'm just not proud of the trip back to Darkhaven, at all. You'd think rising to the challenge of becoming king would mean more than it does now," he whispers, squeezing his eyes shut all the harder. *I'm probably just feeling guilty about Selene. I shouldn't have let her get to me like that. I should have more control of myself by now...it might have been more painful if I did, but I wouldn't be feeling like such an ass right now.* With this, he brings his hands up to dig the heels into his eyes in frustration: "Staying in your own high esteem shouldn't be this hard."

As soon as the words are out of his mouth, there is a knock at the door: "Vachel? Are you alright?" "Maybe," he replies, dropping his hands to gaze at the closed door.

In response, the door slips slowly open, and Crystal makes her way in, closing the door behind her quickly, as she is still just as bare as he is now. Sinking to the floor just inside the door, she brings her knees up to her chest and wraps her arms around them, whispering slowly: "The bleeding has stopped." "So, it seems being a faerie has perks sometimes, too," Vachel remarks with a twisted smirk, as if he has to force it to come to his face.

Gazing up at him, she asks, "What is it that is really bothering you?" "All the people I killed today...I'm really regretting some of them," Vachel whispers as if he does not really want her to hear. Her gaze drops back to the floor as she asks, "What do you mean by 'regretting some of them'?"

"I could have killed those men without so much blood and gore," Vachel explains, "I could have even had my revenge without killing them. That's sad to know." Sighing, he closes his eyes again, frowning as if thoroughly disgusted with himself. He is concentrating so hard on his dilemma that he does not realize Crystal has moved until she places a small kiss on his forehead. He opens his eyes to look at her and finds a smile perched on her lips. The confusion must have shown on his face, because she explains, "I am still grateful for your help, dearest." At this, a small smile peaks onto his face.

"Good. Now then, if you are not going to use this water for scrubbing, I need to," she remarks, climbing into the water so that she rests lightly in his lap and giving a small wince as the hot water gets into one of the outer wounds. He gives her a teasing frown as he replies, "I was going to use it eventually." "I do not have until eventually to wait, you little demon," she counters, jabbing him in the chest with one of her fingers. He just gives her a sly smile as if to say this was all part of his plan.

Shaking her head, she grabs up the soap on the side of the tub, throwing him a small glance before she takes up the task of cleaning all the unsavory things she has collected on her skin from it. She is about to finish with her face when she feels a small tug at her ear.

"What is it?" she asks without turning around. "What do you mean?" he asks all too innocently. Turning her head so she can look at him out of the corner of her eye, she replies, "You know what I mean. You pulled on my ear." "I did no such thing," he protests in feigned shock, a smirk slipping to his face. Shaking her head again, she resumes her task.

It is not long before she feels him tug her ear again. "Stop doing that," she demands, turning to look at him this time. Crossing his arms and giving her a fake frown, he protests, "I haven't done anything." She frowns hard at him before turning back around. She has not even got the soap repositioned when he tugs her ear for the third time. Without a word, she spins around and flings the soap at him.

It collides with his head as she tackles him, forcing them both under the water. In response, he pinches her sides, causing her to push away, giggling. He forces his way up above the water with a loud gasp, droplets streaming from his chin and hair. "Now try to tell me you did not do anything," she remarks, crossing her arms. He is about to answer when another knock sounds at the door. Both go silent as Ven calls through it, "I've got some things for you two to wear when you're done." "Well, bring them in here, child," Vachel replies quickly. There is a pause in which silence drifts over all three before Ven slowly opens the door.

Crystal places a hand over her mouth as she giggles at the sight of Ven hiding his face behind the pile of clothing. "Where do you want them?" he asks, even his voice sounding embarrassed. "Well, out from in front of your face for starters," Vachel replies, a smirk on his face. Peaking around the bundle just enough to see the demon, Ven whispers in a pleading voice, "Vachel...she's not wearing anything."

"One usually doesn't when one takes a bath...so, yeah, she isn't wearing anything. What of it?" Vachel replies, leaning forward to rest his elbow on the edge of the tub. He watches Ven for a moment, his chin resting in his palm before the Hybrid gets up the nerve to speak again: "It isn't really appropriate for me to see her this way."

"Maybe you should ask her what she thinks about that," Vachel suggests, his smile taking a sly turn. He knows just how embarrassed Ven is, but he is still determined to see the Hybrid's face light up red with it. Hiding his face again, Ven replies, "Why do you have to make this so difficult?" "I'm not," Vachel begins, focusing on the bundle in Ven's hand. Before the Hybrid can protest his statement, Vachel directs his wind, jerking the clothing from Ven's hands.

A smile on his face, Vachel finishes, "But now I am."

Ven stands frozen, his hands still before his face where they were positioned when he still held the clothing. His eyes widen immediately, fear slipping in with the embarrassed blushing. To compound the effect, Vachel raises his hand, calling on the Shiku Hara before Ven can regain the use of his limbs. Immediately, the chain responds, jerking Ven forward so it can rest in Vachel's open palm. Using the Hybrid's momentum and the chain, Vachel pulls him head first into the water.

Ven pushes his way back to the surface, every inch of him and his clothing soaked. "What was that for?" Ven demands, jerking his head in Vachel's direction. Releasing the chain, Vachel explains, "I just thought we should get used to being a group. I've decided to make the nickname permanent."

Ven gives him a confused look as Crystal reaches forward and helps him to a sitting position between she and

Vachel so that he is facing the demon. He manages to keep the flush from his face now that he has to look at Vachel. "I call you 'child', right?" Vachel asks, crossing his arms. Ven nods, still confused. "So, what do you think it means when I say that I've made it permanent?" Vachel prompts, giving Ven a raised eyebrow. Swallowing hard, Ven finds he has lost the use of his voice. Crystal reaches forward and wraps her arms around his waist in a hug as she whispers, "Your new title will be Prince of Darkhaven." "I overheard you talking about being king," she adds at the sight of Vachel's questioning look.

Discovering his voice again, Ven asks, "Why me of all people? My magic helped them catch you." "And your blood helped me cure the curse and kill Rust. I think it's the least I could do to ensure you are your own master in the future," Vachel explains. Ven bites his lower lip against the tears threatening again. "It is alright, little one. You can cry if you wish," Crystal whispers in his ear, slipping her arms away from his waist. Ven's lip quivers for a moment before he jerks forward, wrapping his arms tightly around Vachel's waist. The tears stream steadily down his face as he digs his fingers into Vachel's back: "Thank you...thank you. You don't know how much this means to me."

Crystal rests her head against Vachel's chest, the tears streaming after having told him a full account of her capture and imprisonment. "If you had not gotten there when you did, they would have killed me," she whispers, trembling.

His arms around her, Vachel strokes her hair as he apologizes again, "I'm sorry for not being there for you, little one. I didn't think anyone knew." "It seems one of the women in the kitchen overheard your talk with Riko," Crystal suggests. "That doesn't make sense," Vachel responds, "Riko said she placed a charm over the subject." "A sorcerer might have been able to get past the magic," she offers, looking up at him. A spark of realization lights in his eyes before he whispers, "...or a Sister." "You mean- -" "Yes. High Sister Selene," he replies, a glare perching on his face.

At this, she lets her head drop back against his chest: "I am scared. What if she tries again?" "Then, I'll teach her what for," Ven responds from his place between them. His arms are crossed even as he curls up into a ball.

Vachel reaches down beneath the blanket to muss his hair, having to reach down to his waist to find the top of Ven's head. It is less of the Hybrid's idea and more of Vachel's they sleep like this. He wants Ven to feel safe for the time being, and it is part of the Darkhaven tradition to have one's child sleep with him until the first century is under his belt. Ven might be much older than that already, but the tradition still stands. At least for a little while.

"That is sweet," Crystal remarks, running her fingers over his cheek. A hidden smile on his face, Ven presses his cheek against her fingertips. Vachel is the first to give a real yawn as he whispers, "I don't know about you...but I'm bushed." At this, Ven quickly wraps his arms around the demon's waist again, snuggling in against Vachel's bare stomach. The black pants are a little scratchy against the skin of his chest, but Ven is looking for safety, not necessarily comfort. Taking the hint, Vachel pulls Crystal close, so her weight is pressed against Ven's back, like when they were still in that dungeon.

Because she is back in the short nightgown, Crystal's legs are what truly touches Ven. It does not bother him this time, now that he considers having been jerked into a bathtub with her. Crystal smiles up at Vachel for a moment and is about to let her head fall back when Ven whispers, "You don't have to save the kiss just because I'm here, you know."

"I know," Vachel answers, taking her head in his hands as he gives her the kiss. It is considerably shorter than the others, but the message is still sent to either side. Finally, he tucks her head underneath his chin before closing his eyes and letting sleep slowly take him.

The True High Sister

The next morning, they all wake with the intent to see to business and leave for Darkhaven. Vachel is still in all black, but the shirt has a collar and long sleeves. He has tucked it into the tight pants and left the first two buttons open so the chain with the crystal can be seen as it slips forward to the middle of his chest. Crystal made him pull his hair back again, so he let her tighten it for him. At his shins, the pants slip into a pair of black boots.

So they match, Crystal wears one of Mikya's long black dresses, complete with the low cut, but not quite as low as the princess usually wears. Even she agreed her hair would look strange pulled back with nothing but the thin straps adorning her shoulders.

Inviting only a slight change of pace, Ven wears a sleeveless, red shirt, loose at his waist. A thick, black belt holds the black pants in place. At his shins, the pants slip into the mouths of his usual boots, still folding over the rim. His hands are adorned with black gloves again, and he pulled the black cloak over his shoulders, now because it has his sister's scent on it. In his ears are diamond studs attached with a chain to triangles bearing small, decorative flames.

Their trek is actually in search of Mikya; however, the first person they encounter is Gilden. He is decked out in his usual white, the medallion visible again and the gloves removed. Giving a small sigh, he bows to Vachel and greets, "Good day, your highness." "Don't call me that," Vachel replies, not even bothering to nod, "And enough with the formalities. We went on a long and harrowing journey together, killing a king along the way. I think it's safe to say we're somewhere along the same authority rung." "I can see gaining some height on this ladder hasn't affected your attitude any," Gilden observes, his voice tired even with the small smile on his face. All three hear it plainly, but Ven is the first to comment on it: "What's the matter?"

"If the new High Sister has her way, I won't have a position amongst the Elders anymore," Gilden answers in a defeated voice. "Why not?" Ven presses, his eyes narrowing. Sighing again, Gilden explains, "For the same reason she sent Crystal to be punished: I sympathized with Vachel. She can't do anything to Mikya, so she's picking off everyone else. Do you know if she's tried for Riko, yet?" "Yes she has. I had the pleasure of snapping the soldier's neck, too," Vachel replies, anger slipping into his features again.

Hugging himself for a moment, Gilden whispers, "Selene is going to ruin our hierarchy if she keeps this up." "Not if *I* have anything to say about it," Ven growls, slipping one of the fresh gloves from his right hand, "She's just going to have to bring her complaints to the hierarchy of Darkhaven where they belong." At this, he stalks off down the hallway, the glove gripped tightly in his left hand.

"What's he planning, Vachel?" Gilden asks, gazing after Ven.

"You'll see, sorcerer. You'll see."

⟐

They do not have to wait long until Ven bursts around the corner again, laughing as he gazes back over his shoulder. It seems he did not have to search very hard to find the High Sister.

Stopping before Vachel and pointing a thumb over his shoulder, he explains, "I think she's on her way to make her complaint now." The laughter is still on his face moments later when Selene makes her way around the corner, clutching the blue robe of the High Sister tightly around her. There is a furious flush to her face made all the brighter by the silver hair that frames it.

"Rotten little imp!" she yells after Ven as he moves in next to Vachel, "How dare you lay a hand on me!" "It was easy. You had my sister attacked, and you had Riko attacked. None of the people you're going after have done anything to you," Ven replies calmly.

Stepping forward with the glare perched on his face, Vachel interjects, "Besides, if you have a problem with the royalty of Darkhaven, you should take it up with someone from Darkhaven." "Royalty?! What sort of gibberish is that?!" Selene demands, her anger spiking. "I am the new king of Darkhaven, Selene. You should keep that in mind as you throw stones at my allies," Vachel warns, the glare deepening. Her eyes go wide for a moment before she growls, "Fine then. You should learn to keep your little freak of nature away from people. It's dangerous."

"What did you do to her that was so horrible?" Vachel asks, turning his gaze to Ven. Ven is about to open his mouth when Selene shrieks, "He tore open my dress and laid hands on me! I know he's a filthy Hybrid because his power burnt his handprint into my skin!" "You whine an awful lot for a High Sister," Vachel replies, wrinkling up his nose at her. Her eyes widen again as she demands, "You mean to tell me you're not going to do anything about this?!"

"Actually, I think I'll get a second opinion on the situation," Vachel reasons, "I mean, I trust *her* judgment far more than yours, so if she agrees with you, then I will punish Ven as she sees fit." Selene stares at him in shocked fury as he smiles back at her. "Selene, High Sister of Darkhaven, I call you to come to me," Vachel whispers finally, closing his eyes. In response, the air thickens with the resulting magic.

Their gazes fall on one of the walls as a pinpoint of red light appears on the surface. The light grows into a spiraling mass of energy, clinging to the wall like a doorway. Once it has stretched to reach from floor to ceiling, a pale hand grips the edge. Next, High Sister Selene steps through, a long, pale leg slipping in first. Her hair is slightly disheveled around her scarred face as it slides over her shoulders. As soon as she spots her audience, she reaches for the sash at her waist, tightening the front of the silk robe around her obviously bare frame.

"You are the only man I know who could call me out of something like that for business and...feel nothing...Vachel," she remarks with a small frown, brushing some of her hair behind her ear, "Hmm...I am quite uncomfortable with using that name."

"But, I thank you for the effort," Vachel replies with a smile. Shaking her head, the High Sister asks, "Now, what is it that I can do for you?" "You're going to have to tell her about it, *High Sister*," Vachel replies, turning to Selene who is still huddling behind her blue robe. The High Sister gives a slow blink before she asks, "This is the High Sister of Dehurst? What is your name, little girl?" Even the blink lets them know she does not believe a word.

"I'm not a little girl," Selene protests angrily.

Narrowing her eyes, the High Sister observes, "I can tell you are nowhere near 5,720, child. Do not argue with me on the matter of age and how I speak to you. Give me your name and I will address you with it." "My name is Selene," Selene replies, her glare deepening just slightly. The High Sister's eyes go wide as she turns her gaze to Vachel: "You cannot be serious! This little prude is much too pure for such a name! Do you even understand what that name means, child?" Still glaring, Selene gives a small shake of her head.

The High Sister gives a small humph before she replies, "I thought as much. You cannot possibly be a creature of passion...no, you are much too...innocent, child." "Are you trying to imply that I'm too innocent to have even a lover?" Selene demands, her anger spilling up onto her face. That she came to that conclusion immediately lets everyone know she is just looking for a fight. Shaking her head in emphasis, the High Sister replies, "Not at all, child. I am implying that your lover is sorely cheated with the faulty toy he has gotten his hands on."

Ven begins to snicker softly at this as Selene's mouth drops open in shock and anger. Gilden has to look away to keep them from seeing the smirk spilling onto his face; Vachel, on the other hand, doesn't even try to hide it. Even Crystal has to place a hand to her mouth to keep some of the giggling from escaping her.

"How dare you speak to me this way!" Selene exclaims. Crossing her arms, the High Sister responds, "Simple, child, it is the truth. You are a faulty piece of craftsmanship if ever there was such." Before Selene can retaliate, Vachel interjects, "What say we put you two to the test?" The High Sister turns her head slowly, as if to say she is listening, while Selene remains absorbed in her anger. "I propose a match between you two...the one to survive is the winner...and the True High Sister," Vachel explains, his smile taking a scheming turn.

Clasping her hands together and gazing up at the ceiling, the High Sister remarks, "I remember a time before when I was put in such a test to prove myself worthy of another position...perhaps we should do that again, too, love." "Selene..." Vachel warns, his eyes narrowing.

Crossing her arms again, the High Sister protests, "There are too many syllables in your name. If it had just one, I would not be so hesitant to use it." "I use your name, and it has more syllables," Vachel counters. The High Sister shakes her head as she replies, "But, you have found a new pet, love. I have not." "You do enough interviewing to have found one," Vachel remarks with a raised eyebrow. The High Sister gives a small laugh before she answers, "None of them were up to par, love. No one can even meet you halfway. I have been thoroughly disappointed during all of my...interviews, as you call them."

"What do they have to do for this match?" Crystal asks, breaking into the conversation and forcing it in a different direction. Turning to her with a somewhat demonic smile, Vachel answers, "Try to kill each other." "My money's on the High Sister of Darkhaven!" Ven declares with glee, rushing over to stand behind the High Sister. "Why, thank you for the support, little wolf," the High Sister remarks with a smile, "I thought you did not like me."

"I don't...well, not enough to French you, anyway. But either way, I already know you're more powerful than this pathetic excuse for a sorceress," Ven answers, sticking his tongue out at Selene. It is a lie, but he isn't ready to tell her the truth just yet. She is about to snap at him when

Vachel turns to her and asks, "So, *High Sister,* what do you say?"

"I'll wipe the floor with her!" Selene yells, the anger flaring out again. Just as the words are out of her mouth, she is slammed back on the ground, her head colliding hard with the floor. "Rule one, child. Never let your opponent leave your thoughts, you will not be on guard for an attack," the High Sister corrects, her arm raised from the attack. In response, Selene jerks up, sending a wave of ice daggers at the High Sister.

Shaking her head, the High Sister holds her hands, palm up, directing a wall of flame around her. The wall melts the ice as soon as they touch. It is only after she lets the wall down that the High Sister realizes Ven is still at her back. His fingertips are digging into her back through the thin cloth of the robe, and she can feel the slight tremble in his hands. "Perhaps you should get out of the way, little wolf," the High Sister offers, gazing down at him.

Nodding, Ven makes a dash toward Vachel, Crystal, and Gilden only to have his legs swept out from under him by Selene's next attack. He lands hard on his palms, making his arms curls up beneath him. "Rule two, be ready for anything your opponent might use against you," Selene declares, mocking the High Sister with a triumphant laugh to her voice. To emphasize her point, Selene sends a burst of flame at Ven's back: "This should teach him not to mess with me." Ven curls up in anticipation of the blow, but instead, he feels magic lashing out above his head.

Raising his head ever so slowly, Ven sees the High Sister holding the fire within a wall of her own magic. "Have you no honor, child?" the High Sister demands, glaring at Selene, "You are battling me, not the wolf." "I'm claiming vengeance for what he did to me!" Selene counters angrily. In response, the High Sister uses her magic to hurl the flames back at Selene. They only make contact with Selene's shoulder because she manages to slip to the side. Still, the impact of the attack spins her around before she falls forward onto the floor. The cloth of the robe and dress beneath is ripped, exposing her torn, bleeding shoulder. It is only now that Ven takes the time to scramble to his feet and rush over to Vachel's side. He latches on to the demon's hand as he watches.

"That should teach *you* to be better behaved when you enter a battle, especially with me," the High Sister remarks, raising her hand for the next attack. Selene makes it to her knees, anger flaring off her like aura, before the High Sister unleashes her next wave of magic. This sends her crashing against the wall. Jerking to her feet, Selene roars in fury, sending another wave of fire at the High Sister. She narrows her eyes and raises both hands to catch the flames in a circle of her magic, remarking: "Did we not just discover this does not work?"

Selene rakes a glowing, red hand through the air, causing bleeding scratches to blossom on the High Sister's face. "That is the best you could come up with?" the High Sister demands, not even reaching up to wipe away the blood. Selene raises her hand to repeat the gesture only to have the High Sister pin her hand to the wall with a dagger of ice. Simply dropping the flames to the floor, the High Sister moves forward, careful to keep the hem of her robe from the fire. "I think continuing from here will be a waste of both our efforts, do you not think, child?" she remarks, smirking at Selene. Anger flaring up in her face, Selene jerks her hand and the dagger from the wall, opening the wound all the more.

This time, she sends an entire wall of ice hurtling toward the High Sister. Frowning as if she is getting bored, the High Sister lets a violet light slip around her, and the ice simply slides through her, as if she is not even standing there. Desperate by this time, Selene rushes forward and tries to hit the High Sister with a tightly clenched fist. This succeeds only in landing her on her back on the floor, clutching her stomach.

"You cannot defeat a demon that way, child...especially in this condition against one such as myself," the High Sister remarks, narrowing her eyes at Selene. Blood spills from her mouth as Selene yells, "Go to hell, demon!" "Actually, I think I would rather send you first...you know, make certain it is suitable," the High Sister replies, her smile slipping wide enough to flash fangs.

Selene's eyes go wide as the High Sister raises her arm to strike. However, before she can release the magic, Mikya rushes around the corner, her face flushed from running. "What's going on, here?" she asks breathlessly, gazing more at Vachel than any of the others. Smiling at her, he replies, "Oh, just a test to see who's more worthy to be High Sister."

"What has she done to deserve a beating from the High Sister of Darkhaven?" Mikya asks, gesturing to Selene on the floor. "She had Riko attacked...she's trying to strip Gilden of his post with no just cause...I hate her...you know, the usual," Vachel explains with a demonic smile, "Besides, with one High Sister between the two countries, we'll have more of a reason to talk to each other."

"This is certainly new to me...I'd never have thought of strengthening ties between our nations by killing someone," Mikya responds, the distaste in her voice obvious even as she seeks to stifle it. Shrugging, Vachel answers, "Vengeance can be a strange dish, princess." Mikya is about to say something further when Selene cries, "Erdma!"

The High Sister's eyes widen at the sound of the spell and the dread welling up inside her. Everything around her goes black before she feels the ground disappear from beneath her feet. A small cry of fright escapes her just as she lands hard. Slowly she blinks to clear her head. After several hard blinks, she can finally focus on the room that has appeared around her. She gasps at the sight of Vachel sitting across the room from her. *He wears a black, sleeveless shirt, tucked neatly into black pants. At his waist, the black belt forces the tight fabric of the pants harder against his skin. Around his neck, on a gold chain bearing a medallion, is the symbol for*

death[9]. *The black boots slide over the pants to his shins. Around his shoulders is a black robe that falls to the floor around him.*

His eyes are held at half-mast as he rests his chin against his left hand, so his thumb and middle finger cradle his chin and his index finger rests against his lips. It is a posture she has seen him use many times when he is either thinking hard or upset about something. The right arm is folded on the table before him. Beneath the wood plane, he has his legs crossed, and there is an impatient sway to the dangling foot.

The High Sister recognizes the clothing and his pose perfectly. This is the moment when he got rid of her. Just as the thought passes through her mind, the door to the room opens, and a younger version of her steps inside. There is a smile perched on her carefully reddened lips. The black dress is purposely tight in just the right places, and there is a slit from ankle to waist, exposing all of her hip. At her waist, the gold, cloth belt is still rightfully in place.

"It has been quite a time since you came to see me, love," she remarks as she steps forward to kiss him. Vachel pointedly avoids the touch as he answers, "There's a reason for that, Selene." "What reason?" she asks, a confused frown slipping to her face. Getting to his feet, Vachel answers in a dangerous whisper, "I'm not here to play games with you, Selene. What you're doing here is wrong!" "I do not understand," she replies, taking a step back. Slamming his fist onto the table so a crack appears in the wood, he yells, "You and your girls are torturing people!" "That is our job, love. I thought you understood that," she responds, her eyes

---

[7] This symbol consists of a skull in profile.

Yossa's Crystal

narrowing. "Bullshit! Torture is only one means to an end! There are other ways to do it," Vachel growls, towering over her.

This time she does not back down as she counters, "You mean like killing? That is your angle, love." "Don't you call me that! You don't even know the meaning of the word," Vachel hisses, his eyes shining with fury, "You lied to me!" "I merely bent the truth. I only said that I would be gentler. That has nothing to do with stopping or making the girls ease their fun," she protests, crossing her arms. At this, Vachel throws his hands in the air in disgust, "Fine! Have it your way! Goodbye, High Sister!" As soon as the words are out of his mouth, he pushes past her, marching for the door.

"What do you mean, 'goodbye'?" she demands, fear in her voice as she spins around and grabs his arm. In response, he jerks his hand from her grasp and backhands her around the face: "Just what it sounds like! I'm putting some major distance between me and your bloodthirsty hide!" It is the first time he has ever struck her, and it will be the last. Tears of hurt well up in her eyes as she watches him storm out the door.

The High Sister has to wipe a tear away from her own eyes as the scene goes black again. She has only to remember she got her revenge for that day for the black around her to take the form of another room. *It is one she knows quite well, and gazes around to find the other version of herself curled up on the cushion of the throne, fiddling with the ends of her hair. She is depressed, nothing much else can be said about it. She is about to turn over and perhaps cry again when the door bursts open.*

Vachel scrambles in with two Sisters flanking him. There is something she never expected to see on his face: fear.

Sitting up, she asks, "What is this all about?" "High Sister, this man insists on seeing you. He told us you would help him," one of the Sisters explains, the skepticism obvious in her voice. When she smells something a little off about him, she takes a moment to get a feel of his aura to find it severely lacking. Someone has done a number on the Great Death's powers. The first tendrils of a plan start to drop in her brain. "I will see to this matter...you two may see to your other charges," she responds with a dismissive wave of her hand. With a nod and smile each, the Sisters turn away and rush from the room.

As soon as the door closes behind them, Vachel explains in a pleading voice, "He's stolen half my power, Selene. I really need your help. I have to get it back." "Poor, poor baby. Is Death not being treated well?" she remarks, rolling her eyes at him. The tendrils are slowly working their way into an intricate web of pain and vengeance. Dropping to his knees, Vachel pleads, "Please...please help me. I can't do this by myself." "I suppose I could help...but you must repay me as is the custom of the Sisters of Darkhaven," she responds, speaking their title as if they were as high as the king and crossing her arms.

"I'll do anything...please just help me," he begs, letting the desperation flow into his face. The scheming smile is held back in her mind as she holds her hand out to him, "Come, love. Be with me once more." A relieved smile spills to his face as he gets to his feet to take the offered hand. Pulling him up beside her, she immediately steals her kiss. In the end, he does not disappoint,

despite the fragile state of mind he entered with. Before his return to Darkhaven, this was the final time they were to be together.

Just before dawn of the next morning, she turns to his sleeping form beside her and gently shakes him. He wakes immediately, blinking a few times as he asks, "Is something wrong?" "Oh no, love. Everything has gone according to plan," she explains, finally letting the furtive smile slip to her face. His eyes widen as he slowly lets his gaze slip from her to the crowd of Sisters standing ready around them. "Selene?" he asks, a slight whimper to his voice as he gazes out at them all. "Do not fret, love," she whispers, "This is merely payment for what you did to me." He has just enough time to swallow hard before the first pair of hands jerks him from his perch beside her.

"Selene? What's going on?" he demands in fear, trying to pull away from the hands that reach for him. She does not even make a sound as she watches his progress through the crowd. As they push and shove him toward the center of the mass, she can see the panic plainly in his eyes. The smile never wavers on her face as she watches them shove him to the floor and secure his wrists. It does not even twitch as she watches each and every one have her way with him, knives, magic, biting, and all.

However, toward the end, after listening to him screaming nothing but her name through the entire ordeal, there is a small wrinkle in the smile. From that point on, whenever she takes such revenge, that smile with the wrinkle is what appears on her face.

Only when each of them has had her turn does she call for it all to cease. Two Sisters reach down to release him from the shackles. He does not dare even move from his position, let alone try to seek escape. As she makes her way from the throne, she slips *the dagger from her dress on the floor, holding the blade in front of her as she moves forward. He stares up at her, pure terror on his face as she gives him that wrinkled smile.*

After a moment, she turns to a Sister and directs, "Turn him over." The Sister does as she is told, and then the High Sister takes the dagger in her hand and presses it against her own wrist. With a swift, stroke she stains the blade crimson. All eyes are on her as she steps forward and kneels beside him. "I will now mark him as my own," she whispers before beginning the first stroke of the etching that rests just above his waist. Once the work is finally done, she declares, "Whoever can reach him may do the same, but once there is no more available skin, the deal is done."

As soon as the words are out of her mouth, Sisters in a ring around him rush up to make their own carvings. She remains to make certain they heed her instructions and then send them all away. When he is the only other person in the room, she bends down and makes certain her mark is deeper and bolder than the others.

At last she is finished, and she tosses his clothing at him, declaring: "Get out of my sight!" He is quick to pull on the boots and pants, but leaves the shirt because of the wounds. As he scrambles out the doors, she calls after him, "You will only escape our wrath once you are out of Darkhaven, Death!"

Suddenly furious, the High Sister jerks up from the floor as Selene brings the dagger down to pierce her heart. There is an impact in the air, sending waves of magic spreading out to the others. A cloud of violet smoke billows up around the two High Sisters, obscuring them from view.

Vachel narrows his eyes at the scene, having no doubt what the spell caused the High Sister to see.

As the waves wash over him, Ven cannot help but give a small whimper in protest. Crystal keeps her gaze forward on the cloud, but her arms are firmly wrapped around Vachel's right. Hugging herself at the thought of what the spell might have revealed, Mikya's eyes flick from the floor in front of her to the cloud, and back again. In something close to shock, Gilden just stands staring.

Another impact rushes through the space before Selene is thrown backwards out of the cloud with the High Sister right behind her. Landing hard on her back, Selene does not have the time to avoid the attack. The High Sister's furious fist crashes into her jaw, sending her head crashing into the wall. Now unable to get her body to do anything for her, Selene can only lie helplessly as the High Sister makes her way forward. Before she goes in for the final blow, the High Sister demands in a yell, "What kind of cruel bitch are you?! Do you think I am proud of that?!"

"Seemed pretty proud to me," Vachel whispers, his eyes narrowing further. Spinning around and jabbing her finger at him, the High Sister bursts, "No one asked you!" Inside she would rather have asked him how he could think her capable of truly enjoying something like that. Tears have added to the reddening face to make her look more like a raging beast than the composed person she has shown before.

Jerking around to face Selene again, she raises her hand again. "This time you die, bitch! Not even the King of Darkhaven himself could stop me!" she cries, sending the ball of flames screeching at her prey. They are about to slam into their target when every last one disappears.

"You were saying, Selene?" Vachel remarks, holding the flames in their ball above his left hand. Gritting her teeth for a moment, the High Sister demands, "Now what are you doing?! Why did you stop me?!" "You challenged my power, Selene. I can't leave that," Vachel replies, soaking up the energy in the flames and causing them to dissipate. "Fine! I will do it without magic!" the High Sister cries, rushing forward.

This time Vachel does not even speak as she reaches forward and takes a handful of Selene's hair. Rage filling every muscle, she slams the girl's head once into the wall, splattering blood, bone, and gore. "Are you quite satisfied?! I can't even finish what I started, now!" the High Sister demands, wiping furiously at her tears and smearing blood across her face. With a raised eyebrow, Vachel asks, "And why can't you?"

Crystal gives him a look that plainly asks, "What are you doing?"

He pays it no mind as he stares at the High Sister.

She has every intention of screaming at him again, but she remembers herself and the advantage she still has at the last moment. She can make him regret this once everything has settled for a moment and she has a clear head. Her fists at her sides, the High Sister turns on her heel and declares, "I am going home!" "We'll see you on our way, pet," Vachel calls after her, a triumphant smile on his face. He didn't have to lift even a finger to insure his revenge on her for making him forget Crystal was carried out to the fullest. The words make her jerk to a stop and slowly turn her head to face him as she asks, "What did you say?" "We'll see you on our way back to the castle, pet," Vachel explains as if nothing is wrong with his words. She stares at him for a moment longer before she whispers, "I will be waiting."

With that, a burst of black flame engulfs her frame and she disappears.

Unions

Ven sits in a corner, shoveling eggs into his mouth as the women of the kitchen staff dash about the room doing various tasks. Inside, he is smiling to know Riko has been able to bring everything back into order after the attack by the soldier. And speaking of Riko, she just makes it past him when he asks, "Can I have some more bacon?" Smiling and rolling her eyes at him, she points across the room at a girl in the process of making bacon: "If you beg, Mia might give you a piece or two." Ven grins at her before climbing to his feet in the hope of getting the bacon.

As Riko moves farther into the room to tend to a girl in distress over a piece of dough that refuses to do anything she wants it to, Crystal makes her way into the room, her eyes darting around. When she spies Ven and his now bacon-filled plate, a smile slips to her face. He has sat down and is about to dig into the pile when she slips down beside him and asks, "Were you hungry, little one?" "I've never had the choice to eat until I was full," Ven answers, shoveling in more bacon.

Placing a hand on his shoulder, Crystal explains, "We need to be leaving soon, little one. Vachel's getting anxious." Ven lets his gaze drop to his full plate with a disappointed frown. In response, Riko drops a clean cloth on top of it: "Take the food but leave the plate. We're running short on china since the incident with the former

High Sister." A bright smile spreading onto his face, Ven scoops the bacon and one remaining egg into the cloth and ties it, handing the plate back to Riko. "What kind of aunt would I be if I let my nephew go hungry?" Riko remarks, giving him a smile of her own as she turns away.

With that, Ven lets Crystal lead him out of the kitchen, both making certain to give Riko a departing wave. After all, considering she doesn't wish to follow them to Darkhaven, it will be some time before they see her again. They do not get very far when Vachel rounds the corner to meet them with a calm frown on his face. Crystal has a hunch he is trying to assume his role as king and keep his emotions for the current situation under wraps.

"Are you going to say goodbye to Riko?" Crystal asks when he approaches. Nodding but remaining silent, Vachel continues around them before popping into the kitchen. He does not get a chance to speak at first because Riko shoves a spoon between his lips and demands, "What do you think it needs?" He rolls it around in his mouth for a moment, just to humor her, as he could tell the moment it touched his tongue "Onion," Vachel answers, pulling the spoon away after swallowing. Nodding, Riko remarks, "I thought so."

In response, the girl dashes away to see to the onion.

Riko pulls the spoon from his grasp before crossing her arms and asking: "So, what can I do for you, your highness?" "Stop calling me that," Vachel answers, "And, I wanted to tell you goodbye. We're leaving for home." Riko casts a glance around the room for a moment before she wraps her arms around him in a tight hug. "I'll miss you, ya big jerk," she whispers as he returns the embrace.

Kissing the top of her head, Vachel replies, "You complain too much. It's not like we'll never see each other again." "And it's not like I can just patter over to Darkhaven to see you any old time I please," Riko counters. Vachel suppresses the urge to tell her to come with them in that case. Releasing her, Vachel pulls one of the lead spheres from his pocket and places it in her hand, curling her fingers around it: "When you want, just give it a squeeze, and I'll come see you."

"Immediately?" she asks skeptically. Vachel gives her a knowing look as he answers "With as much haste as I can muster. I'm going to have to see to the business of ruling, too, you know." "And to the business of a ruler with needs," Riko adds, crossing her arms. Smiling at her, he whispers again, "You complain too much."

Gilden dashes around the corner, the stone held tightly in his fist as he seeks to catch up to them before they leave. He enters the front room out of breath to find only Ven and Crystal here. "What's the big rush?" Ven asks with a smile, making his way over to the sorcerer.

Gilden has to take three deep breaths before he can answer, *I'm getting too old for this,* "I'm so glad I got here in time. The princess wanted me to give this to you." "Give what to us?" Crystal asks, stepping up behind Ven. Gilden straightens, breathing heavily for a moment more before he holds out his hand, revealing the glittering, black stone balanced in his palm. "What is it?" Crystal asks, gazing at the stone over Ven's shoulder. "This is a communication stone," Gilden answers, "It'll allow Mikya and Vachel to stay in touch without the threat of being overheard."

"Great. Between her and Riko, I'm never going to get anything done," Vachel remarks, stepping into the room behind Gilden. *Or have any fun* he adds in the back of his mind. Ven dashes over to latch onto the demon's waist as Gilden asks, "What do you mean?" "I've given Riko something to contact me with, as well. She isn't too fond of Darkhaven or anything in it," Vachel explains, slipping his hands into his pockets and gazing off at the wall as if in thought.

"How sweet, you old softy," Crystal and Ven tease together. Crossing his arms and turning up his nose, Vachel counters, "I've never been soft in my life." "The High Sister might say something different," Ven mumbles. Grinding his knuckles into the top of Ven's head, Vachel answers, "No one asked you, child."

"But I would have to agree," Gilden chimes in, "She probably knows a kinder side than the rest of us will ever see." "I doubt that, sincerely!" Vachel counters. If anything, Selene probably saw the hardest side there is to him: the side that protects what he holds dear. Nodding her agreement, Crystal adds, "I am sure I have seen something incredibly soft in him." Vachel's confident air slips away, revealing a slight flush to his cheeks. She, on the other hand, has seen something soft: the gentleness he has for a mate of which he wishes to take care. This gets the other three to laugh.

"Tell all why don't ya!" Vachel counters, reacting to the thought that she is talking about the night they spent alone even though it wasn't what came to mind first, "You act like I'm not allowed to enjoy myself anymore." "We never said that. We're just saying that you have a soft side no matter how much you try to hide it," Ven replies, smiling up at him.

As promised, once in Darkhaven, Vachel steers them all toward the Sisters' towering structure of crystal. Even with Vachel at his side Ven still has to swallow back the fear creeping up his throat. However, this time it is the fear of what he will say to the High Sister in gratitude for saving him and to get her to give him a chance now that he doesn't have Rust to deal with any longer. He wants the chance for one of those mate interviews she's been giving everyone else.

When Vachel places his hand on the doors, a Sister dressed in the usual black appears once the doors open. A near squeal spills from her lips, bringing several others to her side to share in the joy of having their favorite toy to play with. Vachel feels Crystal's grip on his arm tighten for a moment, and he has the urge to smack every last one of them. That is, until the High Sister makes her way forward and introduces them: "Girls, I would like you to meet the new king of Darkhaven."

Every jaw drops open as they all stumble over themselves to apologize to him. Dismissing the insult, as hearing them fall all over themselves has made him feel more like laughing, Vachel moves forward with Crystal and Ven, silently demanding the girls give them all space. They do it without a word.

"I will personally show you to your rooms for the night...but, for now, would you care to share a word or two?" Selene asks, keeping her calm despite an edge evident in the way she stands. She is simply not comfortable with having Crystal all but attached to Vachel's arm, especially this soon after having to relive what has separated them. Vachel catches this, but keeps it to himself for the time being. There will be plenty of time to use it later.

"It is good to see you again, little wolf," Selene adds, looking at Ven with an unconcerned stare. She is trying to hide her tension and sadness, but it is not working well. Tilting his head a little to the side, Ven asks, "Are you alright? You look tired." "Do I? I would not know...I have not the time to gaze in a mirror as often as need be at this time," she explains in a flat tone, pointedly keeping her gaze on Ven. Every word makes her sound lifeless.

In response, Ven lets his eyes slip to Vachel for a moment. Had he the ears of his demon third, they would have been pressed to his head. This time, from worry. He has a feeling he knows exactly what has the High Sister so depressed, but he would not be the one to change it to help her. Instead, he would rather give her something to divert her attention from the demon she has lost to a much more willing admirer.

"We can go elsewhere if you need to talk about this," Vachel observes, keeping his frustration at her behavior to himself. It is not that she is doing anything wrong. It is that he cannot do anything he is willing to do to make her feel better. It was fine to get her back before, but now that he sees how hard she is taking the whole thing, he regrets the desire to get back at her even sprang into his mind. Nodding absentmindedly, she replies, "Yes..." before turning to lead the way.

Once in her room, Selene all but flops onto the cushion with no real thought to how ungraceful the movement looks to the others. Dropping back into it, she makes her posture seem all the more unchecked. "Now I know something's wrong," Ven declares, crossing his arms with a frown, "What happened to the High Sister who kicked that bitch's butt earlier?" "She is still here somewhere...perhaps you could help me find her," Selene answers, her voice a dismal whisper as she gives an unconcerned wave of her hand.

A small, frustrated growl escapes Ven's lips before he can stop it. He had hoped to start things off on a brighter note, but it seems he's going to have to work his way up from the bottom. This day is going to end with him getting what he wants no matter what he has to say to her to get it. Crystal glances over at him for a moment before her gaze returns to Vachel. The demon lets nothing slip through his cool exterior.

In addition to the growl, Ven keeps his tight frown on the High Sister as he stalks across the room. Once beside the throne he demands, "How can you do this to yourself?! You're not even trying!" *I'm right here! Look at* me, *dammit! Me!* "How would you know?" Selene whispers dangerously, slowly sitting up to face him. It is the first real emotion she has shown since they arrived. Fists at his sides, Ven growls, "The True High Sister of Darkhaven wouldn't mope around like this...she knows there are better fish to catch than the ones uninterested in her bait." *But I am. Toss it to me!*

As Crystal watches, a smirk begins to slip to Vachel's face.

He can't believe he didn't see it all earlier.

You're such a little liar, Ven.

"Perhaps I am tired of having to maintain such a façade when it does me no good," Selene answers, crossing her arms as her eyes take on an angry shine. "That's just an excuse!" Ven counters, "You're better than this drab little she-demon you've let yourself become! Rejection hurts but you're acting like you've been killed! Dammit! I won't let you do it! I won't!" "And what sort of say do you think you have in what I do, little wolf?" Selene demands, getting to her feet to stand over him.

Unions

Without so much as a word of warning, he leans up and kisses her squarely on the mouth, making certain his hand comes to rest on the left side of her face. Selene's eyes go wide as she pulls away, demanding: "What is the meaning of this?!" "I didn't give you one after Rust was defeated...you didn't give me a chance to overcome the natural fear," Ven explains, a small flush coming to his face. Now that their mouths are no longer connected, he finds himself losing the confidence he has when he first saw what Vachel's turning away from her has done.

"I thought you said you did not like me enough to 'French me' as you so eloquently put it," the High Sister points out, crossing her arms. Letting his gaze fall to the floor as the flush brightens, Ven whispers, "Well...that wasn't entirely the truth." "Oh, really. Then what exactly is, little wolf?" she asks with a raised eyebrow.

Ven takes hold of the edge of his cloak and starts twisting it but refuses to speak. At this, Selene lets her gaze pass over to Vachel, who is about to burst out laughing from the look on his face. At his side, Crystal has a similar look, but she is doing a better job of trying to hide it.

When he spies her gazing at him, Vachel puts in his two cents, "I think the little one would like some auditioning time, pet." "Hmm. Is this true, little wolf?" Selene asks, letting her gaze fall to Ven again. As if feeling her eyes on him, Ven squirms a little before swallowing hard and giving his head a small nod.

At this, Vachel finally tosses his head back and laughs. Crystal tries to stifle hers with her hand, but the giggling rings out into the room just as loudly as the demon's. Instead of the laughter, Selene lets a smile slip to her face as she reaches down to turn Ven's head back toward her: "Why the change of heart, little one?" "You're not as cruel as you want us all to believe," Ven answers, a small smile on his face underneath all the blushing.

"That is very sweet," Selene remarks, giving Vachel and Crystal a side-glance. When Ven understands what she is doing, he looks over his shoulder and gives one of his own. Vachel catches the looks immediately and answers, "All right, we're leaving already. Don't get so upset." Crystal spares them another smile as Vachel starts leading her out of the room. However, before they can make it outside, Selene calls, "Your room is my first."

Sitting Indian-style in the center of the bed, Vachel frowns out at the room, mumbling curses under his breath. He understood Selene enough to get here, but he still cannot believe she left it the way it was after they got through with it the last time. All this crap has been sitting her for a good five hundred years. The blankets of midnight blue are still bunched at the foot of the bed, and the trace bloodstains remain on the sheets.

He can still remember the rivets she worked into his shoulders.

Tossed about the floor are the various articles of clothing she left behind after he left. Scuffmarks appear in the carpeting.

He can remember the rug burns, too.

One of his medallions as Death is hanging from the lamp, although he has yet to understand how it managed to get there precisely in the first place. Sadly enough, it still retains the smell, too. He can remember enjoying it before. But now it is just embarrassing, and Crystal's crooked grin is not helping.

"She did this on purpose," he concludes, the anger obvious on his face. Finally making her way across the room to him, Crystal suggests, "Perhaps she is trying to repay you for your neglect." "She wouldn't know neglect if it came up and bit her on the ass," Vachel responds, crossing his arms. Sitting next to him, she rests her head on his shoulder as she whispers, "Do not let it get to you...this is a simple tactic." "I know...but it still irritates me that she would go to such lengths," Vachel answers, letting his arms fall to his lap as he sighs.

Reaching for his left cheek, Crystal turns his head to face her and gives him a small kiss before she suggests, "We could always make an effort to leave our own marks." "Most of them are already mine," Vachel answers, averting his gaze. *Why in crimson did I just admit that?* Turning his head back around, Crystal presses, "I meant that belong to you and *me*. I am trying to give you a way to get her back."

"You would do that in the midst of all this?" Vachel asks with a skeptical eyebrow. Smiling, she replies, "With you."

"I'd have to agree," he answers, lifting his hand to cradle the left side of her face in it. Crystal leans forward as he does to meet the kiss, opening her mouth to allow him to push his tongue inside. Absentmindedly, she kicks off her boots and scoots up farther onto the bed. Pulling slowly away, Vachel reaches down to toss aside his own boots only to have Crystal push him over onto his back and do it herself.

Taking the hint, Vachel lies still as she proceeds to unbutton his shirt. She takes her time untucking it and pulling it from his shoulders, trailing heat from her fingers onto his skin. With a hand resting in the center of his chest, she reaches up to slip the ribbon loose from his hair. The belt buckle gives her a small amount of trouble, as her fingers are now trembling slightly. Feeling this, Vachel reaches down to take hold of her hand. Slowly, she lets her gaze rise to his face. The smile is still there as he observes, "This isn't an earth-shattering discovery, little one. You don't have to be so tense."

"Tense is not the word I would use."

"Really? Then, what's a better one?"

"I tremble with anticipation."

"Like I said...it isn't anything all that special."

"You got to see me last time...I think this only fair."

"You're telling me not to spoil your fun, then?"

"Precisely."

"Just remember to be gentle, little one...I'm fragile."

The smirk on his face lets her know he is full of shit, too. Shaking her head, she whispers, "I need my hands back." Vachel makes no response other than to release her and return to smiling up at the ceiling.

Finally getting the belt loose, she tosses it up to him. His fist jerks up with speed she really did not expect, snatching the leather from the air just before it has a chance to hit his chest. He lets his gaze fall to her with a look that is part smirk, part what-do-you-think-you're-doing. Sticking her tongue out at him, she pulls open the button of his pants and slowly opens the zipper. He is pointedly keeping his gaze away from her face, but she has the feeling he can still tell there is a red flush to her cheeks even now.

She devotes her attention to getting his pants off and out of her way before she actually takes the opportunity to look at him. Framed in the darkness of the sheets below, he looks all the more pale. The color makes her think of something hard and immovable, despite having had him hold her before. Letting her gaze travel over his stomach and chest, she spies the smile on his face as she whispers, "The power is even in your skin." "I would hope so," he answers, slowly sitting up and bringing his left knee up, "I don't want anyone to think me weak."

Crystal does not remark on this as she reaches for his hand. Bringing it up to rest her cheek in it, she finally whispers, "I am still waiting." In response, Vachel lifts his other hand to her shoulder as he slips the one she holds to the other. As he slips the thin straps from her shoulders, she lets her arms fall to her sides. Just as she did, he keeps his gaze away as he slips the dress the rest of the way down. However, he lets his gaze remain on her eyes as he leans back. A small laugh, akin to a giggle, slips from her mouth before she tackles him back into the mattress.

Blood creeps around her fangs from the wound in his shoulder. She is keeping his muscle deep in her mouth, preventing her from keeping the blood in at the same time. Digging his fingertips deep into her back, he hunches forward into her jaws even as he tosses his head back. The gasping and small cries are not pain sounds even though the film of tears in his eyes is.

Rising up to meet her, he is shoved back deeper into the cushion again. His neck snaps forward again as he seeks to catch even part of his breath. A flush from this very problem has control of his face as he breathes heavily against her shoulder. He can feel the ache in his hands and fingers as the magic is slowly burning into her skin. It was actually his suggestion to give the trust sign first, but she would have none of it. She gave him a rushed explanation about wanting a bit of pain before this all began.

When she gives the wound a jerk with her fangs, a surprised gasp spills from his mouth along with a breathy version of her name. Pounding down on him causes his head to jerk back with a loud moan as the wound tears a little more. His entire frame shudders with the spike of pain.

He is taking it considerably better than she first estimated.

Perhaps she was mistaken to share him over the years.

Just as the thought enters her mind, his hands slip in the blood on her back, finding new skin to react with. This sudden, sharp pain gets her to sink her teeth farther into his shoulder. In response, he shoves most of his body back up against her, finding the next stepping-stone toward that final spot.

A line of tingling down her spine pushes a burst of speed in her already insane movements. Almost involuntarily, he hunches up again before shoving all his strength back against her power coming down. Finally, he finds that final point.

She has the mind to open her jaw as she jerks back up so she does not tear loose the flesh she just had clenched tightly in her jaw. A scream half pain and pleasure erupts from her lips as his fingers slide down her sides with the blood. His own scream echoes hers. They let the room ring with the sound for a while before she collapses back into a heap with him.

Their hearts beat madly against each other as they seek to catch their lost breath. Finally, she slips off of him to collapse at his side, a small smile on her face. Once he has the air to speak, Ven asks, "So…how'd I do?"

Even now, their mouths are locked together, and neither is bothering to try and sort out the tangle of limbs and hair. All he can really tell is they are both on their sides. He managed to get them that way on purpose, but she is determined not to allow him rest just yet. Of course, with a license to go exploring, he isn't ready to give up yet, either.

At last, she pulls away from his mouth to seek air and then doesn't bother to resume her attack. Convinced he has finally gotten her to give it a rest for the moment, he doesn't try to take up where she left it.

She tries to get her hands free only to find her fingers have become entangled in his hair. He happens to be pressing the other firmly between their chests. "I am stuck," she whispers with a small frown. Easily pulling his own hands from around and under her arms, he reaches back to gently slip her fingers from his hair.

Shaking her head, she replies, "You have had much more practice than I have." "You make that sound like a bad thing, little one," Vachel points out, returning his arms to their positions around her. "It is not a bad thing," she replies, "But I would like to be able to do something better than you for once."

"I don't see you with claw marks on your arms," he points out, lifting his for her to see. A frown slips to her face at the sight of the scratches: "That is nothing...anyone could do that." "But, you did it to me, and that makes it different," he answers, pulling her closer, "And...you make me feel safe."

325

"What do you mean?"

"I've missed having someone to love me."

"What about Riko? She does."

"Not that kind of love, little one."

"You could get that from anyone."

"Not *that* kind of love, either."

"Then what sort?"

"The kind a mated pair has out amongst people."

Understanding finally, Crystal presses her lips to his chest as she whispers, "I love you, too."

She wakes to a warmth hanging around her that she at first attributes to being tired still. However, once she realizes that this warmth is breathing she lets her eyes pop open to their fullest extent. It is only now that she spies the bloodstains in puddles everywhere. Finally, it begins to click in her mind. Now, she remembers what happened the night before. Thus, she knows what and *who* the warmth is.

Gazing down, she lets a smile slip to her face as she spies him wrapped around her waist, cuddled in as tightly against her as he can get. She reaches down, stroking his hair, and he whispers, "You didn't answer my question." "Question?" she replies, lifting her hand away for a moment. Nodding against her, he asks again, "I asked: how did I do?" "That all depends," Selene answers, her voice going serious. Ven turns his gaze to her face as he asks the next question with his eyes: what does it depend on?

"Will you be back willingly?" she replies. A smile wide enough to flash fangs slips to his face as he answers, "You can count on it." "Even if I told you never to return?" Selene presses. Digging his fingers harder into her back, he responds, "I'd like to see you get rid of me in the first place." "In light of this new information..." she whispers, giving him a look as if she actually has to think about it, "I would say that you passed, love." "That's good to know...but what do you want me to call you?" Ven answers.

"I think you know that answer to that, love."

"I thought that was taken."

"He has found another."

"I see...hmm, hmm. I love you, pet."

"We shall just see how long that lasts under the strain of my personality, love. Wait until then to say that," Selene corrects. Shaking his head, Ven pulls his arms from around her waist and scoots himself up so that they can look each other in the eyes: "Love and lust are different animals, pet. I thought you knew that." "It seems I have forgotten," she answers with a small laugh. Ven leans forward as he whispers, "Then, let me help you remember." With that, he presses his mouth firmly against hers.

Keep of Darkness

Vachel lets the hot water pound against his back and shoulders as he stands with his head back and his eyes closed. Crystal is still in the other room sleeping. It seems demons have even this sort of recovery advantage over the other races. The thought brings a bitter smile to his face.

Even with the nail marks stinging along his arms, he is still having trouble believing she let him. Especially in a bedroom that still reeks of him and Selene. At that thought, his eyes open a fraction as he hunches forward. His hand slides up to cover his mouth as he slips down in a crouch. *She does not deserve to have to do that. She doesn't deserve to have to be reminded that she was chosen second.*

"What have I done?" he whispers, gritting his teeth.

"You have made me a very happy woman, Vachel," she answers, sliding in behind him. The tension in his shoulders slips away as Crystal wraps her arms around him and rests her head on his back. Letting his hand fall away from his mouth, Vachel whispers, "That wasn't fair to you, at all." "What was not fair?" she asks, gently running her fingers over his wet chest. Vachel pulls his fingers through his hair before he explains, "You shouldn't have had to settle for that...it's not fair."

"If anyone settled...it was you."

"What?"

"I will never match your Selene in beauty."

328

"And she will never match you in love," he answers, turning around to scoop her up in his arms. Crystal gives him a gentle push and he slips away, a wounded look on his face. Out of the corner of her eye, she spies his hand wrapping around the crystal. Still, she has to ask, "Then...you admit I am not a beauty to you?" "That's not true," Vachel responds, his head jerking up with a shocked look on his face.

Refusing to meet his eyes, Crystal whispers, "But...you did not deny when I said that I would never match Selene." "I didn't mean that you weren't beautiful...I was pointing out how I make measure," he replies slowly, as if not certain she will believe him, "Beauty is nothing without the love to back it up."

"It still remains that I am not."

"Stop saying that!"

Crystal goes silent looking at the pain on his face.

"It's not true," he adds in a more subdued tone.

"Why are you protesting so much then?"

"I haven't had anyone...care about me for anything but power before."

"And?"

"And I...I don't want to lose the one person who does."

"You know...I don't think the magic's going to work on you by itself anymore," Ven observes, sliding his bare fingers over her hip as the dress exposes it. She is lying sated and calm before him, her hair spread out on the cushion. With his head propped up on his palm and his elbow digging into the cushion, he rests quietly behind her. Turning her head to look at him, Selene asks, "And would you use it if I asked?" "Only if you asked," Ven answers, giving her a small kiss against the scarred side of her face.

"You enjoy them, too, love?" she asks, giving him a skeptical look. Lifting his free hand up, he runs his knuckles across the scars as he answers, "I enjoy all of you, pet. These are proof of the raging fire within." "Oddly sentimental for a demon, love," she responds, shaking her head with a smile. He laughs softly and whispers, "Guess that's the faerie talking or something." "Or something," she agrees, taking his hand and entwining their fingers.

He is running his tongue over her knuckles when the door bursts open.

Vachel rushes in, his hands over his head with a giant smirk on his face. Crystal chases after him, a furious look on her face as she raises her arm back to toss her boot at him. It crashes into his shoulder, and he grips it but continues to run. However, when the second catches him in the calf, he stumbles forward onto the floor. He has the time to roll over onto his back before Crystal slams into him.

She slams her fists into his chest as she demands, "Apologize you jerk. That really hurt!" Vachel bursts out laughing, but refuses to speak. Crystal hits him harder and cries, "Do not laugh at me! Say you are sorry for tugging on my ear!" "Why?" Vachel demands through his laughing,

"I'm not sorry." "Then I will make you be sorry," she counters, taking hold of *his* ear and pulling.

Ven and Selene's combined hands have fallen across her stomach as they watch this performance, smirks coming to both faces. When Vachel protests against her pulling on his ear and Crystal simply sticks out her tongue, they both have to give a small laugh. Of course, seeing him try to wrestle an apology out of her gets each to laugh openly at their antics.

It is only once they hear this laughter that Vachel and Crystal remember there are others in the room to see them. A bright flush appears on Crystal's face, and Vachel has to avert his gaze to keep from laughing with them from embarrassment.

"You'd think you could get along better than that, being lovers," Ven remarks once he finally has enough control of his mouth. Squeezing his hand, Selene counters, "But remember our 'fight', love. It is not a good idea to point such fingers after that." "I hate to break it to you, scratch that I love it, but I actually had fun 'fighting' with you, pet," Ven answers, giving her a how-do-you-like-that look.

It is not until they hear this exchange that Vachel and Crystal truly see the bloodstains spread out around the pair. He has to narrow his eyes slightly, but Vachel is then able to see the bite wound still open in Ven's shoulder. It has ceased to bleed for the moment, but it is still deep enough to show the red flesh below the surface of his skin. Still, it is the sight of their fingers interlaced that truly catches his attention. He would have felt the surge of power had Ven given her a trust sign, meaning Ven has found his other exemption to the magic rule. Only family and a chosen mate can escape a Hybrid's power.

Vachel's stomach cringes at this news. *Of all the demons, why did he have to pick Selene? After all the fear he showed earlier, it makes no sense.* Vachel has to stifle the urge to ask as he lifts Crystal's boots from the floor. *Then again, from that bite mark, maybe it was fear of Rust's reprimand if he paid her mind that kept him away. Well, at least she won't be pining after me anymore.* Crystal tries to pull them away from him, but Vachel refuses to let her do it. Even with Crystal's hands on his shoulders, and his hands working to get her boot on her foot, Vachel's eyes are for Ven.

Sensing the demon's question in his gaze, Ven leans over Selene's shoulder and runs his tongue along her jaw. With his eyes gazing back at Vachel's Ven cannot see it, but Selene's eyes drop closed at having his tongue on her skin, especially with Vachel watching.

Vachel has Crystal's boots in place and is about to show the little shit how things really work when the doors burst open. A young woman in black dashes past him and Crystal without even looking at them. There is a full flush to her face as she scrambles before Selene's throne. "Forgive me, High Sister, but the sorcerers have come calling without notice," the woman reports, bowing as she does. Jerking to a sitting position, Selene commands, "Keep them out of here! This is not a place for their filth to tread!"

Just as the command leaves her lips, a man steps into the doorway, flanked by three others as he greets, "Good morning to you, baby sister."

Even with his true black hair slipping down from the base of his neck, Vachel recognizes him instantly by the look in his red eyes: Nark. *Dammit, I should have known that snake was too slimy to be human!*

He wears the full wardrobe of the High Elder Sorcerer of Darkhaven. His shirt and pants are now a black to match the shined boots slipping up to hide the fabric to his knees. The belt at his waist bears a gold buckle with a violet dragon raised on the surface. A gold medallion with the same dragon and sapphire for its eye hangs around his neck. The gloves covering his hands are gold at the seams. His black robe, which falls to the floor around him, is trimmed in gold, and he wears a gold dragon over his heart on the black fabric.

Behind him, the three men are done in black, as well. Over each of their hearts is a violet dragon. The one on Nark's right looks to be no more than thirteen with short blonde hair and blue eyes to freeze the room around him. There is a jagged scar running along the length of his jaw. The man to Nark's left is a good three inches taller and built with more muscle than he knows what to do with. His brown hair falls in curls to his shoulders as he glares out at the room through green eyes. At Nark's back is a man whose skin is ghostly pale. His hair is jet black as it falls just past his shoulders. Not even a pinprick of light shines from his black eyes.

"Get out of here! I told you already that you and yours are not to set foot in my domain without proper arrangements, Nark!" Selene demands, a flush of fury spreading across her face. The smile on his face still cool and irritating, Nark answers, "Am I not allowed to visit my own sibling when I so choose?" "You lost the right to call me kin long ago, Nark...get out of my territory!" Selene snaps, jerking to her feet. Instead of doing as she demands, Nark steps away from his men, leaving them to block the exit as he makes his way over to Selene.

Before Nark can pass, Vachel jerks Crystal to him, burying her face in his chest. He hasn't any desire to give Nark another target to try to manipulate against him. Oddly enough, Nark pays him no mind as he continues on his way. Spying the fury running along Selene's every limb, Ven climbs down to stand next to her. She takes some small comfort at having him at her back this time around.

Instead of pausing at the bottom of the steps like most others would, Nark makes his way up to the top. There is a dark look on his face that makes Ven want to tear his throat out. No one but he can look at her that way and get away with it. Nark's smile widens to flash fangs as he asks, "What did you run into this time, little sister? It certainly made a ruin of your face." "You should know...you were the one who told her I was after her mate," Selene hisses, her hands in fists at her sides.

"Hmm, hmm. True...but then, where has your taste gone...to associate with such trash?" Nark presses, leering at Ven. In response, Ven bares his own fangs and growls deep in his throat. Nark gives him a condescending look as he replies, "And just where did you get this mongrel...it isn't even broken in enough to know when to heel for its betters."

The burst of power that shoves Nark off his feet and down the stairs surprises everyone in the room but Ven. Untangling himself from his robe, Nark gazes up at Ven with mingled shock and fury. "Watch how you talk to me, dog, or you'll get worse than that," Ven growls, stepping out around Selene. Jerking to his feet, Nark counters, "Just who's the one with the collar, Hybrid?" "Last time I checked, the loser didn't have much room to gloat over being purebred," Ven answers, looking down his nose at Nark.

In response, the sorcerer vaults himself back up the stairs, catching Ven's injured shoulder in his grip. There isn't even a wince on his face as he retaliates by taking the whole of Nark's face in his hand. Immediately, the bare flesh reacts, burning the imprint into Nark's face. A frustrated scream erupts from Nark's mouth as he jerks away from Ven's grasp. In the same instant, both Nark and Ven jerk their hands up to strike. However, just as the bursts of energy form in each hand, Selene jerks in between them.

Ven closes his hand the moment he sees her, but Nark isn't in the backing-down mood. The energy swirls larger, and every second begins to take hours to tick by as Ven reaches forward. It feels as if he has all the time in the world to pull her out of the way, and yet he knows there's no chance of him making it. Nark almost has the ball formed when Ven takes hold of Selene's arm. In a moment of desperation, Ven is prepared to launch himself into Nark's arm when it suddenly explodes in a rain of blood, bone, and muscle.

The look on Nark's face is one of shock and pain as what used to be his arm and hand splatters to the stone. Ven is unable to understand it for a moment before he spies the black chain withdrawing from Nark's flesh. When he looks up at Vachel, the demon gives him a fanged smile as he calls the chain back. A snarl on his face, Nark spins around and orders, "Take them down!"

Simultaneously, all three of the men at the door spring forward.

As Nark turns around with a triumphant smile, he finds the heel of Ven's boot in his nose. His hands encased in a swirling, black fire, Ven charges after his prey as the sorcerer tumbles down the stairs to land in a bleeding heap.

The largest of the men charges Crystal only to find the faerie is a little faster than first estimated. Even in her heels, she leads him around the room three times before he can get close enough to even touch her. When he does, she kicks him as hard as she can in the groin. He doubles over and she kicks his feet out from underneath him.

Pointing at his back with the index and middle fingers of her right hand, she calls, "Gnin Thgil!" A huge bolt of lightning appears from her fingers, crashing through his back as it splatters blood up in an arch toward her. She cringes at the feeling of his blood all over her face as she whispers to herself, "I must remember that is such a messy way to kill."

Both the blonde and black-haired demon tries to pass Vachel in route to catch Selene, but find themselves blocked by Vachel's magic. "Sorry to disappoint, fellas, but I have all this pent up energy, and kicking your asses should do just fine," he remarks, cracking his knuckles with a fang-flashing smile on his face. Snarling, the blonde sends a mass of flames in Vachel's direction. Vachel gives him a pitying smile as he catches the flames in a ball over his palm. Spinning it in the air a few times, he observes, "Your master didn't tell you I'm a magnet, did he?"

From the looks on their faces, Vachel has to guess not.

Adding his own flame to the sphere, Vachel spreads it back out before sending it right back. "Sorry man, not enough postage," he adds as the flames wrap their way around the pair. They shriek in unison as the flames consume them, and Vachel remarks, "That's what you get for messin' with my postal system. Tsk. Tsk."

Ven chases Nark about the room, slashing at him only to have the sorcerer evade his attacks by barely a hair's width. Running himself into a corner, Nark jerks around and sends a wave of ice at Ven's face. Ven takes an involuntary step back before he jerks to the side, giving Nark the chance he needs to escape. Growling deep in his throat, Ven tears after him.

A burst of energy over Nark's shoulder nearly takes Ven in the shoulder before he ducks, sliding slightly on the floor. He scrambles to his feet to hear Selene yell, "Be careful, love!" At the sound of these words, Ven's eyes flash bright violet. A smile spills to his lips as he forces himself forward faster. This burst of power allows him to catch up to Nark. Tackling the sorcerer, Ven rolls with him. Nark ends up pinned to the floor on his back. His eyes are wide as he spies the look on Ven's face.

"Being the victim not much to your liking, dog?" Ven taunts, licking away some of the blood from his fingers. A knowing, frightened look appears on Nark's face as he watches this. Ven gives him a small laugh as he asks, "You know what this means then?" Nark stays silent. "I thought so," Ven replies, "This means you are beneath me...literally and figuratively. I'm the alpha male here, and you should know that before I kill your ass."

"All I wanted was Yossa's Crystal!" Nark yells, a red flush spilling to his face. Tilting his head to the side, Ven whispers, "Well, you ain't getting it." Nark opens his mouth to say something further, but Ven snatches up his head and slams it into the floor. It takes several more of these before Nark's head gives way, and he ceases to be.

Getting up, Ven growls, "Now who's worthless?"

Just as he turns around, Selene jabs him in the chest and yells, "Do not ever do that to me again! I thought he had you for certain!" "Your confidence overwhelms me, pet," Ven answers, giving her a crooked smile. He couldn't help but steal the line from Vachel. She jabs him once more in the chest before wrapping her arms around his neck and demanding, "Only I am allowed to cause you pain. Swear it to me." "I swear, pet. But...can *I* have the crystal?" he answers, returning her embrace. She stiffens in his arms before whispering, "Is that all you wanted?" "Nope...*you're* all I wanted...it's Vachel who was looking for the crystal. I just don't want him to have it," Ven whispers in her ear, knowing full well Vachel can hear him.

Selene can't help but laugh for a moment before she slips away from him and makes her way back to her throne. Crouching before it, she reaches beneath the cushion and pulls out a black box. She presses her fingertips against it and whispers. Immediately, the box clicks open. From inside, she pulls a crystal the color of a midnight sky, including the stars, hanging from a silver chain.

As she takes it back over to Ven, neither Vachel nor Crystal makes any sort of protest. Ven doesn't have to bend for her to place it around his neck, but he does anyway. Once he is standing up, Selene is ready to say something else when the crystal flares to life. It glows black light into the room, making Selene cringe slightly away and Ven close his eyes slightly. It glows this way for a few moments before there is an audible click. Each person in the room is confused when nothing seems to have happened. However, when Ven reaches up to touch the chain, his fingers brush the Shiku Hara, and it falls to the floor in several pieces before turning to dust.

A smile bursts out on every face, and Selene wraps her arms around Ven's neck again to share a lengthy kiss.

Conclusion: Reunion

"I wanna go faster!" he demands from his perch on Vachel's shoulders. His green eyes are as frustrated as the frown below them. At the base of his neck, the black hair is taken over by tips of red. Around his neck is a chain bearing a gold medallion with his name carved into it: Dred. His shirt is black like his pants and the boots beneath. Gripping two fistfuls of his father's hair, he demands again, "Faster! Faster!" "Hush, we'll get there when we get there," Vachel answers, reaching up to tug gently at one of the boy's ears.

"Mama, make him go faster," Dred whines over at Crystal, giving her his best sympathy face. Shaking her head, Crystal answers, "I cannot do that, little one." Frowning, he simply hunches back against Vachel's head with a huffed look on his face. No sooner than he stops demanding speed do they make their way to the front gate of the castle. The guards snap to give them a bow, which both Crystal and Vachel answer with a nod.

Inside the castle, Ven greets them with a wave of his hand. Dred wiggles around until Vachel sets him down on the floor. Dashing over to Ven, he reaches up to be lifted, and Ven complies. Ven pulls him up in the air over his head and greets, "How ya doing, jerkface?" "I'm big now, big butt, you better watch it," Dred answers, still laughing.

Shaking his head, Ven looks over at Vachel and Crystal as he asks, "Doesn't he look kinda scrawny to you?"

Conclusion: Reunion

"Not too much so," Vachel answers, stepping toward them so that his natural power pushes open the black cloak around his frame. Beneath are his usual black and the crystal; however, he wears a band of gold around each wrist. Carved into each is a dragon.

Crystal's black dress caresses the floor around her. Now, her red hair falls past her waist. A necklace bearing a glittering diamond is secured around her neck. Just as Vachel makes it to Ven's side, a brighter smile slips to her face, and she rushes across the room. All three boys follow her, confused until they spy Selene moving into the room with Gilden and Mikya right behind her. The smile on Crystal's face is as much for seeing them together as it is for the baby girl cradled in the crook of Selene's arm. For the moment, she's sleeping, cradled deep within the folds of a soft blanket.

Hugging her around the shoulders so as not to disturb the little girl, Crystal whispers, "This is great news. How old is she?" "Six months, but it feels more like six years have been taken off my life," Selene answers, sighing even with a small smile on her face. It seems she has finally learned what it really takes to make magic.

While they are speaking and fussing over the baby, Mikya slips around them with Gilden at her heels. When she makes it about an arm's length away from Vachel, she places a hand over her heart and bows low, greeting: "Strength to King Vachel of Darkhaven." "And good day to you, Princess Mikya of Dehurst," Vachel answers, giving her his own bow as a smirk spreads out on his face. She's going out of her way to try to unite their countries as allies when it is already done as far as he's concerned.

"Riko and the girls have been working nonstop since yesterday to get everything ready even though it's only going to be a few of us," Mikya explains, shaking her head. Gazing up with his smile still in place, Vachel responds, "That's just like her to fuss over something like this."

"Don't you want me to?" Riko asks suddenly as she makes her way into the room, "Crimson knows no one else is going to do it." Her eyes are stern, but there is a smile spread out over her face. A happy cry escapes Dred's mouth as he scrambles over to her: "Auntie Riko!" She bends down to wrap the boy up in her arms before lifting him up in a tight hug. Vachel can't help but smile at seeing the two of them together. Perhaps things are actually returning to the way they should be. For once, he can look on a family enjoying their time together without the threat of being torn apart never to meet again. It seems so long ago he could claim he felt the same, and now things have come back full circle after all this time. It seems history does repeat itself, the bad and the good.

Scribe's Note

Strength to you, good reader!

Or, if you prefer, Good day to you, dear reader!

If you can't see it, I'm bowing really low.

Here I would like to take a moment to thank you all for reading my debut work, *Yossa's Crystal*. I'm working really hard to get the sequel up and running. I'd be exceptionally pleased if you would read that one, too. Anyway, I would also like to thank everyone who's cheered me on during the creation process. My mom has been wonderful help in telling me just how great she thinks I am and giving me the confidence to take that next step and keep writing. A friend of mine has been doing a great deal of the editing, and I've tried to catch every mistake I can by reading this same story about seven times. I don't know it by heart quite yet, but I like to think I'm pretty close. I'd also like to thank one of the maintenance workers at the mall where I work for letting me pick on him in exchange for getting to read the manuscript before anyone else.

Once again, I give my thanks to all who have read this. May the memory of Vachel and the Crystal of Yossa wander on.

Darkness Cares![10]

Sarah Scott

---

[10] I hope to make this my very own catch phrase. ☺ Whether it catches on or not, I'm still going to go around saying it to the people who know what it means.